Criminal Zoo

a novel by

SEAN McDANIEL

Crimina

Zoo SEAN McDANIEL ————————————————

THIS IS A GENUINE DEFENESTRATION BOOK

A Defenestration Book | Rare Bird Books
453 South Spring Street, Suite 302
Los Angeles, CA 90013
rarebirdbooks.com

FIRST HARDCOVER EDITION

Set in Dante
Printed in the United States

10 9 8 7 6 5 4 3 2 1

Publisher's Cataloging-in-Publication data
Names: McDaniel, Sean P., author.
Title: Criminal zoo : a novel / Sean McDaniel.
Description: A Genuine Defenestration Book | First Hardcover Edition | New
York, NY; Los Angeles, CA: Rare Bird Books, 2016.
Identifiers: ISBN 978-0-9974407-0-6
Subjects: LCSH Serial murders—Fiction. | Psychopaths—Fiction. | Jails—Fiction.
| Prisoners—Fiction. | Suspense fiction. | BISAC FICTION/General.
Classification: PS3613.C38682 C75 2016 | DDC 813.6—dc23

Prologue

T
HE DISCOVERY OF A skeleton just outside of town baffled
the authorities. That's what the *Clemensville Chronicle* said,
anyway. A man and his dog, braving the dusty winds from
the nearby plains, stumbled onto the body—or what was left of
it. It caused quite a stir.

Clemensville, Texas, festering along Highway 349, was West
Texas exposed. No makeup. Dry, desolate, no natural structures
taller than a pump jack for a hundred miles. The pump jacks
were everywhere, no matter which direction you turned. I used
to pretend they were mighty Tyrannosaurus rexes lowering their
giant black heads, chomping on some poor little dinosaur and
then rising to swallow their meals. Up, down, up, down, all day,
all night.

Strangers were a rarity in Clemensville. Mostly just motorists
passing through on their way to either Rankin or Midland,
depending on which direction they went. Railroads crisscrossed
the state, just nowhere near us; no bums or drifters to speak of
and everybody knew most everybody. That's why the discovery
was so unsettling.

Clemensville was quiet. Boring, even. With the exception
of the boy murdered in his own backyard—every town had its
blemish—almost a decade ago, nothing exciting happened here.
Okay, there was Old Man Jennings going missing last year. They

ended up finding his ninety-year-old carcass less than a mile from his house. Heart attack.

This was different, though. The paper said foul play was suspected. That made pretty good sense; not likely someone walked out there buck naked to die. There wasn't a stitch of clothing found near the remains. The police called in a Midland-area dentist to take dental imprints and the results were circulated to surrounding communities. Nothing came of it.

Everyone talked about the skeleton. In a Bible Belt town with a population of just under 1,500, other than God and football what else was there? Television crews came from Midland, Odessa, as far away as Lubbock. People stood around and watched the newscasters do their on-the-scene reports like they were watching a circus act.

My wife, Carla, was nervous as hell. Before the discovery we weren't all that worried about the boogeyman. Afterward, Carla made me go through the house latching windows and locking doors. Then she did her own walkthrough to make sure I did it right. I'm not sure if she thought I was an idiot or if she was just paranoid. After everything was locked, checked, and rechecked, Carla brought up the same stupid subject—buying a mutt. She said she always wanted one when she was a kid, but her dad said no. I had a problem—I didn't care for dogs. Not since being bitten as a kid. Even bigger problem, Carla wasn't concerned about my problem. With strong proof of a murder not far away, she decided I could learn to like them. I interpreted the discussion as meaning she didn't feel protected. I guess I wasn't much of a man in her eyes. That was fine; she wasn't my dream girl either.

My argument against a mangy, flea-bitten mutt dirtying up the house obviously wasn't very convincing because we added the security she wanted. He was an animal shelter rescue. And to really make her point she went big. Must've had St. Bernard

For Tiki. You once bought me an office chair for Christmas and told me to write you a story. Oh my, have I a story for you.

"Man is at the bottom an animal, midway a citizen, and at the top divine. But the climate of this world is such that few ripen at the top."

—Henry Beecher, *Proverbs from Plymouth Pulpit*

"There is no beast more cruel than man."

—Leonid Andreyev, *Savva*

in him. He was a hundred pounds if he was an ounce. Carla named him Brutus, believing it made him sound like a dog to be reckoned with. Like his size wasn't already getting it done. But he obviously had his own name because that dumb shit never once answered to ours. Carla thought he was cute; I thought he was a big ol' pain in the ass. A walking rug of smelly black and white fur.

So Brutus took over the role of "protector" and Carla lightened up. She had her dog and no longer feared getting raped, stabbed, beaten, and killed in the middle of the night. I figured she didn't have too much to worry about, dog or no dog. We'd been married for a few years by then and I'd never seen her get hit on. Not once.

I tolerated the beast as best I could, but I have to admit, when the Brutus chapter came to a close, I wasn't all that sad to see him go. I suppose I should've been more comforting to Carla, but really—the way she acted, like she just lost baby Jesus, irritated me.

After the buzz about the discovery quieted down and all the reporters left, everything got back to normal. Until more bodies showed up.

S OME TIME AGO, A bigwig from Colorado, gu
Or so everyone thought. But put a passic
of a nation in front of a camera, and bi
is the governor. Yeah that's right, the governo

Something to Think About

amed Jon McIntyre, came up with a pretty far-fetched plan.
e, good-looking guy on a mission to ease the frustrations
! Anything's possible. Especially when the son of a bitch
the great state of Colorado. And boy did he have a plan.

Because a bunch of pansies thought the death penalty was
too cruel, a whole new kind of punishment was about to be
unleashed.

I don't remember how long ago the newspaper ran the story
about the guy's wife disappearing, but it sure gave him a crusade.
Put his suit of armor on and ran with it.

His wife, and mother of their kids, vanished on a weekend
road trip. Paper said there was definitely a crime scene. But no
leads. Apparently first ladies at the state level don't have much of
a security detail.

The governor believed his wife was the victim of a horrible
crime. He got all righteous about it. Stood on his soapbox and
decided anyone who committed a violent crime should be
punished equally violently. Real "eye for an eye" shit.

Although the idea was extreme, it got real popular real fast.
I guess the good people were finally ready to give the bad people
something to be scared of.

A nation of individual complaining didn't do shit. And then a really pissed-off guy, who happened to have some executive power behind him, declared, "We are not going to take it anymore!" He rallied the people and his cause took off. First Colorado, and then everywhere else. His looks certainly didn't hurt any. Not that I look at men, but even I noticed. He seemed tall—but when you're barely five feet seven, everyone seems tall. And I'd bet he wasn't originally from Colorado, either. He had more of a California look about him: blond hair, green eyes, a decent tan. He must have spent a lot of time in the gym—not just on the treadmill, but in the weight room, because he filled out his shirts in all the right places.

I wasn't jealous. I probably could've looked like that too, if I had time to work out. But I was busy doing other things, like trying to figure out how to keep the bills paid and gas in my car. Even if I did work out, I don't think anyone would've paid attention. My small frame, brown hair, and average-Joe looks didn't turn many heads.

But Governor McIntyre was different. The *Chronicle* followed him closely, printing multiple articles about his cause. He also appeared on the news and hit some talk shows. His movement was a subject of conversation across the nation, whether in the grocery store, barbershop, or on Capitol Hill.

Got to admit, he fascinated me. I recorded a daytime TV program with him as the guest. I thought maybe if I studied him, maybe I could someday draw such attention. I'd always thought it'd be cool to be famous.

"A while back," the governor said on the program, staring the clean-shaven, silver-haired host straight in the eyes, "an illegal alien from Mexico murdered a lady cop in Dallas. She was also a wife and mother, killed by a man who should've never had the freedom to commit the murder."

"What happened?" Silver Hair asked. He was too fancy. Obviously rich. I didn't like him.

"The immigrant had been convicted of molesting a little girl," the governor began. "So what'd we do? We deported him, as if Mexico would take care of it. Mexico? Yeah, right. The guy simply walked back across the border. Can you believe that?"

"That is rather odd."

"Not odd at all. Happens every day. Someone reported that a young girl had been assaulted where the man was staying. An officer responded, only to be gunned down. Now we have a dead mom because our judicial system doesn't know how to take out the trash."

"Yes, there are breakdowns here and there, Governor, but wouldn't you agree our legal system is doing everything it can to protect our citizens?"

"Protect our citizens? Are you kidding me? You watching what's happening in the world today?" the governor asked. "People are killing people at will. Not just a few. A lot. New York. Benghazi. Madrid. London. Nairobi. Paris. Bad people are raining terror down upon good people everywhere. And our leaders want to *talk to them*. You know—have a conversation with them."

"Sir, I'm talking about American citizens in our great country. Do you not believe the legal system is doing everything it can to protect them, in their own homes and neighborhoods?"

"You're a fool if you believe what is happening around the world isn't coming to your front door. And when it does, when someone blows up someone you love at a football game, how are you going to punish those people? Talk to them? Tell them we're actually good people and they shouldn't be so mean to us?"

"Again, Governor, I'm talking about reasonable punishment for those committing crimes in our hometowns. Now. Right this minute. What would you do differently? Other than what our criminal system is already trying to do?"

"Fine. Let's talk about the convicted pedophiles walking our streets and preying on innocent children every day. Let's talk about the violent offenders who live in our midst. Here's a good one for you: an Illinois judge recently revoked a restraining order filed by an abused woman against her husband. The guy complained about it infringing on his rights. Afterward, he used his rights to set his wife on fire."

"Yes, but," Silver Hair began, "the husband was intent on harming his wife. Even if the restraining order was left in place, a piece of legal paper wasn't going to stop him."

"Exactly. We need to come up with something tougher than a piece of paper."

"What do you suggest?"

"A place where the punishment fits the crime," the governor said. "I'm sick of hearing how a mom can drown her children and not face severe consequences because she's found *not guilty by reason of insanity*. Of course she's insane! She killed her kids!"

The host eyed his guest. "Are you saying not guilty by reason of insanity is not a valid defense?"

"You're not really asking me that, right?" The governor shook his head. "We're supposed to jeopardize lives while trying to figure out what to do with a woman who doesn't know the difference between buttering her toast and butchering her baby?"

"Should we not differentiate between those who kill with intent and those who kill because they don't know any better?"

"Why? Whether you are mentally ill or not, if you're wired to kill, you kill."

"I don't necessarily agree," the host responded, "but let's say it's true. How would you handle it?"

"I see the problem from a different angle. If a person is diagnosed with cancer, the malignancy is removed, eliminated from the body for the sake of survival, right?"

"Right."

"Our society represents a body—the body of civilization. Violent individuals are cancer cells. We need to cut them from the body of civilization for the very survival *of* civilization. When we try to rehabilitate these people and then set them free, we are causing irreparable damage. When cancer relapses, it often results in death. Society relapses every time a predator is released."

"So you do not believe a person can be rehabilitated?"

"Whether you want to believe it or not, there is no cure for pedophilia. You are defective. Period. You go to prison a pedophile, you come out a pedophile."

The governor's declaration sounded about right. And apparently I wasn't the only who felt that way.

Governor McIntyre proposed creating a place where violent offenders would truly pay for their crimes. He mentioned a newspaper article about an experimental exhibit at the London Zoo, one featuring humans. The Zoo's intent was to showcase man as just another member of the primate family. People across Europe visited the exhibit. Some found it fascinating, others found it stupid. But it made everyone think, especially the governor.

"I say we follow the lead of the London Zoo," he suggested. "We should create a place where we display violent criminals as what they are: animals."

"You're saying we should build a *human zoo?*"

"We spend millions upon millions of dollars every year on our prisons. I'm tired of rubber-stamping the costs of keeping malignant humans alive. The zoo for criminals—"

"The Criminal Zoo?"

"Sure, I like that. It's catchy. Anyway, it could be funded through admission, not our tax dollars. And for an additional fee, it could be visitor interactive."

"You mean like a petting zoo?" Silver-Haired Fancy Man asked, eyebrows raised.

"Yeah, like a petting zoo. A person could interact with a chosen criminal. The criminal's biography would be posted at his exhibit—his age, place of birth, job history, hobbies and interests, and most importantly, his criminal record, in full, gory detail."

"What kind of visitor interaction do you propose?"

"Let's say the criminal beat someone to death with a baseball bat. For a fee, you could take a bat to the guy."

"Ah, Dante's *Inferno* brought to life. Are we talking about a free-for-all beating?"

"No. There'd be restrictions, limits to how bad you could hurt someone. You could hit the guy in the arm or the leg. If you break a bone, the exhibit would be closed while medical attention is given, allowing the human animal time to heal."

"The *human animal*?"

"That's what he is. Say we have a child abuser. A visitor could burn him with a cigarette. Cigarette burns are easy to recover from. Just ask any number of kids. Or maybe we could allow a rape victim to take a police-issue nightstick and sodomize her attacker."

Silver Hair shook his head. "Why revenge? Why not forgiveness?"

"Seriously?" The governor laughed. "Forgiveness will get you killed these days."

"Should we also cut off the hand of the thief or stone the adulterer, Governor? Aren't we supposed to be more civilized than that?"

"The longer we try to figure out how to deal with the psychopath in a civilized manner, the longer the psychopath feeds on us. When the punishment for killing a person with an ice pick is getting stabbed with an ice pick, only then will justice be *just*."

"You're saying 'justice.' But sir, you're talking about vengeance. Sharia law has no place in this country."

"Call it what you want. I'm talking about punishment for people who don't understand anything else. Let's rewind here. Seventeen-seventy-six. The birth of our great nation. How did we punish criminals back then? Floggings. Whippings. Firing squads. Public hangings. Let's get back to giving the guilty something to think about."

The host stared at the governor, tilted his head, looked at the man like he had just spoken in Chinese. "Sir, that was two and a half centuries ago."

"How long has the wheel been round?"

"What?"

"The wheel was invented round, right? A lot longer than two hundred and fifty years ago. And it's still round today. If it works, don't change it."

Mister Fancy Man shook his head. "I'm not even sure how to respond to this argument. Brutality against mankind compared to the shape of a wheel?" He shrugged dramatically. "Let's move on. Say this human zoo of yours was put into place. Who pays for the expensive surgeries to repair all the broken bones and puncture wounds?"

"No expensive surgeries. The bones are set, the wounds are cleaned and sewn up, and antibiotics are given. Heal the criminal and get him back on display."

"Does the guy at least get pain medication?"

"I don't know. Did he give his victim any?" The governor stared at his host.

"And how long would the Criminal Zoo sentence run? Until they die?"

"The Criminal Zoo would pull those who want to hurt us off the streets and never put them back. Live, die, a year, a decade, I don't care. I only want to protect the people who elected me. It is my job to keep them safe."

"Harsh, Governor. Very harsh."

"No, harsh is having to tell your children their mom is never coming home. Never going to tuck them into bed. Never going to kiss them goodnight, ever again."

"Sir," the host replied. "If we allowed something like this to happen, could we still call ourselves civilized?"

"The answer lies within each of us. For those whose hearts have been ripped out by animals with no regard for life, it's an easy answer."

"And you honestly think you could get anyone to take you seriously about this?"

"Just watch me." He paused, then added, "And you want to know the best part?"

"Dare I ask," the host replied.

"The guy is going to ask to be sent to the Zoo."

"Governor McIntyre, please don't take this the wrong way, but you've lost your mind. No one would choose such an atrocity."

The governor smiled. "Depends what's in it for them."

A Frightening New Chapter

THE NATION HAD GOTTEN soft on crime, starting with the president and working down. Too many years of left-wing appointees made the Supreme Court "criminal friendly." Suddenly the bad guys were getting pardoned left and right. Then the justices went too far. They reevaluated the argument against capital punishment, declaring it unconstitutional.

But nobody realized what would happen next. A massive right-wing backlash hit like a tidal wave. People got pissed. Stories like the one about the man cutting off his girlfriend's head and hanging it from his ceiling fan, only to get "life" in prison, infuriated people. Or the woman who read her husband's texts. They must've been bad because she took a machete to him as he slept. Yep, she got life. They all got life.

With the death penalty gone, there was no harsher punishment. TV's constant coverage of one horrible murder after another was overwhelming. The final straw was when a young mom killed her baby girl, cut up the body, and scattered the pieces in the woods for the animals to eat. Life in prison wasn't good enough.

And then a governor's wife disappeared.

At first, the high and mighties in Washington said the whole thing was ridiculous. No one would even discuss the idea of introducing legislation geared toward a Criminal Zoo.

But enough people, stirred up by Governor McIntyre and his nationwide campaign, must have told their representatives that if they wanted to be reelected, they would find a way to make it happen. The first to fall was a Florida congressman. A New Jersey representative was next, closely followed by a fellow from New York. And then Capitol Hill crumbled under the onslaught.

The *Chronicle* reported that not only did the governor muster up a shit ton of support, he also mustered up a shit ton of money. He put together a hardcore legal "dream team" and hired some badass lobbyists to write up the bill. So said the news. It was all everyone was talking about for a while.

Congress finally ran out of ways to sidestep the matter and had no choice but to debate the governor's proposed bill, the *Violent Criminal Human Zoo Act.*

Everyone in Washington moaned and groaned a lot, but eventually passed the proposal. The "Confinement Center" option tipped the scales. Imagine being buried alive, but you could stand up in your coffin, and it would take years to die. That was the Confinement Center in a nutshell. But more about that later.

The president wanted a second term. He went with what the people wanted. He signed the bill. So each night we got a little Government 101 from the news. The proposed amendment went out to the states for ratification. It passed by a wide margin.

Right after that, the president went on TV and gave a big speech about it. He had a serious look on his face while speaking of being "deeply concerned" and said a "frightening new chapter" had begun for the American way of life. He prayed that the Criminal Zoo Amendment would be used with the greatest of care and that "compassion for our fellow man would not become a thing of the past."

Human rights activists went nuts. But it didn't matter. The people had spoken. They wanted the animals to pay the ultimate price.

A multibillion-dollar private company stepped in and offered to build the Zoo. They contracted out with the Department of Corrections and took the reins. Due to the huge cost of building such an elaborate facility from the ground up, the company, along with the DOC, decided the Zoo would be created at an already existing site—Florence, Colorado, home of the "Alcatraz of the Rockies."

Right in the governor's backyard. I'll bet no pockets were lined for that.

The 562-bed prison known as "Supermax," would house the Criminal Zoo. It was already home to some of the worst criminals in the world. But since they were not sentenced to the Criminal Zoo, they were shipped to other locations.

Supermax boasted state-of-the-art security and had never allowed an escape. And it was centrally located, which was a heavy consideration for visitor appeal. Less than a year later, Governor Jon McIntyre's demented baby was born and physical torture became a part of mainstream America.

Because of a man bent on revenge, and the general public's crusade to label me a serial killer, I now reside in Florence, Colorado. I am an exhibit in the Criminal Zoo.

New Friends

A S A KID GROWING up in Clemensville, when the dream of becoming an astronaut still existed, the world was simple. Why an astronaut? What boy didn't want to do that? Think about it. Space: so peaceful. So beautiful. And so far away from my dad.

Back then, things like Criminal Zoos didn't exist. The Bible existed. And everything else existed around that.

There was nowhere to go, nothing for a kid to do, and not a pretty girl in sight. At least not one who paid attention to me. And even if one did, I wouldn't have been able to do anything about it.

My dad had told me long ago that knowing a girl's body before marriage was absolutely forbidden. He informed me that the "eternal tortures of Hell" awaited anyone ignorant enough to fool around with a girl. And if his word wasn't enough, our preacher, standing in front of the congregation and slamming fisted hands against the top of the pulpit, shouted the exact same thing.

I had an older sister, Sheila. I saw her in her bra and panties once. I walked by her bedroom and the door was slightly open. I mean, I hardly even touched it. And I swear I just looked for a second. The way she screamed you would've thought I was posting naked pictures of her on the Internet. I was only like eight or nine. I was curious. That's all. She told my dad. After he was done with me, I couldn't sit down for a week.

So they're different. No penis. Got it. But no one would tell me what the big deal was. The threat of fire and brimstone seemed a little extreme. That just made me more curious. I really wanted to know what sort of wickedness girls hid between their legs. But I'd have to find out on my own. Sex Ed in the Bible Belt? You had a better chance of learning how to drive the space shuttle. Something I would never learn to do, by the way, since my dad crushed the astronaut dream long ago. After he told me, "Boy, you're too stupid to be an astronaut," I never brought it up again.

It wasn't just the way girls looked that intrigued me; I wanted to know how it all worked. Knowing they didn't have the water hose that came standard with boys, I wondered silly things like, *how did they pee?* My questions went unanswered for a long time.

After turning twenty-one, I occasionally went to a place called Texas Jack's—a bar on the northern edge of town—to try to meet girls. I wasn't really a drinker, but it made me feel grown up to hang out there. My normal routine was to grab a beer when I first walked in and sip it for the next hour or so. It didn't matter what kind of beer; they all tasted bad. I grabbed whatever was on special that night. When I was done, I'd drink a glass of water and then order another beer. I wanted to fit in.

They played good enough music at TJ's—that's what the regulars called it. I danced whenever someone would be my partner. I wasn't a very good dancer. But I kept trying because I hoped to eventually find "Mrs. Right" in there. Not that I had a damn clue what that even meant. Someone to cook me dinner every night, served with an ice-cold glass of sweet sun tea?

I'm sure if my dad had found out he would've told me how I would burn in Hell for hanging out there, but I was willing to risk it. Everyone needed some companionship. But apparently I didn't have that certain look the girls went for. It took a few years before I had a real shot at picking one up.

Her name was Starla. Her long red hair caught my attention. The lights were just bright enough to make her hair shimmer, like it was on fire, as she spun around. She wore a short denim skirt, a little pink tank top, and white cowgirl boots that barely touched the floor as she danced.

At the end of a song, she hugged her dance partner, the fourth since I took notice, and walked toward the edge of the dance floor where I stood. She caught me looking. Instead of turning away like every other girl, she smiled. I looked at my feet—cheap tennis shoes, not cowboy boots—afraid to hold her gaze.

"Hi."

I looked up and she stood before me, still smiling.

"Uh…hi," I stammered.

"What's your name, cutie pie?"

Cutie pie? I got lightheaded, even a little disoriented. "Uh… I'm…uh…I'm Samuel."

"Nice to meet you, Samuel." Her smile weakened my knees. "I'm Starla. Care to buy a drink for a thirsty girl?"

"Uh yeah, sure." This was a rare occasion where I actually had money in my pocket. I'd had a pretty good week with my landscaping business. Mowing extra lawns, clearing shrubs, and trimming trees had given me an extra hundred bucks.

We walked to the bar and grabbed two stools.

"Hey, Greg, a couple of drinks over here!" Starla shouted to the big guy behind the bar.

The bartender, wearing a black cowboy hat on top of equally black curly hair and a matching leather vest over a red T-shirt, approached us. He had a Coors Silver Bullet in hand. "Way ahead of you, baby." He smiled as he set the can in front of her and then turned his gaze to me. The smile remained. "What about you, boss?"

"Uh...yeah, sure, I'll take the same." I made a big production of pulling out a wad of money. A fifty, two twenties, two tens, a five, and three ones.

I slapped the fifty down with authority. Greg nodded and retrieved another beer from the cooler. He set the can on the bar. "Coors is the special of the night. Only seven bucks for the both." I pushed the fifty forward. "Here, keep a dollar for you."

"A dollar? Thanks," Greg replied, grabbing the bill. He shot Starla a look I didn't understand. He returned his gaze to me. "Be back with some change." He walked away.

Starla sat on the barstool next to me, put her hand on my thigh, and started talking. I could feel her touch right through my jeans. It made me nervous but I don't think it showed. Hopefully she didn't notice me sweating. Her skirt was short enough that if she moved just right I could see her white panties.

She caught me looking. I braced for the slap. She only smiled. "Let's do a shot!"

"Okay." The word escaped my lips without my consent.

"Greg, two Cuervos over here!"

Greg returned with my change. "Forty-three bucks back at ya, buddy. Except one for me!" He pulled a dollar out of the money, gave me the rest, and then spun around and shoved the buck into his tip jar on the back bar. He turned to Starla. "Two Cuervos coming up!" He grabbed a square, yellow-labeled bottle from the shelf behind him, grabbed three shot glasses, and filled them with golden liquid. He set them before me and said, "You need salad? Or you a man?"

"Salad?" I hesitated. "No, I'm a man. No salad." *What the hell was salad?*

"Those are on me. Now let's get this party started!" He grabbed one of the shots and slammed it. He shook his head, growled. "Medicine for the soul!"

Starla's hand slid up my thigh. I almost fell off the barstool.

"To new friends," she said, picking up her shot.

I picked up my shot. "Yeah, to new friends."

I was with a pretty girl. The bartender was buying us shots. I was having fun. Maybe this was when the world finally decided to give me a break.

In My Wildest Dreams

THAT SHIT BURNED ALL the way down to my guts. I almost threw it right back up.

"You okay?" Starla asked. "You look a little pale."

I nodded, momentarily unable to speak. After a moment the wave of sickness passed. "Yeah, I'm good."

"Wanna get outta here? Let's go to my place. We can drink a beer and you can tell me about yourself."

"Really?" *Is this really happening?*

She nodded, smiling the whole time. "Sure. How else can I get to know you?"

The day I had been dreaming of was finally here.

Starla grabbed my hand, and we climbed from our stools.

Greg looked over. "You guys outta here?"

"Yep," Starla answered.

"Have a great night." The bartender smiled. "See you again soon, huh?"

Starla turned toward the door. "Let's go, Romeo."

In my wildest dreams, I couldn't have imagined an encounter like this.

"I'll just jump in with you," I said, as we walked into the warm Texas night, facing the parking lot. I drove a beat-up old Subaru wagon that I had parked around the corner out of embarrassment.

"Honey, don't you know it's against the law to drink and drive?" She pulled me away from the parking lot and down the sidewalk.

I wiped sweat from my brow and took in a deep breath. I looked at our interlocked hands and then up to her.

"What?" she asked.

"Nothing."

We arrived at her house—a single-wide trailer—in only minutes, yet my heart beat as if I had just run a marathon.

"I have cold beer in the fridge. You up for one?"

"Yeah, of course."

Once inside, Starla motioned me to a faded red couch facing a small flatscreen TV on a cheap-looking stand. Worn carpet covered the floor.

A single framed picture hung on the far wood-paneled wall: a large painting of what was possibly a horse walking out of a barn. Or maybe it was a cow. Hell, for that matter it could've been a dog. "Who's the artist?"

"Me," she said, smiling. "Watercolor. It's an original. You like it?"

"Yeah, it's really good."

A small air conditioner rattled within the confines of a windowpane to my left. Despite the cooled air drifting across me, I was in a sweat. *I'm actually in a girl's house!* I was a grown man. It was time to stop fearing my dad's stories of Hell.

Starla went into the kitchenette, reached into the fridge, and returned with a couple of cans of Coors. She dropped onto the couch beside me and cracked one open. "Here you go."

"Thanks." I grabbed the beer.

"I don't see a ring," she said, looking at my left hand. "You gotta girlfriend?"

"Nah, not right now. I'm in between. Just kind of waiting for the right girl to come along." I took a big chug of beer.

A car pulled up outside. Or at least it sounded like it through her trailer door.

"You have a roommate?"

"Neighbor." Starla took a long pull of her beer and then asked, "What about me? Could I be the right girl?"

I started coughing. I fought to regain my composure. "I don't know." I shrugged real casual-like. And then I burped, and it was kind of loud. I was going to apologize, but I decided it might be more manly if I didn't. "All depends. I like to live on the wild side. You know, have a little fun now and again. Can you handle that?"

"Yeah, I can handle just about anything." She took another drink of beer. "So I guess we should get to it, huh? You didn't come over here to play Monopoly, right?"

"Monopoly? Uh, no..."

She set down her beer and dropped to the carpet, kneeling before me. She grabbed at my belt, undid it, and unzipped my jeans. All the blood rushed from my head, traveling due south.

Starla tugged at my jeans. "Stand up."

I did. On shaky legs. She pulled down my pants. My boner fought for freedom from my underwear.

"My goodness, Samuel, excited to see me?"

My legs buckled. I fell back onto the couch.

"You okay?" She looked up at me. "You got that pale look again. You get sick, you still gotta pay. You know that, right?"

"Wait...what?"

"Yeah, you've already taken up a little over an hour of my time." She stared at me, her face taking on the serious look of a businesswoman.

"I...uh...I gotta pay?"

She stared at me, her head tilted. "Yeah, you gotta pay. I'm not free."

I wiped sweat from my forehead and stood. I pulled up my jeans and stared at her, still kneeling. That's when the anger hit. More like rage. Fury from deep inside. I wanted to punch her in the head as hard as I could.

Starla must have sensed something in my look. She jumped up and walked to her front door. She opened it and motioned for someone to come in. I heard a car door open and then slam closed. Seconds later, Greg the bartender entered. "We have a problem here?"

Everything was happening too fast. "What's going on?" I asked.

"Shift change," Greg answered. "I'm off now. So I decided to come over and see how my girl's doing."

I looked at Starla, my mind reeling. "You're a hooker?"

"Hey now," Greg jumped in. "Let's not get nasty. She's an escort. And she just accompanied you for the last hour, so you have to pay, cowboy."

My whole body shook. I clenched my fists.

"Little buddy," Greg said, "it looks like you're contemplating doing something really stupid. I wouldn't, if I were you. Just empty your pockets on top of the TV."

The room felt thirty degrees hotter. I swayed a little.

"Let's go! Get out your money!" Starla demanded.

"Come on, buddy." Greg stepped closer to me.

All I wanted in the world at that exact moment was to be six inches taller and eighty pounds heavier. I would've beat Greg down. My hands shaking, I pulled out the wad of cash and set it on the TV. Greg scooped it up.

"Okay, so what do we have here?" He counted it. "A hundred and ten. Is that it?"

"It's all I got." I was sick to my stomach. That was all I had to my name.

Greg handed the money to Starla. Except for one dollar. He handed it back to me. "Here, keep a dollar for yourself."

I could barely breathe. I wanted to hurt them so bad.

"Hey, my friend," Greg said, "trying to buy sex is illegal. Starla and I both saw you do it, so it's two against one. Something to think about if you decide to go to the police. Now get the fuck outta here."

I never returned to Texas Jack's.

Honeymooning In Midland

I MET CARLA NOT TOO long after the Starla incident. Carla, Starla—I know. Maybe it's a Southern thing, because I also went to school with a Darla.

Carla was in front of me in line at Dairy Queen. She pulled money from her jean shorts pocket and a ten-dollar bill fell to the ground. It automatically drew my attention from the whiteness of her fleshy thighs. I won't lie, my first thought was, *This girl's about to pay for my lunch.* If she didn't notice the ten spot lying there, of course. I looked around; no one seemed to notice the bill on the ground, so I casually bent down to grab it. Just as I pulled it from the floor, Carla turned and looked down. Our eyes met and she gave me a funny look, like maybe she thought I was a dog in heat, sniffing her butt. And then her eyes moved to the money in my hand. I stood and pushed it in her direction. "Here. You dropped this."

She smiled. "Wow, thanks. DQ charges enough as it is. It would've been a serious bummer had it cost me ten dollars more." She grabbed the money and stuffed it back into her shorts. "Can I buy you a pop for your effort?"

"Okay. Large Coke, please." I wasn't sure if she was serious, but she'd asked.

Turns out she was serious, because next thing I knew she was placing a large Coke in my hand. We ended up eating lunch together. Sure, DQ would've been a pretty boring answer if people asked, "So where'd you guys meet?" But I didn't really have any friends to ask that, so it wasn't much of a concern.

Carla wasn't all that pretty, but she was okay. She didn't look like she'd been burned in a fire or anything. I think a lot of guys have probably done worse.

If I had my choice, I would've taken Starla's body over Carla's, but I didn't have my choice. I didn't have enough money to afford Starla's body. So I went with Carla. She was a little heavy—actually, she was pretty fat, but she seemed nice. At the end of our lunch together, I asked her out and she accepted. We saw each other for about six months and during that time she never acted psycho, never asked for money before we had sex, so we got married. Other than church and high school football, it's about all there was to do in Clemensville.

We went to a hotel in Midland for our honeymoon. Pretty exciting stuff. But it was all we could afford.

Shortly after the Midland trip, she quit her job as a cashier at the hardware store. Her friend Irene had told her about an opening at the convenience mart, with a possible management position in the near future. A little more money now, a lot more later. That's what Irene said, anyway. The store sat at the southern end of town, smack dab on 349. It was the last gas stop until Rankin. If it was after midnight, it was the last stop for a hundred miles, which was why the place stayed open all night. The graveyard shift was definitely not Carla's first choice. Irene told her it would only be temporary, and that soon the two would be working together. It never happened. At least not while I was there.

In general, Carla was all right to have around. When she wasn't complaining, we got along just fine. But then her stomach problems started not all that long after we got married. And then the sex happened less and less. Maybe I should've starting paying her. When she bitched about not feeling good, and I had needs, I did my thing with magazines in the bathroom after Carla fell asleep.

It was Carla's complaining about how I never took her anywhere that really got on my nerves. She wanted to go to exotic places, do the vacation thing. Once, she even brought up Hawaii. All I could do was laugh. Only rich people went to Hawaii. Or the Caribbean. Don't even get me started on places like Europe. To most in Clemensville, Europe was a fictional place, one that only existed in movies or books. I told Carla that. Not only were we not rich, we didn't even *know* anyone rich, so I couldn't seriously discuss a trip any further than Lubbock or Midland. Or I don't know, maybe head west all the way to Hobbs, on the New Mexico–Texas state line. I hear they have good high school basketball there. But I didn't think that would be a big draw for Carla.

Unfortunately, landscaping didn't pay any better than cashiering. And there was no "possible management position" anywhere in my future. So, whether Carla liked it or not, our destinations would be limited to really cheap places within driving distance, none of them worth being stuck in a stupid car for hours on end. Not on a dusty, desolate Texas highway baking in the middle of yet another hot summer day.

As a kid, I had done more than my share of suffering in a car. The sun blazing above, cooking to death all things within ninety-three million miles, yellow road lines blurring beneath our oven on wheels, and time melting into oblivion. *Oven on wheels*—I made that up, because it was hot enough inside to cook a cake. I thought it was clever, but I never told my dad. He didn't think anything I did or said was clever.

Whether my dad had tried really hard, or it just came naturally, he made certain I hated every single second of our road trips.

Inside the Oven

"**G**ET IN THE DAMN car!" my dad yelled. He had the same look in his eyes that he always had—pissed off. His stupid flattop haircut didn't soften his look any. He wasn't in the Marine Corps anymore, but he still played the part.

He pushed me in the back, almost knocking me down. It wouldn't have been hard to do. I was only eight. He herded me toward our two-door, teal green Toyota. Yeah, teal green. Nothing says *real man* like teal green. I lost my balance and landed on my knees, my jeans offering little padding against the gravel. I tried not to cry out, but it hurt.

He grabbed me by the back of my neck, yanked me to my feet, and then spun me around. He leaned down, moved his clean-shaven face close to mine. The scent of Old Spice soured in my nose. He squeezed my shoulder hard and said, "Boy, you better get moving before I make you sorry you were ever born!"

I fought the tears back. A show of weakness in front of my dad was like bleeding in front of a frenzied bull shark. I wondered if my grandma was watching through the window.

We had just visited her in El Campo, Texas. Actually, she wasn't *in* El Campo, but it was the closest town to her farm. Usually Mom came along, except she wasn't with us this time. She had to work at the old folks' home in Midland. I'm not sure what she did there, but it must not have been very much fun because she complained about it a lot. She told us to go and have a good time, and that she'd be waiting for us when we got back.

Dad pushed me toward the car again. I wasn't sure if he was just anxious to get home or if he was mad at me because of the accident. Like it was my fault. I couldn't control what my cousin Jeremy did or didn't do. And I sure as heck wasn't the one who left the pitchfork lying in the hay.

I knew the interior of the car was going to be unbearable as the morning grew hotter. I had no desire to get in the oven on wheels. Traveling on hot days was impossible to endure, since my dad never ran the air conditioner. "It uses up too much gas. Maybe you should quit being such a little girl like your sister and toughen up," he always said.

I looked at the car with dread. "It's going to be way too hot, Dad. Why can't I wear shorts?"

"Short pants make you look stupid, like you're a clown or something. If you want to look like a clown, go join the circus."

"But pants are too hot!"

He rapped me hard on the top of my head with his knuckles. "Did you just raise your voice to me?"

I stared at the ground, rubbed my head.

He grabbed my jaw and forced my chin up. "Boy, I asked you a question. Did you raise your voice to me?"

"No, sir."

"Really? Must have been my imagination then, huh?"

My eyes betrayed me, tears escaping down my cheeks.

"You crying?"

"No, sir." I quickly wiped my cheeks.

"Son of a bitch, you are crying, aren't you? I barely touch you and you cry like a little baby." He stared at me. "What the hell would you do if I really gave you a reason to cry?"

My heart beat rapidly. There wasn't a good answer to his question.

"Don't know?" he asked. "Let's find out." He slapped me hard across the face. "You like that? How about another one?" He struck me again. "Now you have a reason to cry."

My cheek burned like it was about to burst into flames.

"Honestly, boy, why do you make me do that? You stupid or something?"

I pulled up the bottom of my shirt and scrubbed my face, trying to remove the tears, along with the stinging skin.

My dad shook his head. "I swear, Samuel, you must be retarded. Now get in the damn car before you really make me mad."

Through blurry eyes, I looked at the car. The oven door stood open, awaiting me. I could feel the heat radiating outward. There would be no joy in this trip. Only survival.

I climbed inside the oven.

Shut Up and Listen

WE DROVE FOR MAYBE an hour before the rain hit. Heavy and angry, like God was trying to rinse us off the road. It seems to do that in the Bible Belt.

The radio had trouble delivering its music over the pounding of the raindrops. That was okay, because Dad listened to a mix between country and the golden oldies. Maybe we were listening to the "golden crappy country" station. Whatever it was, it sucked.

The windshield wipers raced across the glass like they were playing tag and neither was winning. The rain got worse and my dad smacked the steering wheel with an open palm. It looked like we were driving through a swimming pool.

"Shit! I can't see a Goddamned thing!" He slammed on the brakes. I flew headfirst into the back of his seat. Sheila screamed just before I heard her hit the dashboard. Seatbelts weren't important in my family. My head and neck started hurting immediately. We slid to the side of the road, coming to a complete stop. My dad spun around. "Goddamn it, Samuel, pay attention back there! Quit hitting my seat!" He turned back to the front. "Son of a bitch! How the hell are we going to get anywhere? I can't even see the damn road!"

Complaining of my pain wasn't an option. I should've been ready for anything. Sheila, too. My dad had taken these kinds of sudden actions our whole lives.

Sheila cried. I imagine her impact was about as jarring as mine. My father glared at her. "Don't start with me, Sheila! I swear to God, now's not the time! Stop that crying right now!"

Sheila's sobbing grew louder. Dad grabbed her by the shoulder and pushed her back into her seat. "Stop crying or get the hell out of the car!"

Sheila looked at Dad. Fear radiated from her eyes.

Right then God must have found someone else to bully on another stretch of road, because the rain suddenly let up.

"About damn time," Dad said. He faced the front, stepped on the gas pedal, and lurched back onto the highway.

We soon came to a small town. I don't remember its name, but it had a gas station that I'll never forget. A vending machine hung in the middle of the dirt and grime on the bathroom wall. I didn't know what it contained for seventy-five cents, but the pictures on the front of it—naked women with black lines drawn over their chests and crotches—gave me a funny feeling in my stomach. We always stopped at that gas station during our trips to my grandma's house. One time, I made sure I had three quarters in my pocket—stolen off my dad's dresser a few days before the trip.

The small package that dropped from the machine didn't mean much. I tore it open, examined its milky white, rubber-like content, and threw it away. I would not know what a condom was until the eighth grade, and then only because I overheard some other kids talking about it.

I stood in the bathroom a moment longer, studying the pictures of the nude women, visualizing what was underneath the black lines, and then headed back to the car. Sweat ran down my butt crack and inside my thighs.

Sheila had not yet finished her business in the bathroom. Seriously, how did that all work? My dad stood in front of the car, his phone up to his ear. "Goddamn it!" he exclaimed, and then shoved the phone into his pocket.

"Who'd you call, Dad?"

He turned, glared at me. "None of your damned business!" He paused a second and then continued, "Samuel, while it's just you and I...I know what you did back at the haystack. And so do you."

"Dad, I didn't—"

"Shut up! Shut up and listen! You will never ever talk about it. Do you understand? You will not ever say a word about it. I swear to God, if they come after me for what you did, I'm done with you. No one better blame me because you're my Goddamned kid. Jesus Christ, Samuel, he's dead! Because of you, he's fucking dead! Shit, God Almighty!"

"But Dad, I didn't—"

"Stop talking. Just listen. If anyone asks, you don't remember a thing about it. Not one damned thing. Got it?"

"Yes, sir."

Sheila came out of the bathroom, we all climbed into the car, and Dad sprayed gravel behind us as he pulled back onto the road.

We drove for another hour, without conversation, and arrived at a new town. Dad pulled over. "Stay here," he ordered. He climbed from the car, slammed the door, and pulled his phone from his pocket. He hit a button and held it to his ear.

"Who's he trying to call?" I asked.

"I think he's calling Mom," Sheila replied.

Dad pulled the phone away from his head, screamed something, and then shoved it back into his pocket. He climbed in and didn't speak a word as we shot onto the highway.

So it went the whole trip. A stop here and there, a phone call, cursing the wind. I didn't understand why he kept getting out of the car. I'd seen him talk on his phone driving all the time.

Our speed seemed to increase in relation to each call. The foul energy coming off Dad was reason enough to match his silence. Finally the faded green sign with white print declaring CLEMENSVILLE CITY LIMITS, POP. 1,497 flew by, almost unreadable.

Mom said she would be waiting for us when we got back. She lied. The note on the kitchen table proved it.

Moms Don't Lie

SHEILA WALKED INTO HER room. I followed. She moved to her bed, where a second note lay. She picked it up and started reading. I tried to grab it, she pushed my hand away. Suddenly I was struck by the notion that a note awaited me on my bed. I left Sheila's room and went to mine. I walked to the bed. Nothing. Not knocked to the floor. Not under the bed. I dropped to my hands and knees, peered under the frame. Nothing.

Sheila and I stayed in our rooms the rest of that night.

We had climbed out of the car hot, tired, and hungry. Dad hurried through the front door of our apartment. He saw the single sheet of paper immediately, snatched it off the table, and read it with shaking hands.

A moment later, his hands fell to his sides, the paper cast to the floor. His head slouched forward, his eyes closed. He stood motionless for a long time. I looked at Sheila and shrugged. She shook her head as if my shrug had asked a question and the answer was no. I was confused, not really getting it. And then a look of rage shot across Dad's face. He roared, slammed his fists into the front of the refrigerator, and then down onto the kitchen table. The floor shook from the blow. He picked up the table and threw it sideways. It slammed into the cabinets, dislodging two table legs.

That's when we headed for the bedrooms.

It took a little while to sink in. *Mom's gone.* What I knew instantly was that Dad was to be avoided at all costs. We could hear him throwing and smashing things. We heard several loud crashes and glass breaking. I think back to it now, and wonder why the neighbors didn't call the police. But then I remember the neighbors were afraid of my dad. A couple of brief altercations with him had been enough to ensure that.

Despite my stomach grumbling, it was not safe to leave the bedroom. Not for a while, anyway.

Later that night, after Dad went to his room, I snuck into the kitchen. Sheila must have fallen asleep in her room, but I was so hungry I felt sick. I had to eat something, even if it was just peanut butter and a few crackers. And that's exactly what I ate, as quietly as I could.

After my snack, I walked into the living room. The ugly blue drapes usually covering the glass slider were open. A courtyard light shined through. Torn-up books littered the floor and the TV lay next to its overturned stand in front of the couch. The picture screen of the TV was shattered and pieces of glass shared worn carpet space with shredded pages of my dad's King James Bible. Framed pictures, busted up like the TV, were everywhere. The bookshelf my dad built in the living room—one-inch-thick by ten-inch-wide wood planks spanning upright cinderblocks against the wall—were mostly barren. He had spray-painted the wood white and the cinderblocks blue, staring at it after he was finished like he had just crafted something pretty cool. He built it as a place to keep his war books. The bookshelf didn't match anything else in the house, but then again, neither did any one piece of furniture.

The war books looked like they had just been through a war.

I sifted through the stuff, careful not to cut my fingers on glass, and found the contents of the only photo album our family possessed. I picked up the pages and looked at each. If you didn't know any better, looking at the pictures you would almost think we were a normal family. Generic snapshots were stuck in the album pages—pictures of this holiday or that one, a birthday here and there, a trip once in a while. Nothing really stood out. Well, maybe one did, I guess. It was a picture of Sheila and me on a hotel balcony in San Diego, Mom standing behind us, her arms around us. We all smiled, like we were actually happy.

Dad had just returned from active duty with the Marines. Came back from maybe Iraq? Or maybe it was Afghanistan. Or hell, it could've been Alaska for all I cared. Mom had driven us out, but I was too small to remember much of it.

In the photograph, Mom wore a flower-print summer dress. She was pretty, for a mom. She had curly brown hair, brown eyes, and she had the softest skin I've ever felt. She always smelled like she had just climbed out of the shower, clean like Irish Spring soap.

Mom's gone.

Why would she leave us alone with Dad? And why didn't I get a note? Dad got one. Sheila got one. But I didn't get shit. I asked Sheila what hers said. She told me it was none of my business.

And then I understood. Mom wrote me a note, but forgot to leave it out. It was probably in her pocket right now. Wherever she was, she was about to find it and realize she forgot to leave it. And then she'd feel so bad, she'd come home to give it to me.

Tears ran down my cheeks. Even though my dad wasn't watching, I wiped them away quickly. I studied the picture. Like my mom, Sheila wore a flowery dress. I wore swim trunks and a T-shirt with a picture of a shark on the front. I liked sharks. My brown hair was messy from swimming in the hotel pool. I don't remember much, but I remember having fun that day. Dad hadn't gotten there yet.

I pulled the picture from the album page, returned the page to the mess, and tiptoed back to my bedroom. I stuck the picture under my pillow, pulled the covers over my head, and fought hard for sleep. It took a long time.

The next morning I jumped out of bed, thinking that maybe things weren't as bad as they seemed the night before. Dad always made things seem worse than they really were. I was sure Mom was home, smiling, my note in hand. She wouldn't leave us—not for good. Moms just didn't do things like that.

I headed into the living room. Sheila was cleaning up and putting everything away. My dad sat in a chair in the corner of the room, silently watching. I stood motionless, waiting for Mom to step into view. But Dad's look said it all. Mom wasn't coming back. And I wasn't getting a note. Tears ran down my cheeks as I hurried back to my room.

Mom had promised she would be there waiting for us when we got back from Grandma's. But she lied. Why would she do that? Moms don't lie. At least they're not supposed to.

After a full morning spent under my bed sheets looking at the San Diego picture, hunger overwhelmed sorrow. I knew it wasn't advisable to be anywhere near my dad, but I couldn't take the emptiness in my stomach anymore. Once again, I slid the picture under my pillow and ventured from my room and into the kitchen. As I passed through the living room, I chanced a glance at Dad. He hadn't moved from the chair. He looked at me; his eyes told me today would be a good day to stay outside.

Later that night, with the door to Dad's room shut, I stood in the empty living room and looked around. Other than a couple of holes in the walls and no TV, it looked pretty normal. Sheila did a good job of cleaning up and putting everything back where it belonged. The only thing she didn't return to its proper place was the photo album; the shelf where it once sat remained empty.

We never saw the album again.

Landing on a Pitchfork

SPENT A LOT OF my time in my room after my mom left. Dad was too dangerous to be around. Sheila obviously didn't want to be there either. She was always gone, out with her friends.

One day, while I was sitting on my floor, mostly just trying to hide from life behind my stand-up dresser, my dad came in. I was just sitting there, not doing anything, because to do anything would've taken more energy than I was willing to exert.

Dad walked in and sat on the bed, facing me. He stared at me for several long, uncomfortable seconds, saying nothing. Just staring. I tried to maintain eye contact, but it was too hard. I looked at him, at the floor, back to him, back to the floor. Finally he spoke.

"Samuel, life's hard. It's not meant to be fair. It's not meant to be fun. It's meant to be hard. It's cold. It's uncaring. Unforgiving. Life doesn't give a shit whether or not it runs over you like a semi. In a nutshell, life is about survival. About making it out of one bullshit day and into the next."

He stopped, stared some more. I had no idea what to say. I looked at him, at the floor, at him.

He continued. "Your mom left because she didn't care about you. She didn't care about me. She didn't care about Sheila. She didn't care about anyone or anything but herself. But that's life. That's what I'm saying. Life doesn't care." He exhaled loudly. I wasn't sure where he was going with this, but I was cornered. I had no choice but to hear him out. He added, "And life is about death. But you have firsthand experience with that, now, don't you?"

Okay, I knew where he was going with it.

"What you did is already tearing the family apart. Your grandma, your aunts and uncles, your cousins, they all want you to pay for your sins. But you're eight. So there really isn't anything anyone can do. So they think they're somehow going to come after me. But guess what? That's not happening. I'm not going to have any liability for what you did." He shook his head. "This whole thing went down as an accident. But we both know it wasn't. There's something wrong with you, boy. I see it in your eyes. But I don't know exactly what it is. I can't put my finger on it. Bottom line, you're broken inside.

"So here's what we're going to do. We're going to move past all this bullshit that's happened. Your mom is gone. And you're not going to be seeing your grandma again any time soon. So you just sit there on the floor and do nothing. It's probably the only thing you're good at. Stay in your room and stay out of my way. Got it?"

I stared, hatred for him welling in my heart.

"Boy, I asked you a question. You get what I'm saying?"

"Yes, sir."

He stood, stared at me a second, and then walked out. Not one more word.

After he left, closing the door behind him, I thought about not seeing my grandma anymore.

I liked going to Grandma's. No matter what time we got there, she had a bowl of golden hominy warmed and ready for me. I was probably the only kid on the planet who liked hominy. She had Velveeta cheese for Sheila.

Grandma was the only person in the world who made any effort to comfort me. One night, as a young boy lying on a bed of blankets on the living room floor, when I feared the dark—actually, I still fear the dark—Grandma kneeled beside me. It was just me and her. Everyone else had gone to bed. Sheila got a bed, because she was a girl. I got the floor.

"I'm scared, Grandma," I said.

"Of what, honey?"

"Of the dark."

"Listen," she said. "Just listen."

I did for a few seconds, not saying anything. She stared down at me, also quiet. After a moment, I said, "Grandma, all I hear are the crickets."

"Exactly," she answered. "And that's how you know you're safe. If something bad is out there, the crickets will be silent."

She was right. From that moment on, when I heard crickets chirping, I knew nothing bad was out there.

The crickets were silent in the Confinement Center. And they are still silent in the Criminal Zoo.

GRANDMA'S HOUSE HAD TO be seen to be appreciated. Grandpa built it out of rock, mud, and wood from the surrounding area. The roof of the house looked like it was made mostly out of tar paper. Inside was a low ceiling with exposed light bulbs. There was no means of moving air—hot or cold—and it was far longer than it was wide. Grandpa added a new room, lengthening the house, each time another child was born. After nine kids, the place looked more like a broken-down train with its wheels buried in the earth than anything else.

Those in the house, until just recently, relied on ditch water for everything from taking baths to irrigating alfalfa. A plastic container filled with already-boiled water sat in the refrigerator.

If we came in thirsty from playing outside and the container was empty, a refreshing drink was at the far end of a boiling and cooling cycle.

Supposedly, the last room of the house—unoccupied since Aunt Rachel died after getting bucked off her horse—was haunted. That's what my older cousins said, and they swore they weren't making it up. I never slept back there to find out.

Grandpa died when I was still pretty young; I could never remember the name of the disease, but I guess after he got sick, he suffered a lot. I didn't really know him very well, except I remember him being mean. I also remember he had a really scary German Shepherd named Max. He bit me when I was pretty little. Hence my reasons for not wanting a Brutus later in life.

During the days, there were always things to do with my cousins, who lived just down the dirt road. We played in the fields, explored the hills, and chased tadpoles, blue gill, perch, water snakes, and frogs in Grandpa's pond. I have no idea why everyone called it that. Maybe Grandpa dug it, or paid good money for it, or just told everyone it was his.

I hung out the most with my cousin Jeremy, who was closest to me in age. He always seemed to do everything better than me. We spent a lot of time climbing on the haystack in the barn. It had to be at least twenty feet high. The grownups would come out and yell at us to get off. We would climb down, they'd go back into the house, and then we'd climb right back on. That haystack was better than any playground toy ever built.

Then, during an otherwise normal trip to Grandma's, Jeremy fell off the haystack and landed on a pitchfork. He should have been paying more attention to what he was doing, instead of screwing off and laughing at me.

As he fell past me, I swear he did it in slow motion, screaming, his eyes wide, his mouth in the classic O shape. I smiled. I don't know—the moment just seemed perfect.

None of the family members who came to the hospital would sit by me in the waiting room. Not even my grandma. They all just glared, like I'd meant to wiggle the hay bale Jeremy was standing on. I was climbing. It was loose. He stood above me, on the edge, making fun of how slow I was.

But did anyone ask who left the Goddamn pitchfork lying in the hay? No. Not one person asked that.

After a long wait, the doctor came in and gave us the news. "One of the tines penetrated Jeremy's aorta." I didn't even know what an aorta was, but apparently if it gets penetrated, it's bad. "I'm sorry, but he had already lost too much blood by the time he got here. We couldn't save him."

Aunt Ellen, Jeremy's mom, starting screaming. Loud. Everyone ran to her, huddled around her, crying. Everyone but me, my dad, and Sheila. We all just sort of stood there, watching. Well, I was watching. And then I turned to Sheila and my dad. They were staring at me.

"What?" I asked, looking at Sheila.

My dad's look turned hateful. "Shut up, Samuel. Just shut up."

The doctor approached the huddled mass and said, "I'm so sorry for your loss." He gave them a look of deep compassion and then turned and left the room.

I looked at my dad. His look drove my eyes into the floor.

Whoever left that stupid pitchfork lying in the hay really screwed everything up.

A Treat For Brutus

IN THE GOVERNOR'S CRIMINAL ZOO, there were no lawns to mow. No leaves to rake. No hedges to trim. No sprinklers to move. Zoo exhibits had far more important things to worry about. Like surviving another day of torture at the hands of the real animals—the ones bent on hurting you.

I often think back to the days spent in the hot west Texas sunshine, sweating my ass off doing things I once thought were bullshit chores. I used to complain. I wouldn't anymore.

"SON OF A BITCH!"

I slammed down the lever controlling the lawnmower's throttle and the engine shut off. I had just taken another rock to the shin and it hurt like hell. I stared at the garage sale mower for maybe a second before I kicked it. Even with tennis shoes on, that hurt almost as much as getting hit by the damn rock.

I pulled off my work gloves, my fingers hot and sticky, and wiped sweat—along with grass and dirt—from my forehead. My T-shirt was covered with the same. I surveyed the yard. For as much as I watered, it sure wasn't very green. I think I mowed more dirt than grass. I dropped the gloves on top of the lawnmower and went into the house. It was just too damn hot; I would finish the yard later.

Carla was still in bed. That's where she always was when there was work to be done. In bed with that damn beast of a dog sleeping next to her like it was his job. I swear Brutus was every bit as lazy as Carla.

An ice-cold glass of tea—yeah, that's what I needed. I went to the cupboard, grabbed a glass, and slammed the door closed. If it woke Carla and the stupid mutt, good. It was almost three in the afternoon. Just because she worked the graveyard shift didn't mean she needed to sleep all day. I moved to the fridge, filled my glass with tea, and sat at the kitchen table. My mind drifted back to our kitchen table in the apartment. After Mom left, it only had two legs. A victim of Dad's rampage. He propped the legless end up on cinder blocks. Yeah, it looked as stupid as it sounds.

The tea was good, refreshing, unlike the interior of the house. The shitty little window-mount air conditioner wasn't doing a very good job of keeping up with the heat. How could Carla sleep? Even with her little fan on the bedside table, it had to be uncomfortable. And that dog—big, hairy, and smelly—lying next to her? Gross.

I thought about Brutus for a moment, thought how nice it would be to have him gone. I told Carla we didn't need a stupid dog. I told her I could protect her. My thoughts were never too far from finding a way out of the Brutus era. Besides, why should Carla get what she wanted? I never got anything I wanted. Not a Goddamned thing.

Suddenly a pretty cool idea hit me. I rose from my chair and walked to the cupboard where Carla kept the dog biscuits. Brutus knew where his treats were kept. I opened the cabinet door, allowing the creaky hinges to declare my intentions. Brutus came bounding in a few seconds later. He shook his head, flapping his ears back and forth as if it accomplished something more important than sending his flea-infested hair in every direction. Then he stared at me.

"What, you want something?" I stared back.

Brutus tilted his head and gave me a look that I interpreted as saying, "I hear you talking, but I'm barely smart enough to know how to breathe." He wagged his bushy tail, his tongue hanging out of his mouth. Saliva dripped onto the linoleum.

I reached into the cabinet and grabbed a treat for Brutus. I waved a Milk-Bone biscuit in front of him. "Mmmm, sure looks good, huh? I'll bet you'd like this, wouldn't you?"

Brutus barked a deep, baritone bark.

"No barking!" I dropped the box to the counter and grabbed the dog by his big fat snout, holding his mouth closed. "Be a good boy and you can have a treat."

I let go of Brutus, returned the box to the cupboard, and closed the cabinet door. With treat in hand, I walked to the door that opened into the garage. Brutus padded after me. I closed the door behind us. With Brutus at my side, I crossed the cement floor and approached a wooden shelf fastened to the far wall at about chest height. I sat the treat on the shelf, next to a bright yellow jug of antifreeze. I couldn't help but smile as I grabbed the jug, felt its weight, and unscrewed the top. Supposedly dogs were drawn to the scent of antifreeze. It did smell kind of good.

Brutus sat down next to me, tilted his head again.

"I've got a treat for you, boy. And you get to wash it down with a little Prestone punch." I grabbed a plastic bucket from the floor and dropped the dog biscuit into it. Brutus barked again.

"Goddamn it, dog! Shut up!" I swung at the mutt, but he moved his head.

He stared at the bucket, unfazed by my attempt to hit him. I pushed the bucket toward the dog and filled it with a couple inches of antifreeze. The dog biscuit floated to the top. Brutus stepped up to the bucket, licking his chops. He lowered his head and his snout disappeared into the bucket.

"Say goodnight, boy."

"What the hell's Brutus barking at?" Carla's voice swept into the garage.

I spun around. Brutus's head popped up and he turned to the sound. Carla stood there, wearing only panties and a T-shirt. Her milky white thighs, as fleshy as they had ever been, fought one another for space.

"What's in the bucket?" she asked.

"Huh?" I couldn't think fast enough to come up with anything better.

"I'll say it a little slower so you can follow along. What's… in…the…bucket?"

"Oh, I accidentally dropped it. Brutus was just checking it out." I grabbed the dog before he could turn his attention back to the biscuit. "Get out of here, mutt. I've got work to do." I pushed him away.

"Work? Yeah, right, like you'd know anything about work." She laughed.

"Hey, I do a lot of work around here. As a matter of fact, I've got to finish the lawn right after I finish my glass of ice tea."

"Uh-huh, whatever," she said. She looked down to the dog. "Come on, boy. Come back to bed with Mama."

Brutus wagged his tail. She held the door open for him and together they disappeared into the house.

I grabbed the dog biscuit from the bucket, set it on the shelf, and poured the antifreeze back into the jug. "Maybe next time, huh, Brutus?"

I returned to the kitchen table and my glass of ice tea.

A Little Bit About the Devil

SPENT MOST OF MY hot summer days as a kid splashing around in a crowded swimming pool. We lived in an apartment complex called Jefferson Manor. I looked up the word *manor* once. Apparently whoever named our building never bothered to do the same. Our "manor" came with peeling paint, water-stained ceilings, and cracked windowpanes. The complex was made up of two stories built in the shape of a squared-off horseshoe surrounding a courtyard of year-round brown grass. The courtyard wrapped around the heart of the complex: the fenced-in pool. The place would've looked rundown even from space.

The pool was the place to be during the unbearable summer months. It was hardly ever cleaned, but we didn't mind swimming around decaying leaves and floating bugs. Things like centipedes, millipedes, and roaches drifted past once in a while, but they were always dead. It was the yellow jackets you had to watch out for. A lot of times, they were still alive, sitting on top of the water. The coolest thing I ever found in that pool was a hairy black tarantula about the size of my fist. They would occasionally crawl in from the fields bordering town. It was dead and floating against the edge of the pool in one of the far corners. I wanted to keep it, but I knew my dad would just yell at me and throw it away. So I examined it a few more seconds and then splashed it out of the pool.

A faded sign fastened to the chain-link fence around the pool area warned us that there was no lifeguard on duty, so we swam at our own risk. For me, it wasn't so much the swimming that presented a risk; it was the running on wet pavement.

While running around the pool one afternoon, my feet slid out from under me. I fell backward and hit my head. The next thing I remember was being in the emergency room. My throbbing head rested on a pillow. A doctor leaned over me, looking into my eyes. I tried to sit up but it made me sick so I lay back down.

"Take it easy, Samuel," the doctor said. "You have a pretty serious cut on the back of your head. I stitched it up nice and tight, so it should heal just fine. But I also suspect you've suffered a bit of a concussion." The doctor turned to my dad, who gave me with a hard look. "I'm sure he's going to be okay, but we should scan his head and see if there's any serious injury to his brain. Just to be on the safe side."

"Scan his head? With what?"

"CT machine. That way we can make sure there's nothing too serious."

"Is it expensive?"

"Yes," the doctor began, "of course there's a bit of cost associated with it. Scan and reading, you're looking at about fifteen hundred."

"Dollars? Who's going to pay for that?"

"It would be your responsibility, but it would be a good idea. You have insurance, right?"

"No."

The doctor stared at my dad a moment, then said, "Let's not worry about the scan right now. But we should keep him overnight for observation. Just for the night. To be safe."

"You said he'd be okay." My dad held the doctor's stare.

"Right. And I also said he's probably got a concussion. You have to be careful with head injuries."

"If he'll be okay here, he'll be just as okay at home."

I didn't feel okay at all. My head felt like it was going to crack open.

"Mr. Bradbury, you need to appreciate something," the doctor said. "Sometimes with head trauma, small bleeds can occur in the brain, resulting in cerebral tissue damage. If he's not here, the damage could be extensive. Maybe even life-threatening."

My dad was quiet a moment. "Well, if that happens, I'll just bring him right on back."

"He really should stay here. One night."

"You really that concerned about him, Doc?"

"Of course I'm concerned about him."

"Then you'll pick up the tab for his little sleepover?"

"No. Just like the scan, the cost of the stay would be your responsibility."

"Oh, I see. You're only concerned *if* I give you money."

"Mr. Bradbury, I don't get any money if he stays here. The hospital—"

"Samuel, get up. We're leaving."

Despite the doctor's protests, I climbed from the examining table, my head feeling as if a rusty ax were wedged into it. We went home and I was sent straight to bed. My head hurt all that night, the next day, and for a few days afterward.

The part that really sucked about that whole thing was the doctor telling me I couldn't swim while my scalp was stitched together. So during that time I mostly stayed in my room and looked at the picture of my mom, wondering where she was, wondering how she could have left us. And how she left notes for my dad and Sheila, but not me. That still bothered me. Really a lot. I wanted to find her, to hurt her like she had hurt me. I wanted to let her know how bad Dad had become, and that it was all her fault.

A whole week went by before the doctor finally pulled out the stitches. That stung big time, brought tears to my eyes, but I had them wiped clean before my dad saw.

Later that day, after looking at the picture for the thousandth time, I went swimming. Afterward, I pushed water from my face and hair and moved to the sidewalk surrounding the courtyard. I sat on the cement, knees pulled to my chest. The warmth rising off the sidewalk soothed my drying body. I looked straight up and the sun forced my eyes closed. The next thing I knew I was lying on the ground, holding my head, wondering what had just fallen from sky. I opened my eyes and a shadow blocked the sun.

"Samuel, you need to come on back to the apartment." My dad stood over me, outlined by the blinding sunlight. He grabbed me by the shoulder, yanked me up, and pushed me forward. My head felt like it was about to come apart, just like it had the first time. I gritted my teeth and walked. Each step sent an excruciating shockwave through my brain. He led me to the apartment and shoved me all the way to my bedroom. He closed the door behind us and pulled a crumpled-up photograph from his pocket. "What's this?"

I stared at it. *How did he find it?*

"You stole this from the photo album, didn't you?"

I couldn't think fast enough.

He grabbed me by the shoulders and shoved me backward into the wall. My head bounced off its flat surface. The pain that erupted through my skull buckled my knees.

"Goddamn it, boy, answer me!" He lifted me back into a standing position and shook me. "You stole this, didn't you?"

No answer on Earth was going to save me from his blows.

"That piece of shit bitch left us behind because she didn't care about us, remember? We've already had this talk. She dumped us like unwanted trash and you save her picture? You try to hide it from me under your pillow? Do you think I'm stupid?"

His question left me without an answer.

"Samuel, do you wish I was the one who left?"

"No, Dad."

"You know, boy, I bust my ass for you Goddamn kids. I really do. And this is how you thank me? You disrespect me by stealing a picture of the whore that left me and keep it under your pillow like it's some kind of a treasure? Help me understand, because I'm struggling with this one. I really am."

He waited for an answer. I had none. His hand raised into the air. I knew where it was headed. I dropped to my knees, my arms covering my head.

Each strike seemed harder than the last one. I couldn't help it, I threw up. He jumped back.

"What the hell! Have you lost your mind, boy? You know you're going to have to clean that shit up, don't you?"

I wiped my mouth, splinted my pounding head between my hands, and nodded. Dad stood over me a moment longer. He tore up the picture and dropped the ragged pieces on me. "This is trash, just like your mom! And if you want to be with her, you're trash, too!" He shook his head and sighed. "You ever seen the Devil, boy?"

"Yes, sir."

My dad pulled me to my feet. Leaned in close. "Oh yeah? Well then, tell me…what's he look like?"

A father who was once in the Marine Corps. "He's red, has a mustache, a pointed beard, and horns." The words hurt my head, made me want to throw up again. But I knew better; I held it back.

"No, dumb shit, not the stupid Halloween costume. I mean the real one. Let me tell you a little bit about the Devil. He's got razor-sharp teeth, hooves for feet, clawed hands, twisted goat horns, and a forked tongue like a snake's. His breath is rotten, like decaying flesh. Maggots squirming between his teeth and everything."

I fought the nausea.

"He knows your worst nightmares, boy, and he can make them happen."

"He can?"

"Damn right he can. Hell is right under your feet. He walks on a floor made of charred human skin. When he wants to come up, he does it by clawing through the floor under the beds of kids who don't mind their parents."

Many nights after that, I lay in my bed—covers pulled over my head, eyes shut tightly—listening for the slightest sound of claws ripping through the floor.

"And you know what he eats?" my dad asked.

"No."

"Children, Samuel. He eats children. Pulls their arms and legs clean off their bodies and eats them just like you'd eat a chicken leg. That's why there's always maggots in his mouth, eating the leftover meat."

Bile rose in my throat. I willed it back down.

"He eats kids because they don't mind their parents, Samuel. Whether they don't go to bed when told to, or whether they touch things they shouldn't touch—say, pictures that don't belong to them." He tilted his head and suddenly became quiet, like his thoughts had just turned down a new street. "Or if they touch themselves, for that matter." He paused a moment, looked hard at me, and then asked, "Boy, you don't touch yourself, do you? Like some little homo faggot. Not in *my* house, right?"

"No!" A lightning bolt of pain blasted through my brain.

He stared at me a moment longer. "Good. Anyway, some children deserve to be punished. So if you think I'm a hardass, think again. I wouldn't want to be you if *he* comes calling. Now, what do you think? You think maybe you better start minding me?"

"Yes, sir." My head pounded harder and harder. I became dizzy, needing to sit down immediately. I slid into a squatting position, my back resting against the wall.

He stared at me, probably trying to decide whether to hit me for slinking to the floor. I looked up, defenseless. He grinned. "Maybe from now on, when I tell you to do something, or to *not* do something, you'll listen. Otherwise, Mr. Satan's coming to dinner. And you're on the menu. Now, get on into the bathroom, get yourself cleaned up, and then clean up this mess. It stinks to high heaven in here. And Samuel," he looked at me, "when I check back later, there better not be a trace of puke anywhere. Got it?"

"Yes, sir."

He nodded like we had an understanding and left the room. My head felt like it was going to explode. I barely made it to the bathroom before getting sick all over again. Afterward, I staggered back to my room and collapsed onto my bed. I'd clean up the mess. I just needed to rest for a second.

I stared at the ceiling, my hands bracing my throbbing head. Tears made a mess of my cheeks. *One day, Dad, it'll be my turn*, I thought. *I'll be the one hurting you.*

Serving Up a Lesson

N MY DREAMS I can still hear Carla's damn dog barking. It was an explosive, deep-from-within bark. Almost rattled the windows. How many times did Brutus wake me before I was finally forced to take real action?

THE BARKING SHATTERED MY sleep like a crowbar meeting a windshield. I opened my eyes, looked at the clock on the bedside stand—barely five in the morning. *Are you kidding me?* The sky wasn't even lit yet. I dragged Carla's pillow over my head. She wasn't using it; she was still at work. Maybe I needed a lead-lined pillow or something, because the noise wasn't drowned out.

"Shut up, stupid mutt!" I threw the pillow against the wall, wiped sleep from my eyes, and climbed from the bed.

I moved to my dresser, pulled open the drawer second from the top, and grabbed a T-shirt. The front of the shirt displayed a large T. rex skull with DALLAS MUSEUM OF NATURAL HISTORY printed underneath. It was my favorite shirt. I put it on, stretched, and then grabbed a pair of Walmart's finest khaki shorts—clearance, $12.97—from the floor and pulled them over yesterday's tighty-whities.

The barking continued. I slid my feet into my slippers and went in search of Brutus. The infuriating noise led me to the kitchen. I turned on the lights, illuminating the beast. He stood on his hind legs, his front paws braced against the back door, his snout pressed against the glass of the window. He barked like he had information of the utmost importance to relay to me.

"What? You think you're fucking Lassie or something? Has little Eddie fallen into the well? Shut up, you fucking mutt!"

He turned, whimpered, and then looked back out the window. I walked to the door, stood next to him, and looked into the backyard. It was still too dark to see anything, but that didn't seem to bother Brutus. He barked again and again.

"Goddamn it, Brutus! I said shut up!" I kicked him in his backside.

And that's when that damn thing turned and nipped at me. I don't know if I caught him by surprise, or if he was finally showing his true colors, but I wasn't going to stand for that shit. Not in my house. Time to serve up a lesson. And what better for that than an iron frying pan?

I grabbed the pan from the stove and returned my attention to the dog. He had already forgotten about me and had resumed his barking, probably a rabbit hopping across the yard. If Carla had been there, though, she would've been positive it was whoever left the skeleton in the sinkhole.

Brutus paid me no attention. That was his mistake. I swung the heavy skillet down as hard as I could. It crashed into the top of Brutus's head, made a cool cracking sound, and cut off his bark in midstream. The dog dropped like his off switch had just been flipped.

I stood next him, frying pan hanging at my side. "Not so tough now, are you, Brutus?"

Not even a whimper came from the mutt. But was he just knocked out? I debated on how to proceed. *Stupid Carla. This is your fault. You wanted a dog, so you got a dog.* I've wanted a lot of things. But I never got a fucking thing. Not once. Not ever. My whole life could be summed up in three words: "Didn't get shit."

I raised the pan over my head and swung down hard a second time. I stared at the lifeless dog a moment and then concluded the Brutus chapter could now be put in the history books.

There was only a small amount of blood on the frying pan. I rinsed it off and placed the pan in the cabinet under the stove, where it belonged. It irritated me how I was the only one who ever put things back in their proper spot. I was always cleaning up after Carla. And you think she ever said "thank you"? Yeah, right.

I kneeled next to Brutus, trying to decide what to do with him. I couldn't just leave him lying there. I didn't have time to bury him in the backyard. And Carla had the car, so I couldn't take him to the dump.

An idea suddenly came to me. I hoisted Brutus into the air— he was a lot heavier than I thought he would be—and threw him over my shoulders. I was breathing hard before I even got out of the front door.

I walked about a block from the house, my furry kill growing heavier by the step. I probably looked like an Old West trapper who accidentally walked too far, all the way into the present. Then I dropped the dog in the middle of the street. I think I damn near had a heart attack from the exertion.

Carla would come home soon and more than likely be the one to find Brutus. Possibly even run him over. Oh man, that would be classic. Think of the guilt. I could use that against her for years.

I had my story ready. I let Brutus out to pee and he took off like a rocket, leaping the small, broken-down backyard fence, obviously in hot pursuit of a wild rabbit. That was totally believable because both Carla and I had seen him do it. I went after him but couldn't catch him. After losing him, I decided to head back and wait for him to return. Why else would I be up so early? And as the carcass in the street would prove, the poor dog should've looked both ways.

I noticed a few drops of blood on my shorts, but thankfully nothing on my T-shirt. I would've been really mad if that dog had ruined my shirt. It did have a ton of stupid dog hair all over it, but Carla showed me a pretty cool trick once, wrapping masking tape around her fingers—sticky side out—and patting down her hideous brown polyester pants covered in Brutus hair. The tape worked. The hair was gone. If only the tape could've had the same luck removing the ugly from the pants.

After returning to the house, I pulled off my shorts and rinsed them in the bathroom sink. I threw on a clean pair, dropped the dirty shorts into the laundry basket, and headed into the kitchen. I moved to the coffee maker, made a pot, and sat at the kitchen table. Nothing started the day quite like a delicious cup of black coffee.

My White Nightmare

THERE WAS NO COFFEE in the Confinement Center. No iced tea. There was no TV. No radio. No phone. No computer or e-device. No books, magazines. No pen, paper. Nothing whatsoever to write with, or on. There was no clock. No sound. No smell. There were no people. No talking. No singing. No shouting. No whispering. No laughing. But there was crying. My crying. A lot of tears shared with nobody.

Four bright white windowless walls surrounded me. They were padded. An equally padded door blended into one wall. A tiny camera lens, the size of a nickel, watched from inches above the door. They watched me cry. But they didn't care. Did they laugh? Did they point at me and call me a baby, just like my dad used to?

My universe was probably four or five feet wide by maybe eight to ten feet long. But felt smaller. A lot smaller. It was a coffin you could stand in. The ceiling was also white. And maybe a foot over my head. Way too low, like the room was closing in on me. Had a very suffocating effect, like being buried alive.

The floor was white and soft, like the walls. The whole floor slanted slightly downward to a small hole cut into one corner. They had called it an "evacuation port." I called it a shithole. Apparently it emptied into a chemical toilet, so I was supposed to shit and piss in it. But sometimes, in protest, I took a shit wherever I wanted. Only problem, when I did that, a nozzle popped out of the ceiling and sprayed down the entire room with a sanitizing liquid. It wasn't hot. It wasn't cold. It was exactly room temperature. It would spray over and over until either the shit was rinsed down the hole or I physically pushed it into the opening.

The room was bathed in white light. It never turned off. It didn't flicker, dim, or brighten. It was constant. White. Only white. Absolute, unrelenting white. I read in a magazine once of a condition skiers call being snow blind. Apparently the total white obliterates all perception of depth and details. That's what happened in the Confinement Center rooms. They called them Total Sensory Deprivation rooms, or TSD rooms. And they were right.

Even the air had no feeling to it. Not hot. Not cold. Just there. Nothing in the TSD room ever changed. Each second, each minute, each hour, was the same. No day, no night. Nothing. Time didn't just stand still, it didn't exist at all.

Sleep was not easy to come by. No bed. No covers or clothes. The feel of fabric against the skin was only a memory. The last time I had clothes on was right before they stripped me and threw me into my living coffin.

Sometimes I screamed as loud as I could just to hear the sound of my own voice. I slapped my hand flat against the wall as hard as I could just to feel the sting of my flesh. Those were the only sources of stimuli. I closed my eyes, opened them, closed them, opened them so I could experience the contrast of light to dark to light again. Anything to make something different, even if only for a split second.

If I banged my head against the door or walls out of boredom, or a desire to hurt myself, I could accomplish nothing. I tried— dozens, maybe hundreds of times. Barely even got a headache.

Food was served without any set schedule. Sometimes it felt like twenty-four hours between servings. Sometimes ten. Sometimes a hundred. A small slat rose at the bottom of the door. Probably only three inches high. A food bar was pushed in. Not by a hand, but by a mechanical lever that retracted. I had no idea what the food bar was made of. I can only imagine it was comparable to NASA food. Like the shit they ate in the space station. Shit that I one day dreamed of eating, back when I believed good things could actually happen. Like a boy from Clemensville could grow up and become an astronaut.

The food bar was around five inches long, three inches wide, and an inch thick. It had the consistency of any snack bar. It didn't taste bad. It didn't taste good. It didn't taste, period.

A cup of water followed the bar. You had perhaps half an hour to drink the water. I'm guessing. The cup was made out of dissolvable shit, like the stuff coating a pill you take for allergies or something. If you didn't drink the water fast enough, it puddled on the floor.

The room and the food did its job. No stimulation whatsoever. Total sensory deprivation. The only thing that provided any contrast at all in my white nightmare was a bright red button set in the far wall. It was at chest level and about as big as the top of a pop can. It glowed out of the white like a beacon.

I would sit and stare at that button. I knew the rules. Push it and I was out. Gone from the Confinement Center forever. Push it and see human beings again. Push it and hear voices again. Push it and see darkness again. Push it and feel again. See, hear, smell, touch, taste—all the sensations I had been deprived of for who knew how long. Oh, how I would've liked to feel again. Anything. One simple push of the button.

They wanted me to push it. And they said we all eventually did. Fuck them. I wasn't pushing it. I knew what lay in wait on the other side.

Kitty Bowling

WHEN I WAS A kid, back in the apartments, I always wanted a cool pet. Not a dog, but a cool one: like maybe a Komodo dragon or a bald eagle; something that would really make me stand out. Something that would make all the other kids jealous. But it didn't happen. Sheila and I did have a kitten once, but not for very long.

Perhaps it had been a stray, or maybe someone knew that kids lived in our apartment and was looking to give it a good home. For whatever reason, the kitten just showed up one morning on our front doorstep.

My dad must have thought if we had a pet we wouldn't bother him, because he totally surprised us by letting us keep it. The thing was all gray, except for four white feet, so of course Socks was the only fitting name. Sheila fell in love with the kitten immediately; she carried him everywhere she went. I wanted to carry him around too, but she would never let me. She never let me do anything. She got to play with Socks. I got to watch.

But when she wasn't around, then I got to play. I made up a game that I called "sock face." I'd pull one of my socks over his head and laugh until my stomach hurt while he ran into walls and furniture as he tried to get away. You would think the stupid animal would spend a little more time trying to pull the sock off instead of running around like a retard. But then the game wouldn't have been near as much fun.

And then one day my dad walked into my room, holding Socks. Actually petting the creature like he cared. "Samuel," he said. "Have you ever kitty bowled?"

I sat on my bed, alarms going off in my head. My dad knew what I had done and hadn't done. Was this a trap? A trick question? Usually when I had the wrong answer to his questions, I got hit. But today, something was different. My dad smiled. That never happened. I stared at him, at the kitten cradled in his arms. "No. What's kitty bowling?"

"It's a game I used to play with my cat when I was a kid," he answered. "Come out to the hall and I'll show you."

I was confused. If he wanted to hit me, he didn't have to come up with such an elaborate scheme to get me into the hallway. Usually, when he wanted to hit me, he just hit me. Leery, I followed him.

"Okay, here's how you play," Dad said. "First, you grip the cat real solid around the neck. And then you wind up and bowl it down the hallway as hard as you can."

With that, my father went into a windup that any bowler would be proud of. I watched in fascination as my dad stepped into his swing and launched Socks end over end with tremendous force. The cat tumbled head over tail all the way down the hall, smacking the wall at the other end.

"Bingo!" my dad yelled. He shot me a look. "Get the cat!" And then he laughed. It suddenly occurred to me that I'd never heard him laugh before.

I sprinted down the hall, grabbing Socks before he got his bearings. I scooped him up and brought him back to my dad. My dad looked at me. He was grinning. He was actually no-bullshit

kidding-around grinning! I smiled. So this was what it was like
when a father and son had a normal bonding moment.

"Okay, Samuel, your turn." He nodded. "The object of the
game is to get the cat all the way to the far wall. I wanna hear it
hit with some authority!"

My dad watched. I was actually nervous. I wanted to show
him I could do it. Holding Socks tightly around the neck, I
stepped into my throw and released the cat with all my might.
But it wasn't enough. Socks dug his claws into the carpet about
halfway down and came to a stop.

"Come on, Samuel, you gotta give it more than that! You
throw like a little girl! Get the Goddamned cat and do it again!"
My dad's smile disappeared. My heart raced. I knew the game
was about to turn dangerous.

I tried again. And then again. No matter how hard I threw
that cat, I never did get him to the other end. My dad stared at me
with a look of disgust. Our moment was over.

"You really are worthless," he said, shaking his head. I
braced for the hit I was sure to follow. But he simply turned and
walked away.

I was furious at that stupid cat. It had just ruined my chance
to bond with my father. I held him behind his neck and threw
him so hard it hurt my shoulder. But the damned cat still didn't
make it to the wall.

Socks must have been pretty dizzy from all the tumbling,
because after he got himself stopped, he attempted to run away,
falling over in the process. I would've laughed at him if I wasn't
so mad.

I tried several days in a row to bowl Socks all the way to the
wall. He always stopped himself before he hit it and then tried
running away. Usually I was on top of him before he got far. On
occasion, he managed to escape the hallway. I moved to the next

game: "lion hunter." The apartment was too small for him to disappear for long.

Socks got really mad, even more than usual, during a round of kitty bowling one afternoon. I threw him hard, making it closer to the other end of the hall than ever before—probably missed it by less than a foot. He dug his claws into the carpet, came to a stop, shook his head, and then stumbled away. I tracked him through the deepest, darkest regions of the apartment—looked a lot like Africa in my mind—and cornered him under Sheila's bed. I dropped to the floor, flat on my stomach, and reached for him. For no reason at all, he bit me. He had bitten me plenty of times before, but this time it really hurt. I pulled my hand back, saw blood.

It was time to teach Socks a thing or two about respect. I jumped to my feet, ran to the closet, and grabbed a wire clothes hanger. We had lots of them. They were used to hang clothes almost as much as they were used to beat us. I left the hooked end untouched and straightened the rest. I went back to the bed, returned to the floor, and pushed the hanger toward the cat. He hissed fiercely, which definitely made the game more fun. It took me several tries, but I finally snagged Socks by his collar and dragged him toward me. He put up a great fight, sometimes clawing at the carpet and other times flopping like a trophy largemouth bass. I was proud of his effort.

Once I had him clear of the bed, I grabbed Socks behind the neck and lifted him into the air. I pushed myself up from the floor and moved into a seated position, with my back against the bed. I rotated the kitty so that he faced me and I held him by the scruff of his neck. His ears laid flat; his lips were pulled back, baring his fangs. He hissed at me. It actually was kind of a scary hiss.

"That's the spirit, little kitty. Heart of the lion and eye of the tiger."

Sheila had told me one time if you dropped a cat, it would always land on its feet. She wouldn't have told me that if she hadn't wanted me to test it. So I climbed to my feet and lifted Socks over my head. I swung him upside down and let go. The cat did a neat little flip and sure enough, landed on his feet. I quickly pounced on him, pinned him against the floor, and patted him on the head. "Not bad, kitty. You passed the test."

He hissed again.

Time to make the test a little harder.

I scooped up the cat, closed the bedroom door, and then moved to Sheila's bed. I climbed onto the bed, stood tall, and turned around, facing away from the bed. Once again, I raised the cat above my head. This time, I didn't just let him drop; I wanted to give him a little more challenge. I threw him pretty hard to the floor. I couldn't tell whether he landed on his feet or not because everything happened so fast. Socks let out a goofy-sounding shriek when he hit, and then he literally bounced. He came to rest in a crumpled heap, quivering.

I wasn't completely pleased with the results of the test because I couldn't tell what part of Socks hit first. So I repeated it. I threw him down really hard. It wasn't as hard as I could—I wanted to give him a fair chance—but it was pretty darn hard. I watched closely and I can say with complete confidence he did *not* land on his feet. He landed squarely on his back. So much for Sheila's little saying.

And then Socks became still. I grabbed him from the floor and shook him. His legs swung limply and his head flopped side to side. And then nothing; he just hung from my hand. *Sorry, Sheila, looks like you don't get to play with Socks anymore.* I stuffed him under my shirt and left the bedroom.

Dad sat in his chair in the living room and stared at whatever program was on TV, a TV much smaller than the one we had before Mom left. He paid no attention as I passed. Sheila was still outside, so I headed to the end of the complex that opened up to the parking lot. I dropped the cat in an empty parking space.

The next day I went back to where I had left him. He was flattened into the pavement. Must have been a pickup truck.

A Pretty Cool Idea

WITH SOCKS GONE, I had to find other ways to stay entertained. Exploring the local alleys and kicking over garbage cans was always fun. One summer afternoon, I wandered into an alley not far from our apartment complex and gave several trash cans extra hard kicks. I had some anger issues that day.

Everybody else was at the pool, but I didn't want to go swimming, even though it was like a thousand degrees outside, and almost as hot in our stupid apartment. I had been swimming the day before and I slipped on the wet cement again. I hadn't hit my head that time, but it hurt every bit as bad in a whole new way. One leg shot into the water and the other slid along the cement, smashing my nuts against the edge of the pool. I suppose the scream was probably girlish, but it just slipped out. My dad stomped over and jerked me out of the water. "Samuel, are you stupid or something?"

All the other kids, and even some of the grownups, had laughed. Tears filled my eyes, but I was done letting my dad make me cry. I clenched my teeth, grabbed my towel, and left. I walked to the apartment—it took me a while because every step made me want to throw up—and into my bedroom. I climbed onto my bed, curled into a ball, and cried.

So despite the heat, I wasn't going to swim with those assholes ever again. The sound of their laughter still bounced around in my head. Instead, I took out my frustrations on the trash cans.

I approached another one, executed a wicked karate kick, and sent the can flying. A flash of yellow and black shooting out from under the can caught my eye. Something slithered toward the pile of trash now littering the ground. *Awesome! A snake!* I stepped on it, not hard enough to kill it, but hard enough to pin it. It struck at my tennis shoe, but that didn't do much. *Now for something to put it in.* An empty plastic trash bag lay in the trash heap. The snake hissed as I grabbed it behind its head and lifted my foot. I held the reptile in the air and examined it. A bull snake. Not all that big, maybe two, two and a half feet long, but big enough to keep for a while. Maybe hide it in my bedroom. I dropped it into the sack and twisted the top closed.

I walked down the alley a little further, happy with my catch. That's when a pretty cool idea came me. Why hide it in my bedroom when it could be put to better use? The snake writhed inside the sack, searching for a way out. My grin grew even bigger.

I tied the top of the sack closed and ran back to the apartment complex, my balls barely even hurting. I stashed the snake under the bottom step of an outside stairwell, then went to our apartment, threw on my swimsuit, grabbed a towel, and returned to the stairwell. I laid the towel on the ground and put the sack on top. I opened the bag, dumped the snake into the center of the towel, and quickly balled it up.

The pool was really crowded. Sheila played in the shallow end while my dad sat on a lawn chair next to a blond girl sunbathing in a tiny yellow bikini.

"Careful, Dad, horrors of hell," I mumbled.

No one paid attention as I strolled to the pool's edge. Yeah, it was crowded, but not so crowded a bull snake couldn't take a swim. Everyone was busy swimming, splashing, and screwing around. I climbed in and pulled the towel next to the water.

As if it already knew the plan, the snake shot out of the towel and into the pool. It darted across the top of the water like a torpedo in search of a battleship. I turned away, pretending not to notice.

Things got good in a hurry. People started screaming and trying to get away. It was really funny to watch everyone running through the water, pushing each other out of the way and jumping from the pool like Jaws had just been spotted.

A young boy was knocked down. The kid had always looked a little weird to me, like God made him with a messed-up face, putting his ears too low and making his eyes almost Chinese. And he talked funny, too.

I saw the boy go under. I watched as his little hand reached up, barely breaking the water's surface—his pruned fingers searching for anyone, anything to grab hold of, only to be knocked back under by another panicked body. I wondered how long the kid could hold his breath.

His hand came up again and for a second I thought about grabbing it. But then the memory of everyone laughing at me came back. He might have been one of them.

The boy wasn't breathing when the ambulance got there. Everyone gathered in a circle and watched as one man pushed on his chest while another blew into his mouth. They tried to make him breathe, but he didn't. He just lay there. His mom was on her knees beside him, just screaming and blubbering, carrying on like an idiot. A lot like my Aunt Ellen when the doctor told her about Jeremy. But if the kid's mom had really cared that much, why hadn't she been keeping a closer eye on him? I think moms are all show. Nothing real.

Everyone was talking about a snake in the pool, and they really got mad when it was drained the next day. Had I known they were going to empty it, I probably wouldn't have put the stupid snake in there. If my dad had ever found out I was the cause of all the trouble, he probably would have killed me. But he didn't find out and life went on. Just not for the funny-looking kid.

Slowly Being Erased

THE DEAD BOY IN the swimming pool seemed like a lifetime ago. Since then, the world had grown only meaner. Harsher. Even more unbearable.

Silence roared through my head, sliced through my mind like a meat cleaver. The saying "the deafening sound of silence" had taken on a whole new meaning.

My universe was absent of all noise. I existed in a horrifyingly unnatural quiet. I had for a long time. And then there was the white light. All the fucking time, that white light! No break from it. Ever. White light and nothingness—that was my entire world.

It didn't take long to realize that my sanity would soon become a casualty in the Total Sensory Deprivation room.

I kept closing and opening my eyes. Over and over. I counted each time I closed them, each time I opened them. I counted each time I breathed in, each time I breathed out. In the silence, I could hear my heart beat. I counted that too. I counted to create something out of nothing. To occupy my mind. Counted forward. Counted backward. Started in the middle. Again and again. But it never occupied my mind. I jumped up and down, listening to my feet hit the soft floor. A noise. Slight, soft, but something. I jumped until I was exhausted. Until I could barely stand. Sweat poured off me. And then the sanitizing spray rinsed me. But at least the water felt like something. Almost. Something more than nothing.

I screamed until my throat hurt. I screamed until my voice failed me. I screamed for no reason. I screamed for every reason. I screamed to make sure I still existed. To make sure I could create a change in the universe, no matter how small. I pushed against my skin. It was real. I took up space. I was real. I hadn't disappeared. Not yet.

Sleep didn't happen anymore. It was more like I just passed out once in a while. It wasn't peaceful, restful. It was filled with anxiety and despair. I was going crazy, second by fucking painful second. No sound! No smell! No feeling! I needed to feel something. Anything.

I became obsessed with existing. I launched myself into the walls. The slight sound of my body slamming against the walls gave proof I was still real. I did it again. Harder. And again. And again. And again. Each time harder. In some bizarre way, this was almost comforting. Not quite, but almost. Hearing my body hit the wall, the floor. Knowing I was real.

But to exist, you had to feel. Feel something, even if it was pain. Something was better than nothing.

I looked at the red button.

"Push the button and we'll be here in seconds," they told me just before closing the door and making me invisible to the universe. "Only two ways out. Push the button or die."

They told me there was no medical attention here. If I had a heart attack or massive stroke, it basically took care of the problem: no more me. If I chose to starve myself to death, no worries. Problem solved.

They watched me. They were ready to come get me. Push the button and I would see people. I would hear voices. I would feel their grasp on me. Their touch. And the nothing would go away. But on the other side of the button was the Criminal Zoo. Physical torture—day in, day out. Being the object of other people's pain. People intent on hurting me because they themselves hurt. Because misery loves company and if they hurt, so should I.

But at least in the Zoo, they had told me, there were doctors. Medical attention.

"Serve your time in the Confinement Center," the governor had proposed during yet another talk show. "If you're good there until you die, so be it. But if you can't take the solitude, the loneliness, you have a choice. Choose the Zoo. Make it one year in the Criminal Zoo and you are released into a traditional maximum-security prison. But you cannot be set free. Never. You gave up the right to freedom when you became a killer."

That was the chain of progression. Sentenced to the Confinement Center. Stay there and die, slowly and in madness, or push the red button: next stop, the Zoo. Survive one year in the Zoo, tortured daily, and graduate to a "lifer" in maximum-security prison.

I was told that Zoo exhibits who actually ran the gauntlet and made it through the Zoo and into the prison system were revered by the other inmates. Treated like heroes, real badasses, because they were tough enough to survive the Zoo.

The degree of torture, both physical and psychological, was staggering. How sick was the governor to push someone into getting physically tortured day after day, their only goal for survival being to walk tall in a maximum-security prison for the rest of their lives? The depth of his callousness was immeasurable. And the death penalty was cruel and unusual? You gotta be fucking kidding me. How in the hell did the governor get an entire nation to buy into this insanity?

Push the button, Sam.

"No!" I screamed.

Make the nothing go away.

"I don't want to be tortured!"

You're already there.

I screamed. Screamed until I passed out.

Almost Normal

F THERE WAS A highlight to my life, it was between the ages of maybe ten and fifteen. That's when my buddy Terry Anderson was around. We did just about everything together.

We met right after my dad moved us for the third time, ending up in Terry's neighborhood on the edge of town. He lived two houses down from ours. The neighborhood was generally pretty quiet and shared a border with infinity. At least that's the way the desolate field next to our property appeared to me as a child. It started at our street and ended where land turned into sky.

While unpacking the car, I noticed the boy standing in his driveway beneath a basketball hoop, a ball tucked under his arm. He watched me for a few moments, threw the ball into his yard, and walked over.

"Need some help?" he asked.

"Sure." I nodded.

"I'm Terry."

"Hey."

"What's your name?" Terry asked.

"I'm Samuel. Samuel Bradbury."

"Hi, Sam."

I stopped what I was doing and looked Terry in the eyes. "I don't mind if you call me Sam, but if my dad's around, you better call me Samuel. He gets pretty mad when people don't. He says if he'd wanted a boy named 'Sam,' he wouldn't have put the 'u-e-l' on the end."

Terry held my stare for a moment, probably deciding if I was yanking his chain. When I said nothing else, he replied, "That's really stupid."

"I know, but it's important to him. It's a name out of the Old Testament."

"So who was he?"

"Samuel? I guess he was a prophet or something."

"Yeah, whatever." Terry shrugged and stepped toward the car. He was skinny, a little taller than me, and had pale, freckled skin. The direct sunlight made his hair look like a miniature version of the burning bush. "Want some help?"

"You bet."

He reached into the trunk, and after a brief struggle pulled out a cardboard box. "Holy cow, what you got in here, rocks?"

"That's either the box with pots and pans, or all the stupid books about wars that my dad reads. I think it's the books."

"Hmmm. Feels like rocks."

From that day on, we hung out. He was the only real friend I ever had. With Terry around, it was like life was almost normal.

About the only thing I accomplished without him was to compete in my church's Scripture Challenge. Actually, it was about the only thing I ever accomplished, period.

My dad used to wake me up every weekday morning at five. He made sure Sheila and I were seated in church by six for Bible studies. Afterward, he picked us up, made us breakfast—either burned toast or cold lumpy oatmeal—and sent us to school.

Terry used to tease me, saying, "I know you had to get up at five this morning, but it could've been worse."

"Really? How?"

"It could've been *me* getting up at five!" He finished the line with a laugh. He was the only one laughing.

My attitude about learning the Bible changed one morning when my dad said, "Samuel, no matter how hard you study, you'll never know more about God than me. You want to know why?"

"Why?"

"Because you're too stupid. And to think I named you after the prophet. You don't even know who he was, do you?"

Didn't my dad just say Samuel was a prophet? What else was there to know? I said nothing.

"Yeah, that's what I thought." My dad wasn't one to let things go. "Maybe you should actually read about your namesake. Maybe then you'd appreciate the gift I tried to give you. But you won't, will you? You won't because you're lazy. Lazy and stupid. Everything the prophet Samuel wasn't. Boy, did I call that one wrong."

After I finished my schoolwork each day, I went to work on the word of God. I would know the Bible better than my dad, our preacher, or anyone else. I would prove it was my dad who was the stupid one.

Each year, our church held a competition called the Scripture Challenge. Apparently it was a pretty big deal. Participants were given clues to certain Bible verses, and the first one to find the verse won the point. After several rounds, the points were tallied. The one with the most points won.

An old lady named Edna Johnson was the defending champion. She walked around like she was a heavyweight prizefighter. It was time to take Edna down. But I wasn't after the awards. I couldn't give a shit about a brand-new personalized Bible and an engraved plaque hanging on the wall in the church hallway. I was after something much bigger, much more important. I was after the satisfaction that would come from proving my dad wrong. And him knowing he was wrong.

The day of the contest, the questions were asked, clues given, and verses found. Edna was good, but not good enough. When the Bibles were closed for the last time and the dust settled, there was a new champion. I beat Edna, and I knew more about the scriptures than my dad. I didn't necessarily believe them, but by God I knew them!

What I hadn't taken into account was how Dad would respond. He didn't like finding out he was the stupid one. He came into my room the night after the Scripture Challenge and sat on the end of my bed.

"Sit here next to me, Samuel," he said, patting the bed.

I obeyed.

"God doesn't take any shit. You know why?"

I had no idea where the question was going. And I certainly knew better than to try to force a stupid answer. Stupid answers got you hit. So I shrugged.

"No? Well, I'll tell you. Because God doesn't take any shit. He'll turn you into a pillar of salt if you cross Him. And you know what? That's the way it should be."

I stared at the floor, uneasy about the direction of this one-sided conversation.

"That's why I don't take any shit, either. Especially from you stupid kids. Because I don't have to. In your world, I'm God. I'm the punisher. You know that, right?"

"Yes, sir."

"Damn right you do. I'll smack your asses so hard you won't sit down for a week. And now that you're thinking you're pretty smart and all, thinking you know the Bible more than me, I'm sure you know all about how God told Abraham to kill his own kid."

I nodded again.

"But do you know why?"

Of course I knew why. God was testing Abraham's faith. But I also knew my dad would have his own answer. I shrugged.

"Because He had to put Abraham in his place. Let him know who the boss was. So Abraham raised a knife over his boy's chest and was about to stab it right into his heart because God told him to. But then God told him not to. Once again, He did it because He could."

My dad paused for effect. I said nothing.

"You better hope God doesn't tell me to take you out, boy, because I won't give Him time to change His mind." He laughed.

I had no idea what was funny.

"So the moral to this little story is...you don't mess with God and you sure as hell don't mess with me. You think you're all smart because you won some stupid church contest. It doesn't mean a damned thing. Not in this house. You know that, right?"

"Yes, sir."

"That's good. Because I'd hate to think you might get a little cocky, thinking you're special or something. Just like God does, I'd put you in your place. And I can guarantee you wouldn't like it. Do you understand?"

"Yes, sir."

"Good. That's good. It would be wise for you never to forget this conversation."

I never did. I also never forgot that when he least expected it, I planned on putting him in his place. Permanently.

Uncle Henry

WHEN I WAS A kid, I had a really cool pocketknife. It was an Uncle Henry: Five inches of badass, lethal stainless steel. Hard plastic handle molded to look like polished wood. I carried it with me everywhere I went and used it any chance I got.

My Uncle Henry came in handy when I was hanging out with my boyhood friend, Terry. Following him around, I always seemed to have reason to pull out my knife.

"NICE SHOT, TERRY." I nodded my approval of my buddy's marksmanship.

I moved toward the flopping gopher. Gut shot. But still very much alive. Terry followed me to the animal. He smiled like he was about to open a Christmas present.

"You got your Uncle Henry?" he asked.

"Of course. Always."

I pulled the knife from my pocket and snapped it open. Its beautiful polished silver blade glistened under the Texas sun.

I had found the Uncle Henry back when we lived in the apartments. I had gone to see if a kid named Garrett could play; I guess you could call him a buddy of mine at the time, even though he was kind of a geek. But he lived in the unit next to ours and he always wanted to play when I was bored. Garrett's dad let me in and went in search of his dorky son. While I waited, I saw the knife—folded up all nice and safe—lying on an end table by the couch. I grabbed it, turned it over in my hands, felt its weight and admired its fine craftsmanship. And then I dropped it into my pocket. I didn't do it because I was a thief; it just kind of seemed like the thing to do. The weight of the knife was comforting, like it belonged there.

Garrett entered the living room, followed by his father. I was a little nervous when his father walked right to me. He stood over me, next to the table, which was now missing an Uncle Henry.

"Hey," he said.

My pulse quickened, my face flushed, and I turned my eyes downward.

"After you guys are done playing, let's go down to the Sonic and grab a Coke," he said. "My treat."

I loved the Sonic. "That sounds real good, Mr. Johnson," I said.

Garrett's father nodded in approval. "All right, then, it's settled. Cokes are on me."

I smiled. I didn't have many good days, but that one was shaping up pretty well. I nodded and said, "Cool!" Then Garrett and I headed for the door. On the way out, I patted my pocket and felt the knife's bulk. But it wasn't just any old knife; it was a genuine Uncle Henry. And it was all mine.

TERRY HAD SEEN THE gopher sitting at the edge of his hole, before I did. "Look," he'd said, pointing.

I followed his finger and saw the creature; he sat there like he didn't have a concern in the world. From maybe fifty feet away, Terry calmly and smoothly pumped air into his rifle, took aim, and squeezed the trigger. One second the gopher was standing tall, king of his world, and the next he was on his side, kicking and clawing at the dirt.

"Slit his throat," Terry said, grinning. "Let's watch his blood squirt out."

That's what intrigued me so much about Terry. He was this skinny little redheaded kid, didn't look even the least bit threatening, but he had the heart of a hitman.

I kneeled down to the creature and grabbed the fur behind its head.

"I hope it bites you," Terry said. "Give me something to laugh about."

"How about you laugh about me stabbing you in the stomach?"

He would've probably laughed had I done it, too.

I pulled the animal's head back, its eyes bulged and its lips pulled away from some teeth that could definitely cause harm. I put the blade against its throat.

"Do it!" Terry shouted.

I put pressure on the blade and slid it along the softness of the gopher's throat. A thought struck me as the metal sliced through fur. *Wouldn't it be cool if I were actually opening my dad's throat?* Blood sprayed onto my hands. The creature kicked violently for several seconds, then went limp. I held it in the air, gazing at its now lifeless body.

"Holy crap, Samuel, that was awesome!"

"Oh man, did you see the blood shoot out of its neck?" I looked at my hand, now bright red. I turned back to the gopher, felt in my gut the power that came with ending its life, and then the moment passed. I dropped it into its hole. "Go on home to mommy, little gopher. I'm sure she's got supper ready."

"Oh, man, you are cold-blooded, Sam. I love it!"

I looked at the blood on the knife. I started to wipe it on my pants. I almost did it, too. But at the last second a vision hit me: my dad squeezing me by the back of my neck. In my vision, he held me in one hand and in the other he held my jeans with gopher blood on them. "Boy, you think jeans grow on trees?" he would ask.

"No, sir," I would answer.

"Then why ruin a perfectly good pair of pants?" He wouldn't wait for an answer. Instead, shaking his head, he would crack me hard across the face. And then he'd say, "Samuel, why do you make me do things like that?"

I looked at the blood on the knife and again pictured it being my dad's. *Maybe someday, Dad.* I squatted and wiped the blade in the dirt. *When you least expect it.*

Playing with a Little Risk

WHEN TERRY AND I weren't curbing the gopher population, we were playing basketball in his driveway. The chances of either of us becoming NBA legends with our pictures on trading cards—or even benchwarmers without cards—were not very good. By the sixth grade, Terry and I were barely five feet tall. And, as if our lack of height wasn't bad enough, Terry also had asthma. I didn't know much about asthma, other than what he told me about his attacks. "It's like you need air real bad, but you're trying to breathe through a clogged straw."

I asked my dad about it one time. He said Terry was just being a little girl—that it was all in his head, and a sign of mental weakness.

Despite being vertically challenged and mentally weak, Terry played ball okay. We played one-on-one, lightning, and horse all summer long. We made sure Terry's mom kept a supply of popsicles in the freezer. I would've asked my dad to contribute to the cause, but I didn't feel like being told that popsicles don't grow on trees.

Terry's inhaler was always in his pocket, ready for a quick blast if necessary. He let me try it once. It tasted like medicine-flavored shit.

We always seemed to come up with ways to make our games interesting. Initially, it was as innocent as the loser having to go inside and grab the next round of popsicles. After a while, though, we needed higher stakes, more risk. That ultimately led to Terry running to the far end of the block, touching the fire hydrant on the street corner, and running all the way back, wearing only white Fruit of the Loom underwear and black Chuck Taylors. He had his inhaler in hand, trying to pump while he ran. It was pretty damn funny, until the two older boys who lived in the corner house came tearing out of the front door, yelling, "We're going to kick your ass, faggot!"

Terry screamed like he was being chased by rabid dogs. Suddenly, it wasn't funny anymore; it was downright hilarious. Until I realized he was leading the boys back to me. We ran into Terry's house, locked the door, and decided TV would be a better idea.

The games grew way more competitive, way more intense, whenever the girl from across the street walked by. Angie was a year older than us, making her all of thirteen. She was really pretty and already had boobs. She had long brown hair, eyes that matched, and her butt filled her jean cutoffs perfectly. When she was around, it was showtime.

One day she didn't just walk by; she stopped and asked if she could play. After Terry and I got over our shock, we said, "Sure!"

We played the first game for fun. Afterward, we explained how we usually played. She agreed that playing with a little risk would make things more exciting. So the second game started with the loser getting the popsicles. But Angie said that was boring. It didn't take long for things to get a whole lot more interesting. We played a game where, if Angie was the first person out, she had to lift up her shirt. If one of us went out first, the loser had to pull down his shorts.

I could've kicked Terry in the balls after that game. We moved to the side of the house, where he stood red-faced, displaying his underwear, because he couldn't make his stupid E shot. Like I really wanted to see him standing there with his shorts around his ankles. I hoped he was embarrassed by the yellow stain in the front of his skivvies.

We played again and things went way better; Angie lost. That same tingling I used to get in the pit of my stomach, staring at the vending machine pictures in the gas station bathroom, hit me when I pictured what was going to happen next.

"I lost," Angie said. "Better pay up."

"Yeah, time to pay up," I said, my heart beating rapidly and my voice squeaking.

"Not here," she replied. "Somewhere so nobody can see."

We went into Terry's backyard. I was almost dizzy with excitement. A tree house sat in the middle of a large cottonwood occupying the far corner of the yard. The tree house had a sturdy floor—trapdoor entry, four walls, a pitched roof, and a window overlooking the yard. Terry had decorated its interior with a poster displaying three bikini-clad women, all bent over a red Corvette. The tree house's only furniture consisted of two fold-up lawn chairs.

Inside the tree house, Angie held up her shirt and I stared at her bra. I had seen one before, but it was my sister's and it was a training bra crumpled up in the laundry basket. Sure, I touched Sheila's bra, even sniffed it—just wondered if boobs smelled—but it didn't do much for me. I had never seen one *in use*, though. Angie's bra, and the stretch of the fabric, fascinated me. But not nearly as much as what lay beneath.

"You want me to take it off?"

My knees weakened and warmth rushed to my groin; I hoped my trembling didn't show. I looked at Terry. He stared at Angie with wide eyes.

"Uh, yeah," I said, trying to conceal my excitement.

"Yeah, I'll bet!" She laughed. "Sorry, gotta earn it!" She pulled down her shirt, lifted the trap door, and was the first out of the tree house. "Come on, let's play again."

Never before had I concentrated so hard on making every single shot. In the end, we found ourselves back in the tree house staring at Angie, this time with her bare chest exposed. My heart raced. Terry had his inhaler so far into his mouth I thought he was going to choke on it. Angie's magnificently curved breasts, the dark rings around her nipples, the way they popped out, it was almost overwhelming.

"Can I…uh, can I…touch them?" I wanted to feel her breasts more than I wanted to take my next breath.

"Maybe later. I got to get home now."

The words landed on me like a cement wall. I had never been so close to actually touching a girl—a *real* girl. And not just touching her, but touching her in a forbidden place. Sure, I'd touched Sheila a couple of times, but she had been asleep. And she was my sister, so of course it didn't count.

Both Terry and I insisted that Angie play again tomorrow. She finally agreed and then left us to our imaginations.

Tree House Adventures

After a night of anticipation that could be compared only to the night before Christmas, the three of us resumed play. Out of nerves, Terry and I missed a lot of shots during the game. Yet somehow Angie went out first.

Once again in the tree house, she lifted her shirt, but didn't stop there. She pulled it all the way off. She smiled, unfastened her bra, and dropped it to the floor. I stared. Terry took a big hit off his inhaler and muttered, "Holy cow."

My eyes were locked onto Angie's exposed chest, and God Himself wouldn't have been able to turn me away.

"Wanna touch them?" she asked.

"Uh, yeah, sure. I guess so." *Act like it's no big deal.*

"Go ahead," she said.

I reached for her tits, my heart racing and my hands shaking. Terry did the same. She giggled as three twelve-year-old hands explored her flesh. A fourth hand tightly grasped an inhaler. Her skin was warm, incredibly soft, wonderfully smooth, unlike anything I'd ever felt before. I pushed against her boob and squeezed it like a water balloon.

"Don't grab so hard," she said.

My penis throbbed painfully inside my shorts. I needed to reposition things. I reached down with one hand—trying to divert attention from my movement by clearing my throat—and nudged myself a little to the left.

"What are you doing?" Angie asked.

My cheeks became really hot, like they were on fire. "Uh, I uh…"

She looked down at my crotch. "Something wrong?"

"No, it's just that, uh…"

She looked up. "Your turn, guys. Show me yours."

"R-really?" *Was this actually happening? Did the summer day just grow impossibly hotter?*

"Yeah, really."

I paused a moment. She might be joking. She stared at me, not laughing.

"Okay, I, uh—yeah, I guess, if you really want us to." I steadied my hands, reached for my shorts, and fumbled with the button. After what seemed like hours, I finally got the button undone and the zipper down. And then I froze. I could go no further.

"Don't stop, Sam." She turned to Terry. "Come on, Terry, you too. Don't be a scaredy cat."

Terry turned the same color of red I must have been. "We shouldn't be—"

"You guys are being chickens!" she cut him off.

"No, it's just that my mom might come out."

"Whatever. Quit being a baby!" She reached down and unsnapped his button.

The walls of the tree house briefly wavered like we had just passed into a parallel dimension, one where really cool stuff happened. I was sweating, and it wasn't just because of the heat. Angie must have decided we were moving too slowly; she stepped toward me and yanked down my shorts. If I had been lying on my back, my underwear would've looked like a miniature tent, the tent pole straight as a ruler. I was horrified.

"Ha! Look at you! That's funny!" She laughed.

My face burned. Why was she laughing at me? And then she moved to Terry, doing the same thing to him. His anatomy mirrored mine and his expression confirmed that he shared my terror.

"Let me see your dicks."

I stared at her, my whole body shaking. The sound of Terry's inhaler going off hit me from the right. *Was that three shots in less than a second?* And then, as if someone else controlled my body, my hands slid my underwear to the floor. My penis popped to attention like a little sailor saluting Angie. Terry's did the same.

"Wow!" She grabbed us by our dicks and tugged. That single squeeze felt better than anything I had ever experienced in my life.

She released her grip, unbuttoned her shorts, and pulled them off without hesitation. I stared at her shiny pink panties, wondering if a kid my age ever died of a heart attack. She looped her thumbs underneath her panties and slid them down about an inch. "Want me to take my panties off?"

I couldn't even speak. Apparently, neither could Terry.

"Or did you wanna play another game of basketball?" She tilted her head, waiting for our response.

"I…I want to see," I answered.

She smiled and then slid her panties down her legs.

"Suck me sideways," I uttered in disbelief. Before yesterday, I hadn't even seen boobs. Today, I was staring at a completely naked girl. She kicked off her underwear and stepped to one of the lawn chairs. I decided right then and there that the naked female body in motion was the most glorious sight I would ever behold. She sat on the front edge of the chair and leaned back. She spread her legs. My knees buckled and I barely caught myself before hitting the floor.

"Hey, Sam, you okay?"

"Yeah, sure," I stammered. "The heat just got to me, that's all." I stared at the small mound of dark hair between her legs. My mouth went dry. I couldn't even swallow. My heart pounded hard and fast against my chest. I turned to Terry; his eyes were wide and his mouth was wrapped around his inhaler. He double pumped, and then hit it two more times for good measure.

"Come here." Angie beckoned me with a finger.

Terry looked like a scared little boy. "If my mom catches us, she'll—"

"Shut up about your mom! She won't catch us!" Angie snapped. "Get over here, Sam."

I stepped forward on rubbery legs, ready to buckle again. I was hot, dizzy, and fighting to maintain consciousness.

She leaned toward me, grabbed my penis, and guided me to where her legs met. "Put it in."

I put a hand on each armrest, bracing myself so I wouldn't crash to the floor, and placed my penis against her. She grabbed me around my hips and pulled. I pushed forward and entered her. Though her warmth covered only a few inches of my flesh, it sent an indescribable blast of heat throughout my entire body. I felt as if maybe I was about to melt, like everything I was made of flooded into my penis. Something was happening and it scared me and excited me all at once.

"Oh my gosh, Angie! Oh my gosh!"

She shoved me backward; I stumbled and landed on my butt. I watched in horror as milky white stuff spurted out of my penis, spraying along the inside of my leg. Every square inch of my body exploded in pleasure.

"Holy shit!" Terry shouted. "What's happening?"

I had learned earlier that year what a condom was. *You wear it during sex*, I had overheard a boy telling his buddy on the school playground. I figured it had something to do with not getting your penis dirty. Today I learned its purpose.

Angie started laughing. "Relax, dummies, it's just cum."

I stared at her, my mouth hanging open.

"It happens whenever you have sex. It makes babies. My mom already had *the talk* with me. But if it happens in me, then I'm the one having the baby. And *that* ain't happening!"

"That felt awesome!" I exclaimed, after recovering from my shock.

"That's why people have sex, stupid," Angie said.

Terry stared at her, right between her legs. "Can I…"

"What about Mommy?"

Terry shook his head. "She's probably watching TV."

"Come here, scaredy cat. But if you feel something happening, you gotta tell me."

He pumped his inhaler a couple of times—I wondered if you could overdose on one of those—and moved forward. I watched in fascination as he entered Angie. He didn't last any longer than I.

WHATEVER INNOCENCE TERRY AND I had before that day was forever washed away by the wetness between Angie's legs. We had climbed into the tree house as excited children, wanting to see something we'd never seen before. When our feet touched the grass again, we had left childhood behind. We had become men. But our tree house adventures left our souls contaminated. Tainted by lust.

Once on the ground, Angie said, "If I were you guys, I wouldn't tell anyone about today. Grownups think it's okay for them to do this stuff, but not us. And they get really mad. Believe me, I know." She flashed a smile that said it all.

She had just given us a taste of something we would seek for the rest of our lives. And then she walked away.

On my way home, I thought about a sermon our preacher gave one week: "God gave His life for our spiritual purity. The wicked act of fornication throws God's most sacred gift back into His face. The eternal tortures of Hell await the soul of a fornicator upon his death."

Sometimes a soul doesn't have to die to end up in Hell.

The Button

PUSH THE BUTTON! IN the absolute silence, the voice had grown stronger. Nothing to drown it out. *Push the fucking button and get out!*

I sat on the floor, my back toward the wall, rocking forward, backward, banging my head against the soft border of white oblivion. I was blinded in the whiteout, the only color being the red button that blazed like the sun. It called to me as the light calls to the moth. Sunk its hooks into my soul, pulling, pulling, dragging me into its brightness. *Come to me.*

"But they will torture me in the Zoo."

They are torturing you now!

The voice was right. I couldn't bear this torture anymore. I hadn't seen anyone or heard another voice in what seemed like years. Could've only been days, for all I knew, but it seemed like a decade. I needed to hear something. More importantly, I needed to feel something. Anything. Even pain would be better than this. You can't be in pain if you don't exist.

Push the button! One year! You can survive one fucking year!

Could I? Could I survive one year in the Criminal Zoo? Being tortured daily? But if I was being tortured, then it would be a living person in front of me doing it. A living person talking to me. Touching me. And even if they were intent on harming me, they were still there because of me. Showing me attention.

Proving I existed. And their very presence, there in front of me, for me, because of me—*I am the reason for the season*—would bring me back to life. In my pain there would be life!

Push the button, survive the Zoo, and become a God in prison.

The governor was smart. So very fucking smart. He made you disappear, and the only way back was through pain. He made you choose pain instead of nothingness.

"Brilliant, Mr. Gov!" I cried out. "Bravo, you sick fuck!"

Push the damn button!

"Fuck!" I screamed as loud as I could.

I stood up, swayed, slid toward the button. Reached out. Pulled my hand back.

You want to exist! Push the button!

"No! I don't want to hurt!"

To hurt is to feel! To feel is to live! Push the button to live!

I screamed. Screamed with everything I had. Screamed until I couldn't scream anymore. And then, vision blurred by tears, I reached for the button.

I pushed it.

Exhibit CZ1013

THE GOVERNOR'S CRUSADE FOR the most ruthless method of punishment resulted in the Criminal Zoo. Of which I am an exhibit. That's what we're called in here, "exhibits." Not "inmates," like we're people, but exhibits, like we're animals. I don't have a name anymore—not according to these guys, anyway. I speak my name out loud to keep it alive. To hear the sound of it. But I am the only one. I do not remember the last time I heard my name spoken by another. It was before the Confinement Center. Probably as I was being sentenced by the judge.

Samuel Bradbury is gone. Dead and buried under six feet of hate. Allow me to introduce myself. I am Exhibit CZ1013.

But, whether man or animal, I exist. I feel. I am alive. My first day in the Zoo, I saw people. I heard their voices. I was surrounded by sounds, by smells. I was no longer nothing. I was something. I had re-entered the known world. For a few beautiful minutes, everything was fantastic. And then the guards, wearing their stupid maroon jumpsuits and referring to themselves as "zookeepers," took me through "orientation."

The keepers are mean sons of bitches assigned to our enclosures to keep an eye on us. They know everything about us. We know nothing about them. Who they are. Where they come from. I can only guess, but I'm going to say maybe former military. Or cops. Or hell, mafia hitmen would be more fitting. They are serious assholes with no regard for our well-being.

Orientation is just another word for Hell on Earth. Every new exhibit is required to take a hit from the standard weapon used by the keepers. The weapon reminds me of a cattle prod. "What we got here, One-Zero-One-Three, is a Zap-stick, with a capital Z!" My keeper held up a three-foot-long rod. To him, I wasn't even an exhibit. I was nothing more than a four-digit number.

The Zap-stick had a black rubber handle at one end and two rounded silver probes at the other. The shaft of the weapon was orange.

"That's Z for zinger, baby! As in, it delivers one hell of a zing!" He laughed. "Hell, if I wanted to burn your balls off, I could do it with this!"

When the probes were pressed against the flesh—it also worked just fine through clothes—and a bright red button on the handle was pushed, the results were horrifying. It ensured the keeper had complete control of his exhibit, while his exhibit lost all control of his bladder and colon.

"Your average stun gun," the keeper said, "starts at around twenty to thirty thousand volts. The Zap-stick delivers one hundred fifty thousand volts, making the stun gun look like a child's toy. But the amperage—that's what kills ya, buddy—is pretty low. So, no, it ain't gonna make you dead, but I guarantee it'll knock your dick into the dirt for quite some time!" He followed with a laugh.

I was restrained in what they called a "confinement chair." The chair—a solid piece of hard plastic furniture bolted to the floor—featured thick leather straps fastened to the armrests, the front legs, and the back rest. It looked to be inspired by an electric chair, only without the metal skullcap. The chair's sole purpose was to eliminate all movement on my part. It served its purpose well.

The keeper pushed the probed end of the stick against my stomach. "When I press this little red button, you're going to wish you were never born."

I was really starting to regret pushing the little red button back in the Confinement Center.

"Wait! Please don't!"

He flinched. I squeezed my eyes shut.

Nothing happened. After a few seconds, I opened my eyes and looked at him.

"Gotcha!" He laughed. "You thought I was going to push the button, didn't you? Oh, man, you shoulda seen the look on your face. Classic!"

I stared at him a second. Relaxed slightly. "Yeah, I thought—"

He pushed the button.

The knockout punch hit me like a runaway truck. I woke up, unsure of how long I was out, my body wracked with excruciating spasms, every muscle knotted and fighting against the restraints, my underwear soiled. I'd never been in such pain.

I struggled to speak. "Why…why'd you do that?"

"I know, I know, that wasn't fair, right? You didn't do anything and I'm just being a bully," the zookeeper said. "That's what they all say. But you know what? I did it so you'd have the utmost respect for the Zap-stick. This bitch is for real, baby. Now, when I tell you to do something, you'll do it, won't you?"

I guess I didn't answer fast enough, because he hit me with a grin and then pressed the button again.

The feeling of every muscle tearing away from my bones erased all other reality. I couldn't move and could barely breathe. I tried to scream, but couldn't push enough air from my lungs. I truly thought I was going to die right then and there.

I wish I had.

Father Calhoun's Demise

THE ZOOKEEPERS HAVE TO follow a "no firearms" rule inside our enclosures. The assholes in charge believe that if one of us ever overpowers a keeper and gets hold of a gun, we will kill as many people as possible while trying to escape. They're right.

But if we can only get hold of a Zap-stick, we can easily be stopped by the heavily armed security force, called the "Regulators," that patrols the corridors, keeping the staff and visitors safe. They walk around in their black cargo pants, black army boots, and black T-shirts like their shit doesn't stink. Each member of this terrorist hit team is armed with an assault rifle, a sidearm, a Taser, and a radio.

Not long ago, they killed an exhibit during an attempted escape. I didn't have a visitor that day and was trying to sleep—the only way to pass the time in here—when the ear-piercing sirens shattered the silence. I jump every time that Goddamned alarm sounds. Was the silence of the Confinement Center really so bad?

My keeper told me about the event shortly after. He had a look of envy in his eyes as he detailed how the Regulators blew the old man away. "Had to be two dozen holes in that old bastard by the time they were done with him. Fuck, why do they get to have all the fun?"

His name was Father Calhoun. He had molested numerous boys during three decades of service in the Pope's pedophile brigade. From what I was told, the church had relocated him several times, trying to keep him out of trouble—or ahead of it. They were obviously trying like hell to keep him out of the headlines, too. They didn't accomplish shit. A predator will stalk its prey, eventually acting on instinct and going for the kill. The scorpion will sting the frog, no matter how far across the river it is. Or where the church relocates it.

The priest should have known that one day he would be held accountable for his actions. And that day finally came. He panicked when one of the children, his final victim, tried to run for help. The priest chased him down and struck him in the back of the head with a candleholder. Who needs Professor Plum? *The priest, in the choir room, with the candlestick.* The child died and the old man ended up here. The priest claimed he hadn't meant to hurt the child. He only wanted to slow the lad down so he could comfort him.

I was told of the old man's presence in the Criminal Zoo several times. I was compared to him, to his wickedness. They tried to make me believe I was nothing better than a child-killing psycho. It made me sick to my stomach to even think about comparisons between me and the priest. I don't touch little boy penises.

The Blue-Hair's Tears

ODAY, I SIT SHACKLED to my confinement chair in front of yet another Level 2 visitor. Level 1 visitors, or "L1s," are merely spectators, no threat to us. They come here to observe us like we're zoo animals. But this zoo doesn't allow cameras or recording devices of any kind. Still pictures and video are strictly prohibited. No cell phones, nothing. My keeper told me all visitors pass through full-body scanners like those at the airports. All electronic devices are immediately confiscated. The outside world en masse has never seen the horrors within these walls. Only those who pay to view us in person are privy to what goes on. This ensures that ticket prices stay high—ninety-nine dollars a head, says my keeper—and kills the possibility of public outrage upon footage of a Level 2 visit going viral.

The people who pay Level 1 admittance don't concern me. It's the sick fucks paying the $299 ticket price, the ones who want personal interactions with us, the assholes who want to hurt us. The Level 2 visitors, or "L2s"—those are the ones who make me sick. They're the ones feeding my nightmares.

Right before my L2 entered the room, my keeper placed a pair of clear plastic goggles over my eyes. Look just like swim goggles. But these goggles aren't meant to keep water out of my eyes. They're meant to keep blood out.

"Stupid, I know," the keeper said while putting on the goggles. "If it were up to me, I'd let them cut out your fucking eyes."

The greatest contradiction in here is the concern for my protection while being tortured. Seriously? Eye goggles to protect my eyes while they carve into the flesh of my face?

An L2 once complained to me that he had to read a Zoo-issued pamphlet detailing "proper protocol, techniques, and risk management while engaged in a Level two visit."

"They made me read the damn thing before I could come in here," he said. "I had to sign a waiver stating that I read, understood, and accepted the rules applying to all Level two visits." He first had to read the menu of available torture techniques, then had to declare his method of choice. Afterward, Zoo officials issued an educational booklet for that specific method. He laughed when he told me the booklet stated, "All possible safeguards have been put in place for you, the Level two visitor, and for your participating exhibit."

If this isn't evidence that Zoo policy is strictly dictated by government oversight, nothing is. Bureaucratic bullshit at its finest.

And get this: right after the goggles are put on, a mouth dam is inserted. I am not allowed to talk to the L2. Unless the L2 pays another fifty dollars for "conversational privileges" with the exhibit. Apparently the Zoo knows what it's doing, because most of my L2s pay the fifty bucks. They want to hear how much pain I'm in.

The L2 standing before me now is a frail old woman and, not counting the dark green coveralls, resembles an everyday grandma ready to bake some sugar cookies. But reality is warped in this place. In here, the church helper doesn't pass around the collection tray, patiently waiting for donations; he comes to collect blood. The accountant doesn't arrive to answer year-end questions; he comes to tax me in pain. And Grandma doesn't come to bake cookies; she comes to carve into my flesh.

The blue-hair is here to bury her pain underneath mine. That's why they all come. She stares at me, gripping a small pocketknife. I can't see the handle of the knife but I know what it looks like. Black plastic with tiny white print running down each side. The print reads CRIMINAL ZOO. It's the same knife they all bring. Though the stainless-steel blade is only one inch long, it might as well be a foot. It hurts just the same.

The zookeeper stands behind Grandma. He is also dressed in coveralls—his are always the same ugly maroon. He wears white surgical gloves but nothing covers his all-black sneakers. He watches a moment, turns his eyes to his wristwatch. "Ma'am, you should get started. You have a time limit." He reaches into a front pocket and pulls out a pair of latex gloves. He hands them to her. She pulls them on.

Grandma turns to me. "So, Exhibit CZ One-Zero-One-Three, what's it like in here?"

"My name's Samuel." I don't know her name. I never know any of their names or anything about them. She doesn't know my name until I tell her. And even after I tell her, like all of them, she will refer to me only by my number. As she was instructed upon entrance to the Zoo.

They come in, cause me harm—like it's going to somehow ease their own misery—and then I usually never see them again. Once in a while, however, I have return visitors. They are the people I fear more than Satan himself.

Hatred burns in this woman's eyes. She stands before me in her stupid jumpsuit, booties, and surgical gloves as if the Zoo-issue apparel will shield her from the bad things she's about to do. She's just like every other warped L2.

My wrists and ankles are firmly secured to the arms and legs of the confinement chair. I can do nothing, go nowhere. My keeper stands in the corner of the room, behind Grandma. The high-voltage Zap-stick leans against the wall beside the keeper, within quick reach if needed. I hate that Goddamned thing almost as much as I hate my keeper.

"It's always the same with you people," I tell her. "Someone did something to you, or to someone you love. But I didn't do it. Don't become a part of the evil that exists in here. Go home and forget you ever paid money to get in here."

"Go home?" Grandma responds. "Sorry, dear, but I'm afraid that's not going to happen. I paid way too much. I even had to skimp on my church tithing this month."

"It won't take your pain away."

"How do you know?" she asks. Her eyes narrow. They are blue, probably sparkle in the sunlight. They don't sparkle now. "I lost my daughter to a sick bastard like you."

"I'm a sick bastard? I'm not the one paying money to torture another human being." I try to stay calm; try to use reason. "You're the one holding the knife."

"I have a knife because you're a monster."

"If you do this, you become the monster." I stare at her, unblinking.

"You want to know how it happened?" she asks.

"No." They all tell me their story. It's always the same. Just replace the name and cause of death.

"My daughter went through a painful divorce," she begins. "There were two beautiful children involved, twin boys. It took her a while to get over it. Finally, a year later, she agreed to have dinner with a coworker. She was hesitant to accept. She asked me if she should do it and I said yes." Tears form in Grandma's eyes. "I told her to do it. And I never saw her alive again." The tears spill down her sagging cheeks. "Her body was found in an irrigation canal a week later. He strangled her to death. Can you imagine the terror she experienced as she died?"

The blue-hair's tears don't fool me. I know there is no softness in her heart. "Yeah, terror that I didn't cause."

She wipes her eyes. "Maybe I just want someone else to suffer, too."

"In Job 36:15, it says, 'But those who suffer He delivers in their suffering; He speaks to them in their affliction.'"

"Don't quote the Bible to me, you monster!" Grandma slaps me across the face with a bony hand.

"Don't hit me!" I scream. My cheek stings, just like when my dad used to hit me. "Go visit the asshole who killed your daughter! Go hurt him!"

Grandma looks at me and shakes her head. "I can't. It happened before the Criminal Zoo. The murderous bastard went to prison. That makes you the lucky one. The people you murdered, they were someone's loved one. My actions today aren't only for me—they're for all the victims out there."

Grandma moves the knife toward my face. My heartbeat accelerates. I try to pull away, but the leather straps hold. With the blade, she gently circles the goggle lens around my left eye, teasing my skin.

"I didn't do anything to you, you fucking bitch! Leave me alone!"

"Did your victims beg for mercy?" Her upper lip pulls into a snarl, revealing thin, yellowed teeth. She pushes the blade into my flesh, her hand trembling, and begins cutting around the goggles. She makes a complete lap around the lens.

Searing pain flashes across my face. My hands clench into fists, pulling against the restraints. "Fuck you!"

Grandma pulls the knife back and smiles. "That actually felt pretty good."

"Stop!" I shout. "This makes you just like all the other monsters in here!"

She moves the blade to my right side. Taps it against my cheek. Stares at me, smiling like a demented bitch. And then she stabs the blade into my cheek.

My entire face burns like a hot fireplace poker has just been dragged around it. Blood runs down each cheek and tears fill up the inside of the goggles, burning my eyes. Grandma pulls the blade out and then, laughing, sticks it back in.

"Stop cutting me, you fucking whore!" I scream.

She doesn't listen. Instead, she goes back to work. I push my heels hard into the floor. I fight against the restraints around my ankles, wrists, but I won't win this battle, not now, not ever. I can't escape the chair, or the pain. Instead, I try to hide from the pain in the deep hole I dug in my mind many, many visitors ago.

"Open your mouth," Grandma says.

"Fuck off!" Because of the physical alterations I did on my so-called "victims," most of the L2s eventually go in this direction after assaulting the tissue around my eyes. My tongue is badly scarred.

I once got a small taste of revenge with an L2. The memory of the screaming man who had been stupid enough to reach for my tongue will serve me well the rest of my God-forsaken life. They restrained my body, but not my mouth, not my teeth. I would've swallowed the visitor's severed finger had my keeper not hit me with the Zap-stick.

Grandma wipes the blood from her blade onto my pants. "I said open your mouth."

I shake my head.

She looks at the zookeeper. "He won't open his mouth."

My keeper moves to me, his Zap-stick aimed at my head. "One-Zero-One-Three, I believe you were told to open your mouth." He pushes the probed end against my neck.

I move my head back as far as I can, not wanting to feel the shock of that fucking thing again. My heart pounds and my entire body trembles.

I have no idea how long I've been enduring this kind of torture. All I know is that every day brings more pain. Because of the media's comparison of my work to the cartoon figures of three Goddamned monkeys—"See no evil, hear no evil, speak no evil"—I'm a main attraction at the Zoo. The ridiculous nickname "Three Monkeys Killer" has even been uttered. Words do no justice to my hatred of that name.

I have been stabbed multiple times by the small Zoo-issued pocketknives; my face has been carved on again and again; my tongue has been punctured and sliced, and much of the tissue around my ears has been cut off. After each visitor leaves, I am restrained on a gurney and taken to the Repair Shack. It is a series of rooms—each room having enough space for three beds on wheels—complete with a sink, locking cabinets fastened to the walls, and a strong antiseptic smell. Needles, surgical thread, medicines, syringes, bandages, splints, braces, and medical tools are locked in the cabinets. I dream of one day grabbing a scalpel from the cabinet and exacting revenge on my keeper.

During my first few visits to the Repair Shack, I screamed as loud as I could, making my pain obvious to anyone within hearing distance. But I quickly learned that all I accomplished, besides giving myself a horrendous headache, was giving satisfaction to the zookeepers. That's when I dug my "mind hole." I dug it deep—deep enough to hide in.

If my wounds are bad enough, they push a button in the control room and a plastic cover slides across my viewing wall. A sign is painted on the face of the cover, stating that the exhibit is temporarily closed for recovery. I am allowed time in the Repair Shack to heal and then returned to my enclosure. Afterward, the visits begin again.

Now, the keeper pushes his Zap-stick harder into my neck. "Open wide."

I open my mouth.

Grandma moves closer. A little more and perhaps I can headbutt her.

I keep my mouth open only because a Zap-stick blast to the soft flesh of the neck hurts more than anywhere else, except maybe the balls. One of my keepers told me how a young exhibit went into violent seizures due to a direct shock to the neck. He bit off his own tongue.

The kid was a fifteen-year-old boy who had murdered his baby sister while his parents were in the other room. He'd killed the girl with the claw end of a hammer. According to my keeper, the kid said he did it because his parents weren't paying attention to him anymore. Because of the viciousness of the attack, the kid was tried as an adult and ended up in Colorado.

Grandma pushes the knife toward my jaw. My mouth snaps shut. The keeper's fist slams into the side of my head. Bright pins of light explode across my field of vision. Pain shoots through my temples.

"Keep your mouth open!" the keeper screams.

Dazed, I open my mouth. Grandma stabs the knife into my tongue. I scream and snap my head back, hitting the backrest of the chair. The blade rips into my tongue. My mouth fills with blood. I try to scream again, but I inhale blood and cough violently.

"Time's up," the keeper finally declares. He steps in, pulls Grandma back.

Pain-induced nausea overwhelms me. The keeper is prepared for it, already moving back as I retch.

Grandma scoots to the side, a predatory look in her eyes. She clenches her jaw and closes her hands into fists. "Just a few more minutes, okay?"

"No, ma'am," the keeper says. "I need you to make your way to the door."

"Come on, just one more minute. Please." Without warning, Grandma arcs the knife across the bridge of my nose, opening a deep gash.

The pain is excruciating. I'm now searching desperately for my mind hole, the only place I can escape the pain.

The keeper grabs Grandma by her wrists. The knife drops from her hand. "That's it, ma'am! Your time is up!"

"No!" Grandma fights the keeper, but is no match. "Let me go!"

"Ma'am, please!" the keeper yells. He moves her away, pushes her against the viewing wall, pins her arms against her sides. "You must control yourself."

Eyes grow wide among the L1s gathered outside. Everyone pushes forward, wanting a better look.

She stops fighting and a look of panic flashes across her face. She begins to cry. "Oh my God, oh my God…" She shakes her head. "I'm sorry. I'm so sorry."

"It's okay, ma'am, it happens. You're not the first to lose it in here and you won't be the last."

"Okay," she says. "I'm so sorry."

"Don't worry about it. You're going to be just fine." The keeper turns from her, moves to me, and slaps me hard across the face before I can disappear into my hole. "Stay with us, exhibit! You looked like you were drifting there for a second."

Grandma looks at the keeper. "Can I have the knife? I paid the extra thirty dollars for it. I have my receipt."

The keeper bends down, retrieves the knife, and then reaches into his pocket. He pulls out a small vial. He unscrews the lid, dips the knife blade into the liquid, and swirls it around. He wipes the blade and handle clean with a small piece of cloth from his breast pocket, folds the knife closed, and hands the keepsake to Grandma. "Now, if you'll please follow me," he says as he replaces the vial and cloth in his pocket. He moves to the door in the viewing wall.

The blackness is coming for me and I welcome its arrival. It will take me away, if only for a little while.

Frisbee Football

ONG BEFORE L2S CUT into my skin, before the darkness became my only friend, I spent my days with Terry. That kid's ruthless nature flat-out fascinated me. Whether we were shooting baskets in his driveway or shooting gophers in the field, he made life almost bearable.

When we were kids, all things were possible. Whether it was high school prom king, football captain, or heroes hoisting shiny trophies won in the heat of battle, only time would tell what we'd become. The football thing was probably a bit of a stretch, since neither of us knew how to play. And the trophies were still up in the air, our battlefield still undecided—hadn't gotten that far yet, but by God we were going to win something.

Unfortunately, the only thing time told us was our athletic abilities would never blossom. Neither would our popularity. Trophies and proms were the last things we'd ever have to worry about.

We never did go out for any team sports. We didn't know a thing about cars, weren't invited to stoner parties, so that left us in the only remaining group: geeks. And even geeks were required to go out for PE.

Our sophomore year had just begun and August heat bore down with a vengeance. We were in the middle of fourth period PE, enduring a game of Frisbee football, shirts versus skins. I hated being skins. Apparently, I was on the delayed-development plan. I was the last kid in my class to have a noticeable chest or anything resembling shoulders. Actually, I still don't have a noticeable chest or anything resembling shoulders, but at least I'm a little bigger than I was back then. I was the last kid to develop pubic hair; consequently, the last kid to drop his towel for a shower at the end of PE class. I was the last kid to start shaving—that didn't happen until I was in my twenties. Many of the other boys had biceps bigger than my legs. Even Terry was bigger than me, just barely. But one early August day, with our high school experience freshly blooming, he wasn't big enough.

Terry had been sprinting for the Frisbee, eyes locked on the bright orange disc. He had no way of seeing the blindside hit. One of the biggest kids in our class, Billy Spurlock—fullback for the varsity football team—teed off on him. Terry flew through the air and hit the ground hard. The blow knocked the wind out of him; he couldn't breathe. He lay on the field, his back arched skyward, and his feet kicking against the grass.

I ran to him, knelt beside him, watched him flop like a carp thrown to the bank. My seventh-grade health class had confirmed two things: asthma was real and my dad was an idiot.

The other kids gathered around Terry, eyes wide. The PE teacher ran over. "Give him some room, fellas."

Terry grabbed at his sweaty T-shirt, his throat, his hair, anything he could latch onto. He looked at me, fear exploding from his eyes.

"Terry, calm down," I said, not knowing how bad the situation was. "You just got the wind knocked out of you, okay?"

The other boys watched. Their expressions seemed to show not so much concern for Terry, but excited fascination, like maybe they were going to see something they could tell their friends about later.

Terry reached for me, grabbed me by the collar of my T-shirt, and yanked me to him. He tried to say something but couldn't. The fear that had been in his eyes now evolved into sheer terror. "Where's your inhaler? You just need to take a hit, that's all." I didn't want to panic him further, so I acted as if he was fine. The bluish hue in his lips made me think maybe he wasn't fine. "Terry, do you have your inhaler?"

He frantically shook his head.

I started to panic a little. The kid thrashing back and forth at my feet was the only kid who would hang out with me. I kind of needed him to stay around. I looked up at the PE teacher, Mr. Braxton. He just stood there. He didn't look like the high school football hero he always bragged about being; he looked scared. Suddenly the situation seemed a lot more serious. "Mr. Braxton, do something! He needs his inhaler!"

"Where is it?" the teacher asked.

"It's probably in his locker. He needs it now!"

Mr. Braxton turned from Terry and scanned the kids around him. "Do any of you guys know which locker is his?"

No one said anything.

I looked at Terry, grabbed his hand. "Hang in there, Terry! I'm going to get your inhaler. I'll be right back, okay?"

For a split second, I thought I saw understanding in his eyes. But maybe not. Maybe I was just imagining it, because the look went right back to really scared.

I jumped to my feet and sprinted toward the school. I reached the building, ripped open the doors to the locker room, and ran to Terry's locker. I tore through his clothes, throwing them to the floor, and stared into an empty locker. "No!" I dropped to my knees and grabbed his pants, shooting my hand into a front pocket. Nothing.

I felt inside the opposite pocket. There! I snatched the inhaler and raced back outside. I looked out to the field where everyone was standing, gathered around my buddy.

I ran, not like Terry's life depended on it, but like mine did. I didn't want to go through high school alone. I knew why he didn't have his inhaler. He was tired of everyone giving him shit, calling him weak because he was dependent on the inhaler. He was trying to make a point: he was tough enough to go without it. *Stupid, Terry. Really stupid.*

I pumped my arms, my legs, ran against the clock. I would save Terry. I would be a hero. Only fifty yards to go. Faster. Run faster. "I'm coming Terry! Hang—"

Something caught my foot and I was now headed nose down, straight into the ground. Seemed like it was happening in slow motion, but I couldn't stop any of my movement. I tried to shield my face by putting my hands in front of me, trying to stop the Earth speeding up at me. I hit the ground hands first, my face following. My legs, now in the air above my head, kept going. I planted face first into the ground and scorpioned hard. I screamed as I flipped onto my back.

I lay face up, wondering what had just grabbed my foot. Satan was my first thought. I rolled onto my stomach and pushed myself up onto my hands and knees, frantically searching for Terry's inhaler. It was right there in front of me, lying on the ground. Broken into pieces. "No!" I scooped up the pieces, jumped to my feet, and looked at the crowd around Terry. Everyone was now looking at me.

I ran to the group. They stared at me, shaking their heads. Mr. Braxton was bent over Terry, administering CPR. I was suddenly taken back to a day at the apartments when two guys administered poolside CPR to a funny-looking little kid who'd had a light blue hue to his lips. Just like Terry had now.

And then the hue deepened and began spreading across Terry's whole face. His eyes were closed, his body still. I stared, my hands dropping to my side. The pieces of the inhaler fell to the ground.

I WATCHED THE EMERGENCY medical techs load Terry's body into the ambulance. My whole body shook. I wanted to lash out, to strike something, anything. Every muscle in my body tightened. Billy had just killed my friend *This isn't fair!* I wanted to scream as loud as I could. But my dad's words, *Life's not supposed to be fair,* cut me off. If I'd had my Uncle Henry right then, Billy would've seen just how unfair the world could be.

Terry didn't deserve this. He was only doing as he was told, playing some stupid game with a bunch of fucking assholes hellbent on hurting someone. I looked up.

"This is bullshit, God!" Why did things always go wrong for me? Was it too much to ask that something in my life went right for once? *Life's not supposed*—"Shut up, Dad," I said, silencing the voice.

I looked down at the pieces of inhaler. If I hadn't fallen, Terry might still be alive. I knew I was going to get blamed for this. The kids were already pointing and talking.

But it wasn't me. It was Billy. He stole my only friend in the whole world. *Why?* What did he have to gain?

And then a thought swept through me. Maybe it wasn't Billy who had killed Terry. Maybe it was Satan. Could he really have grabbed my foot? Or who knows, it might even have been God.

My eyes turned skyward. "Is this some kind of joke? You think this is funny? Is it funny when you fuck with someone like that?"

I wondered if God was laughing.

Iniquity

IFE AS I KNEW it forever changed the day Terry died. Lying in bed that night, knowing sleep would not come, I thought about Terry's last day. As he threw on his shorts and T-shirt, without knowing it, he had dressed not for gym class, but for the afterlife. And when his time came, did he see the light—maybe his grandpa or grandma standing in it, arms open, beckoning him forward?

Or was it a guy with cloven feet, horns, and razor-sharp teeth who awaited him, the rotting flesh of naughty children dangling from his foul mouth? Had Terry's soul become dinner for the Devil?

Terry was the only bright spot in my life. He was the only person who ever liked me, accepted me as I was. Everyone else abandoned me. My grandma never looked at me the same after Jeremy died. She issued a distant "Hello, Samuel" each time my dad brought us by her house. There was no more hominy. She expressed no emotion, no feelings toward me when we were in the same room, which wasn't often, because she usually left when I entered. I tried to explain to her that it hadn't been my fault, but she told me to quit talking about it.

Sheila blamed me for Socks dying. She came home in tears after finding his flattened carcass in the parking lot. I knew I should've gotten rid of him better. I tried telling her it was Dad's fault, but she told me to shut up and never talk to her again. She was a serious bitch from then until she left home at seventeen.

My dad got only worse. He acted like we had driven Mom away. He acted like if drowning your children were legal, he'd be filling the bathtub to the rim.

Everyone in my life left me. Including Terry. Thanks to Billy. Or the Devil. Or God. Or whoever the hell took him.

I tossed and turned, visions of demons doing the dance of the dead across my mind. I thought about another time I couldn't sleep: the night before an encounter in a tree house. That was the day Terry and I had allowed the evil between Angie's legs to soil our souls. The more I thought about that day, the more it bothered me. I had been warned time and again about the consequences of "knowing a woman" before marriage. My dad, our preacher, the Bible—they all agreed. You're screwed if you screw. But Terry's and my lust had gotten the better of us; we had contaminated our spirits and, afterward, never did anything to make it right. Unfortunately for Terry, his chance to cleanse his soul was now gone. He was dead. The preacher's voice echoed through my head. *The eternal tortures of Hell await the souls of fornicators.*

If that was true, Terry's actions guaranteed him a ticket straight to Hell, the guy with the cloven feet awaiting his arrival. I shuddered. Was that what awaited me?

The whole Heaven and Hell thing, and how it worked, suddenly became very important. I felt I had a pretty good grasp on the Devil. But what about God?

While I was a child, my dad beat the story of God and his unforgiving, punishing existence into me. Dad never allowed me to forget the Lord had absolute rule over mankind, along with a nasty habit of seeking revenge against those who transgressed against Him. The preacher's voice again: *Vengeance belongeth to me. So sayeth the Lord.*

According to all the stupid scriptures I had to learn, God was about vengeance. He'd turn you into a pillar of salt, drown you in a flood, or strike you down if you ever made Him mad. He was the ultimate punisher. He stated His mood clearly in the Second Commandment: "For I the Lord thy God am a jealous God, visiting iniquity of the fathers upon the children unto the third and fourth generation of them that hate me..." I had to look up the word "iniquity" to really appreciate just what He was saying.

It scared the hell out of me to think God would visit wickedness upon a group of children whose only mistake was to be the descendents of unbelieving fathers, grandfathers, and even great-grandfathers. That seemed a little extreme. What was God so afraid of?

Yet, God also said He'd show mercy on those who loved him. So, if you were His friend, He'd be nice to you. But if you weren't, He'd kill you. That didn't sound very God-like. Matter of fact, it sounded very human-like.

Spite, jealousy, favoritism, anger...even rage. *Human-like.* All the emotions of man. The more I thought about it, the more confused I became.

Throughout the Bible, God is attributed with human emotions. Why? Wouldn't a "true" God be above those emotions? Shouldn't God have eternal wisdom and the ability to comprehend infinite existence? Not the human desire for revenge. You'd think His mind, His awareness, would be enlightened beyond the primitive emotions controlling the human brain.

But God admits to having those human emotions. He says it in His own words: "I the Lord thy God am a *jealous* God." He admits to being jealous and vengeful, not to mention a serious control freak. If you didn't do exactly as He said—like plunge a knife into your son's heart—He'd make you sorry you were ever born. Those were human traits if there ever were any.

I thought hard about the Bible. About the scriptures. What if they were actually true? What if all that Mary and the "immaculate conception" crap was real? And here I always thought she was just too scared to tell her husband she'd been messing around. What if the prophets in the Bible were real? Men who actually spoke to God, revealing His word. Could it all be true?

I stared into the darkness, thought deeply about everything I believed to be real, everything I believed to be bullshit. The night seemed to go on forever as I pondered why I was supposed to worship God if he was going to act like a man. Hell, with those traits, I could've just worshipped my asshole father. I had to be missing something—something about God's tie-in with humanity. Why not hide human attributes from worshippers who believed Him to be all powerful? My dad said emotions were weaknesses. Why give mankind the awareness that He had weaknesses? What was He trying to tell us?

God speaks to us through the verses of the Bible. He teaches us through scripture. I've read the scriptures front and back. I've studied them more than anyone I know. So let's say they're real. What was He trying to teach me right now?

I was restless, far from sleep. The silence was eerie, the blackness almost suffocating. I realized the customary chirping of crickets was missing. When was the last time I had lain in bed without the chirping of a million crickets outside my window?

Listening to the terrifying sound of silence, I mumbled, "There's no crickets, Grandma."

Something was definitely out there, outside my window. But it wasn't the boogeyman. No, I had the feeling it was something far worse. It was God, waiting to see if I could answer His little riddle. My throat tightened. I knew the consequences of not getting it right with my dad. I was willing to bet God was a lot worse.

Think of God's words; think *in* His words. "I am the Alpha, I am the Omega," I uttered into the black. The beginning, the ending. He said it, knowing we would analyze it in human terms with human brains. What did we know about the beginning and the ending? My beginning was when I was born; my ending would be when I died. So what about that was important? A question formed: what physical state was I in during the beginning and what would I be at the end? When I was born, I was human. When I died, I would die human. That was significant.

And then a verse popped into my mind: Genesis 1:26. "Let Us make man in Our image, according to Our likeness."

I needed to break it down word by word, literally. "*Let Us make man in Our image, according to Our likeness.*" Analyze the facts: I am human. I am made in His likeness. Alpha and Omega—beginning and ending. Human throughout. If all that is true then there can be only one conclusion: God is *human*. Or at least He started out that way. Otherwise, I couldn't have been made in "His likeness," right?

Something else about the verse troubled me. God refers to Himself in the plural form. He says "Us" and "Our." Of course I'm familiar with the Trinity—the Father, the Son, and the Holy Spirit, and how they're supposedly three people in one. But seriously, would God speak in plural terms if He were really talking about Himself? Sounded a little schizophrenic to me.

Maybe there was a better answer than just a crazy eternal bastard suffering from multiple personality disorder. Instead of trying to invent our own way of understanding God's words, maybe we should just take them at face value. Maybe He wasn't trying to be clever and cryptic at all. Perhaps He was trying to tell us something very important in very simple terms. Maybe He was telling us that there were more than just one of Him. And if there were more than one…

I sat up in bed and shook my head in amazement. The awareness I had stumbled upon was overwhelming. "Holy shit…"

More than one means there may actually be a *race* of Gods.

A race of Gods. A race of *human* Gods. If that were true, the million-dollar question was how did there get to be a group of Gods? Was there a secret God Kool-Aid? "Hey, kids, drink this and go part the Red Sea!"

And then it hit me—man's ultimate destiny, his reason for existence, even if it takes an eternity, is to elevate his spirit to the level of Godhood. It's written in the scriptures in black and white—*Our image; our likeness!*

Understanding washed over me. I could become a God.

"Holy shit! Holy fucking shit!" I exclaimed. "Can I really become a God?"

But how? What does one do to become a God? I remember watching a movie once about a serial killer who killed because he wanted to be God. The character had said something enlightening like, "To become God, one must do as God does." Could it really be that simple? Could that single line from a TV show really be the answer? Could it be that I was meant to watch that exact show at that exact time? Was it a divine message delivered through my TV? At first it seemed kind of silly, but the more I thought about it, the more sense it made. God speaks to us in strange ways.

Do as God does enough times and become as God is. Do as They do and become as They are.

"That's it! That's really it!"

So what exactly was it that God did? He didn't just go around killing people. Well, actually He did. People like Terry. But He did more than just that. What else did He do? What was His ultimate job? I pondered that until the light of another day—a day holding wondrous new possibilities—introduced itself through my window.

I imagined a job description for the position of God. It would have to read something like: Must be able to decide who suffers and who doesn't, who should be shown mercy and who should have iniquity visited upon them. Must be able to decide who should live and who should die. And must decide that vengeance is, in the end, always best.

Hey, I could do that. I could do all of those things. To the people I decided to show vengeance upon, didn't that make me God? And it made perfect sense to believe that the more people I did that to, the more widespread my God-like powers would be. I trembled with my new awareness. It was the first day of the rest of my life—a life that would culminate with me as the newest member of the God race.

I slid from my bed, having passed a whole night without a wink of sleep. But it didn't matter, because I was going to be a God. And Gods don't need sleep.

Billy Spurlock had taken my only friend from me. Time to visit iniquity upon him. My first act of Godhood.

Swinging for the Fence

ALMOST TWO YEARS. THAT'S how long it took. Almost two damned years before I got the chance to teach Billy Spurlock about God and his vengeance. And unfortunately for Billy, his vengeful God was packing an Uncle Henry.

I watched him. Studied him. Even followed him now and then. I wanted to get a feel for Billy's habits. His behaviors. Where he hung out. Who he hung out with. I needed to know as much about his life as I could. In two years, you can learn a lot.

Billy and I were the same age. As such, we took driver's ed together. Not that I would ever have a car. My dad said if I wanted a car, I'd better get a good paying job so I could buy one. Otherwise, find one growing on a tree.

When it was time to sign up for driver's ed, my dad signed on the dotted line, but I had to mow lawns to pay the fee for the class.

As luck would have it, Billy, a kid named Mark, and I were assigned to the same drive times on Saturday morning. I learned a lot during those Saturday drives. I did it by being cool. Since the day he killed Terry, I wanted him dead. But every Saturday morning, though he was always giving me shit, harassing me, I smiled and took it. Quietly, patiently, listening the whole time. All was good because there would be a day when I laughed. As he died.

He was an asshole. It was up to me to teach him that God didn't like prideful bastards. Job 40:11 said, "Unleash the fury of your wrath, look at every proud man and bring him low." Oh, how I wanted to unleash my fury and bring Billy low.

During one Saturday morning drive, he and Mark, also a member of the football team, talked about a house party. Billy's parents were out of town and he was throwing a party. He invited Mark. "There'll be hot chicks up the ass!" was his closing sell. Mark accepted emphatically. Then Billy turned to me and asked, "So what are you gonna do tonight, dickweed? Sit in your bathroom and beat off to pictures of your mom?"

Pictures of my mom? He could not have cut any deeper. Mark laughed. Billy joined him. I smiled like I was in on the joke instead of the butt of it. Parents out of town? Time to release my inner God.

That night, after my dad and Sheila went to bed, I snuck out of the apartment. It was shortly after midnight: the witching hour. In Clemensville, after midnight on a Saturday, unless you were at a bar, you were either home watching movies or sleeping. Or throwing a party while your parents were gone.

I walked the five blocks to Billy's house, using the dark of the alleys. I didn't see a soul along the way. I hid in the alley behind Billy's house while his gathering of Clemensville High's A-listers partied inside. Peeking over his fence, I watched through his open windows. Everyone appeared to be having a blast. Laughing. Drinking. Flirting. I knew I would never be invited to a party like that. I would never know this kind of fun. Billy hung out with his people, partying hard, while I hung out in the alley alone. It just made me more focused on the job at hand. *Pictures of my mom? You shouldn't have gone there, Billy.*

Finally, a little after 1:00 a.m., people started heading out. Within half an hour, everyone was gone. Knowing he didn't have a dog, I climbed over the backyard fence. Actually, I fell off the top of the fence and into his backyard. I told you I wasn't very athletic. While crossing the yard I stepped on a baseball bat.

I crept to the back door, not sure what my plan was, but knowing I needed to be ready to strike when the opportunity hit. I gripped the bat with both hands. My Uncle Henry weighted down my front jeans pocket.

It didn't take long for opportunity to present itself. Billy opened the door and, with a full trash bag in hand, staggered onto the patio, his back to me. I was ready to swing for the fence. *Swinging for the fence.* I always loved that saying. So cliché. Like everyone stepped up to the plate to hit a homerun every time at bat. I didn't even play baseball and I knew that just didn't happen. Except for me. Right here. Right now.

Billy dropped the bag to the ground, and then, in an unbalanced, swaying manner, turned toward me. His eyes grew wide just before the bat crushed his face.

He went down like he had just been shot. I set the bat down and dug the Uncle Henry from my pocket. I straddled Billy's still body. I had brought the proud man low. I kneeled down, a knee on either side of his chest. Two scriptures popped into my mind. Psalms 59:12: "For the sins of their mouths, for the words of their lips, let them be caught in their pride." And Isaiah 2:11: "The eyes of the arrogant man will be humbled and the pride of men brought low, the Lord alone will be exalted in that day." I used to think the scriptures were full of shit. Not anymore. God was giving me direction. Telling me how I could become like Him. Like Them?

I set the Uncle Henry down on Billy's now flattened forehead and pulled yellow rubber dishwashing gloves from my back pockets. Stole them from under the bathroom sink. One of the few acts of kindness my dad showed Sheila; at least she didn't have to get her hands dirty while she cleaned the toilet. I slid them on.

"Billy," I began softly, holding the Uncle Henry, "for the sins of your mouth. You laughed when you hit Terry. For the words of your lips. You bragged about it."

His face was bloody and a bit misshapen from the bat, but the main features were still discernible. I opened his slack jaw and grabbed his tongue. I was actually surprised at how hard I had to saw to cut it out.

I threw the piece of meat into the yard and then moved to his eyes. "The eyes of the arrogant man will be humbled." I cut out his right eye first. It was kind of like cutting out a grape, but slimier. It kept slipping between my fingers when I tried to grab it, but I finally got it out of the socket. The Uncle Henry slid easily through the optic nerve. I threw it after the tongue and went to work on the left eye. I obviously did something different, because it popped with a wet, squishy, sickening sound. Some of the eye goo shot into my mouth. It tasted rotten, salty. I almost spit it out, but then I remembered a crime show I watched where they caught the bad guy by DNA in his saliva. I swallowed. Almost threw up.

Two things I will never forget: the sound of a human eye popping, and the taste of that very same eye.

The words of another verse drifted into my mind. I couldn't remember exactly which one it was, but it was something about "stoppeth his ears from hearing of blood, and shutteth his eyes from seeing evil."

Okay, the eyes were done. That left only the ears.

Must be cartilage around the ears, because they're not very easy to cut off. But where there's a will, there's a way.

I left Billy lying there, brought low on his patio. I took the baseball bat and went home. I quietly let myself into the apartment. All was well, Dad and Sheila sound asleep.

In the bathroom sink, I washed the blood from the gloves and put them back where I found them. Then I snuck into my room and buried the bat and the clothes I was wearing in the bottom of my closet. It would be safe there for now, because with my dad, if he couldn't see it, he didn't give a shit. Sheila did the laundry each weekend, but she made no effort for me. If I didn't get my clothes to her, they didn't get washed. The stuff in my closet was safe.

I wasn't prepared for the fallout. You would've thought the president had just been assassinated in Clemensville. The police questioned every damn kid in our school. After that incident, I realized I'd better lay low for a while. Put the God thing on the back burner. No need to draw attention to myself.

To Be Desired

O F ALL THE THINGS I miss in the governor's fucking hell, Carla isn't one of them. She never was much of a wife, or a companion of any sort. If I had a redo, I would've kept Brutus and instead hit her over the head with the frying pan. How many times can a guy be told how worthless he is? How many unsuccessful attempts at making love can a guy endure? It was funny how her stomachaches and headaches always seemed to occur at the exact moment I needed her to make me feel like a man. She finally went to a doctor who diagnosed her with irritable bowel syndrome and fibromyalgia. That made me laugh. My dad would've told her she was just being weak.

I used to lie on my back in bed and listen to her snore. I'd interlock my fingers behind my head and stare into the darkness, wishing I'd married someone who wasn't such a waste of a wife. It was usually hot—too hot to be covered by anything heavier than Fruit of the Looms. Usually I ended up climbing out of bed and heading into the living room. I'd throw in an X-rated DVD and take care of business on my own.

One night, instead of watching porn, I remained in bed and thought about the young schoolgirl who walked past my house each day. There were always other kids too, but Jenny usually walked alone.

I met Jenny Nelson as she walked home after the first day of school. Our house was about a block from her junior high. I had just mown the lawn and was putting water to it when she passed. We didn't talk that first day, but our souls shared something unsaid.

She was really pretty and she dressed so sexy I couldn't help but notice. I am quite certain that was her intention. Back when I went to school, skirts had to be past the knees, shoulders had to be covered, and a girl's stomach couldn't be exposed. Times had obviously changed. Jennifer wore a denim miniskirt—frayed at the bottom—that didn't reach much below her butt. Her spaghetti-strap top revealed shapely shoulders and a flat, tanned stomach. I wondered what kind of parents would let their kid dress like that. They obviously didn't care about her. Not like I did.

At first I didn't completely understand why I had developed such deep feelings for her so quickly. She noticed me watching her. She nodded and kept walking. The way she looked at me, you could tell she was thinking about me. She was probably having thoughts that confused her. She made kind of a funny face when I smiled and she continued past, her pace quickening. She didn't have to explain; I knew why she sped up. She was afraid she might stop and nervously say something that would sound dumb and she didn't want to scare me away.

As I lay in bed thinking about her that night, it suddenly all made sense. I hadn't looked for her. She hadn't looked for me. This was bigger than her. Bigger than me. God, the Gods, the universe, whatever power was out there, had brought us together. Had brought her to me.

When I brought Billy low, when I punished him as a God would, I turned the heads of the Gods. I got Their attention, making a statement that I was here and I was to be taken seriously. And Jenny was Their response. Compensation for a job well done. My reward. Why else would she just suddenly be dropped in my lap?

Without her knowing it, I followed her home one day. No big deal; I was just curious. I stayed way back so if she turned, I could've ducked behind a car or a bush. But she never looked back. The reason she didn't was that she secretly wanted me to follow her and if she looked back, hoping to see me, she would've revealed her true feelings. Four-twenty-nine Houston Street. Committed to memory.

Thinking about her, my excitement grew despite my fat, snoring wife lying next to me. Jenny reminded me of Angie. Angie of the tree house. Angie, the thirteen-year-old girl who had made my legs weak, set my heart fluttering, and exposed me to a feeling of ecstasy the likes of which I had never known before, and have never known since.

I thought about Jenny's tan body, her flat stomach. I slid my hand inside my underwear and grabbed myself, massaged myself. Carla's snoring faded away.

Jenny's young skin must have been awfully soft, and she probably smelled really good. Probably smelled really clean, like my mom always had. And I'll bet she didn't just smell clean. I'll bet she *was* clean—innocent and uncontaminated by another man.

I thought about the honey nectar wetness between her young legs, the budding black hair growing there, and I pulled on myself, harder and harder. I pictured her lying underneath me, looking up at me, admiration in her eyes. She wanted me, pulled me in closer, squeezed me, longing for my forceful thrusts. Her fingernails found my back and her groans of pleasure filled my ears.

And suddenly, just as I had in the tree house so many years ago, I gave in to the rapture that came with beautiful young girls. *Relax, dummies, it's just cum.*

My underwear absorbed the residue of my fantasy, and needed to be changed. I lay for a moment more, allowing my breathing to slow, and then climbed from the bed. I felt my way through the dark room to my dresser and quietly grabbed a clean pair of underwear from the top drawer. It was at that moment that the idea occurred to me.

The most incredible thing I'd ever experienced was that day so long ago in the tree house. Now, with the Gods smiling down on me, with their gift before me, I was going to relive it. Jenny would be mine. Of course, there wouldn't be a tree house, but I could improvise. I knew of a shallow cave outside of town— just like the one the skeleton had been found in. Actually, they weren't really caves, more like good-sized holes in the ground. That happened around here a lot. The limestone beneath the soil separated or collapsed and the earth just kind of fell in. It would serve my purposes well.

The magic of that tree house day would once again reveal itself. I would be desired by an attractive young girl, and I would experience unbound ecstasy. And it wasn't like I was contaminating my soul. To reject her would be to throw the Gods' gift back into Their faces.

I returned to the bed. Carla snorted—just like an old sow— and rolled away from me. Good. She was probably all sweaty anyway. I lay in the darkness, wishing it was Jenny lying next to me. I longed for her youth, her beauty, her freshness. I saw the way she looked at me; she wanted me every bit as much as I wanted her. To be desired again. It would feel so good.

I thought about what steps needed to be taken, what bases needed to be covered to develop a relationship with the young girl. I would have to proceed with caution. I knew that if anyone found out they'd butt in and ruin everything. Her parents would tell her I was too old for her. But they didn't feel what Jenny and I had felt that first time we looked at each other. They didn't know the connection we had already made.

Yeah, I'd have to be careful that they didn't find out. And that went for Carla too. No interruptions.

My pulse quickened as I mentally mapped out how our little rendezvous would go. I would have to be very careful and it would have to remain a secret, but that wasn't a problem. I had lots of secrets.

A Nervous Reward

IT WAS OBVIOUS FROM the first day that Jenny liked me. Yes, she was only a teenager and I was almost thirty, but in many parts of the world, thirteen was marrying age.

Each day she walked by and each day I was out front, busy with chores. I made sure my real work, my lawn service, was done early in the day so I could get home, get cleaned up, and be ready for Jenny's walk-bys. I always stopped what I was doing and tried to make small talk, but she never returned much more than a "Hi." I imagine when you're super shy and you really like someone it's hard to reveal your innermost feelings.

I came to realize it was up to me to overcome her shyness. After several days of saying hello, I finally took the relationship to the next level. I was watering the grass when she walked by.

"Hot today, huh?"

She nodded and kept walking.

"Hey," I called to her in a real casual tone.

She stopped and turned.

"If you're ever hot and need to grab a quick drink of water on the way home, the hose is always out front here."

"Okay, thanks," she said. She turned to walk away.

"I'm Samuel. What's your name?"

She turned back. "I'm not supposed to talk to strangers. My dad would be mad."

"It's okay, I'm an old friend of your dad's. He probably wouldn't remember me, but you guys live over on 429 Houston, right?"

"Yeah," she said, giving me a quizzical look.

"He's right about the *strangers* thing. There are a lot of weirdos out there. But since we're practically neighbors, and I know your dad, I think I'm safe."

After a short pause, she said, "I'm Jennifer. But everyone calls me Jenny."

"Nice to officially meet you, Jenny."

"You too," she said. "I have to get home now."

"Just remember, the hose is always here, okay?"

"Okay." She turned and walked away.

I pumped my fist.

SCHOOL WOULD BE LETTING out any moment. I busied myself with details around the yard until Jenny came by. I wore a nice pair of khaki shorts, a polo shirt, and cologne.

Earlier that morning, Carla had informed me she had to work a double. "Irene's having some complications with her pregnancy. I gotta cover her shift today. And mine."

Irene Frye. I liked her. She was nice, always asking how I was doing. You could see in her eyes that she actually cared. At a store picnic last summer, we had done a three-legged race together, because her husband was out of town for work—oil business— and Carla's stomach hurt. We didn't win, but we had fun and we definitely connected. Anything beyond a friendship would be difficult, though. She was married and so was I.

"Is she going to be okay?" I asked.

"She's got too much amniotic fluid so she's going to Midland for some tests." Carla stopped, tilted her head, and stared at me, her hair a mess and her nightgown wrinkled from sleep. "Why you all dressed up? You got a date or something?"

"I'm going to fill out some applications today. With my landscaping business slowing down, I'm looking for a better job so I can help us more."

"Oh, yeah? Why start now?"

Why did she have to be rude? Carla stood in the hallway by the bathroom door and scratched her crotch.

"Actually find a *real* job, huh? That'd be something new."

She made no effort to shut the door before she lifted her nightgown, pulled down her panties, and took her place on the toilet. She farted, peed, and then snapped several squares of toilet paper from the roll. She folded the toilet paper, swiped it between her legs, and pulled up her panties as she stood. She dropped the soiled paper into the toilet and flushed. She looked at me, shook her head, and then pushed past me in the hallway.

"I have to get ready for work. Because I have a real job now."

I dropped Carla off at work. I needed the twenty-year-old Subaru to fill out the apps.

I parked the car, passenger side next to the curb, directly beside Jenny's path—for convenience. She would want to keep our relationship secret for fear of getting into trouble. And I figured if the car was right there, she could jump in without anyone seeing her. We could get to know each other better—get comfortable on our way to the sinkhole.

JENNY WAS LATE. I had been waiting for quite some time. All the other kids had long since passed. She must have had a make-up test or something. At first I was pretty annoyed. And then I realized it was all part of the plan. She was supposed to be late. Just to make sure the other kids were already gone.

Though I knew she was my reward, I knew she would be nervous. She was young. Naïve. Innocent. She didn't have the enlightenment I had. So I would make things easy on her. Time to resurrect Brutus.

As Jenny came down the sidewalk wearing a cute blue skirt and light pink T-shirt, I stood on the curb next to the car, looking intently down the road, projecting the image of a man searching for something important. She walked by and I glanced at her, giving her a soft yet concerned look. "Hi, Jenny. Hey, I don't mean to bother you, but you haven't seen a big ol' mutt tromping around, have you? His name is Brutus. He's big and goofy. A giant teddy bear."

Jenny stopped. She shook her head. "No, I haven't."

"Oh, man," I said. "I'm worried. He's too trusting. Like he would go with anyone if they pet him."

"What's he look like?"

"Like a big ol' mutt. He's an animal shelter rescue. So sweet and so lovable."

"I've never seen him in your yard."

"We keep him in the house. He's always trying to run away. You know, go exploring the world. I just worry that he's not smart enough to come back!" I hit her with a quick, appropriate laugh.

"What did you say his name was?"

"Brutus. But he should be named Pooh Bear." Again with the soft laugh.

"I'll keep an eye out for him on the way home."

"I don't suppose you'd wanna help me find him, would you?"

"I would, but I have to get home."

I nodded. "Oh, sure. Hey, let me give you a picture of him so you'll know if you see him, okay?" I moved to the Subaru. Opened the passenger door. Reached for the glove box. Opened it.

Jenny stepped toward me, held her hand out.

I reached into the glove box, made the motion of retrieving something, and then closed it. Jenny moved closer. I backed out of the car, turned, and did a quick scan of the neighborhood. No one in sight. I snatched Jenny by the wrist. Her eyes widened, and for a split second she appeared to be contemplating the reality of the moment. She opened her mouth to scream. I slapped my hand over it and shoved her into the car, slamming her door. I slid across the hood, just like they did in cop shows, to the driver's side. I thought it might impress Jenny. I checked again for anyone watching.

Jenny was obviously okay with this because she didn't try to run. Of course, even if she had wanted to, she couldn't. The interior door handle on her side was busted.

I climbed in and said, "I know this is kind of overwhelming, but whatever you do, don't scream. It makes me nervous, and sometimes when I'm nervous I do stupid things."

"Let me go!" she cried.

"Relax, Jenny. You don't even know what I've got planned. I think you'll like it."

We pulled away from the curb and headed to the highway. I put my hand on her leg, squeezed it reassuringly.

"Please don't hurt me," she whimpered.

"Oh, honey, I'm not going to hurt you. Just relax. Really, you're going to enjoy this. Just don't scream, okay? Everything'll be fine."

I turned off onto a dirt road only a few miles outside of town, pulled to the side of the road just past the large bush that marked the area of the sinkhole, and parked the car. I grabbed Jenny and pulled her through the car and out the driver's side door. She moved as if she were sleepwalking. Or maybe in a trance. I think, maybe, the Gods were in her mind, telling her to relax.

It only took a few minutes to find the sinkhole, even though we were slowed a bit by Jenny. Her legs buckled a couple of times, but I think that was because she was nervous. I was nervous before being with Angie, so I knew exactly how she felt.

I pulled her down into the hole and forced her to the ground in front of me. I pushed her onto her back and climbed on top of her, straddling her waist. I smiled and told her to relax.

That's when everything went wrong. She starting screaming as loud as she could. She kicked me, clawed at me, became wild, like she had been raised by wolves. She was crying and carrying on like a two-year-old. I grabbed her wrists and laid on top of her, allowing the full weight of my body to rest on her, and I kissed her.

Jenny screamed and somehow managed to get a hand between my face and hers. She tried to shove me away. She almost gouged out my left eye. So I punched her in the side of the head. I suppose I did it harder than I meant to, but she shouldn't have gone for my eye. That could've really hurt.

With my right hand, I pinned both her wrists together above her head. With my left, I pulled her skirt up past her hips. I stared at her pink panties. I got that same wonderful tickle in my groin I had with Angie in the tree house.

Jenny screamed again. She ripped her arms free and dug her fingernails into my forearms. I slapped her hard and then grabbed her by the throat with both hands. I squeezed until she couldn't scream anymore. "Stop! You're ruining everything!"

Had I been mistaken? Was this actually a test, the Gods seeing how I would play this out? A God takes what He wants, right? Even if there is resistance.

Jenny tried to pull my hands off her neck.

"Settle down!" I yelled. "If you do, I'll let you go, okay? I promise."

Her eyes were wide and filled with tears. I let go and she was immediately overcome by a fit of coughing.

"Please don't ruin this." I reached down and pulled her panties to her knees. I couldn't wait to slide into the wetness just beneath her budding hair of womanhood. I would allow my desires to move my body, show her how much I liked her. And when it was time, I would pull out, spilling my seed all over her. "Relax, dummy, it's just cum," she would say. And then she would giggle.

I had obviously underestimated her nervousness. It was quite a struggle holding her down and getting my shorts unzipped at the same time. Even though I had advised her against it, she opened her mouth to scream. I got tired of that shit in a hurry. I slammed my fist into the side of her head again, silencing her. Finally, I got my shorts pushed down far enough that I was fully exposed and fully erect. I positioned myself directly above her.

The pain from her knee driving into my balls erupted through me like an atomic bomb. My entire stomach went into cramps. I screamed and punched her again, this time as hard as I could. And then I did it several more times.

I doubled over, still on top of her, tried to catch my breath. I couldn't believe how bad my balls hurt. And then I got mad. Really mad. It wasn't supposed to go like this. So I dug my Uncle Henry from my shorts pocket. Without even thinking, I stuck the knife into Jenny's belly. She screamed. I was afraid her yelling would attract the attention of someone passing by—not that the road was used much, but you never knew. People would've automatically drawn the wrong conclusion if we were discovered down there.

I put my hand over Jenny's mouth. Her screams, though muffled, were still too loud. I pressed harder. I knew if I could just get her to understand that I hadn't meant anything by stabbing her, she would settle down. It probably hurt pretty bad, but it wasn't like I had intentionally brought her out here to stab her.

I must have covered her nose as well as her mouth, because after a moment of kicking and scratching, she became still. I lifted my hand from her face to tell her I was sorry, but her eyes rolled to the back of her head. Her lips had developed a light blue hue. *Oh, shit.* I had seen that before. Terry had that exact same look.

My mind raced. It was happening again. Son of a bitch, it was happening again! Someone very special to me was about to cross over, carrying with them a spirit dirtied by worldly desires. I couldn't let her go like Terry had gone. I couldn't let her spend her eternity bound to a soiled soul, walking the afterlife alone. We hadn't consummated our relationship, but her soul was tainted. There was a reason she had gone with me to the sinkhole. She wanted this to happen as badly as I did. I learned in church that "in the eyes of the Lord, so as sin is committed in the heart, it is committed in the soul." I had to save her soul.

Do as God does enough times and become as He is. Become as They are.

I'm not sure why that thought popped into my head, but its significance was not lost on me. *Become as They are.*

Jenny's eyes suddenly opened. She started coughing violently. Her entire body shook. Blood poured around the knife still stuck in her stomach. I had heard that just before someone died, they sometimes went into death spasms. Jenny was definitely in spasms. That didn't give me much time.

Jenny had been bad. She had been immoral. Her salvation could only come through her punishment. God punished people. *Do as God does…*

I knew what I had to do. What I'd done to Billy Spurlock was more than just a simple punishment; it was a cleansing. I had sent him into the afterlife not a proud young man, but a clean young man. Through my effort, removing a tongue that spoke evil, eyes that watched evil, and ears that heard evil, I sent him to the Gods renewed. Tainted flesh left behind.

I pushed Jenny's head to the ground, pulled the knife from her belly, and moved it toward her face. Her skin was soft. The knife cut through it like butter. After several minutes, I looked at the Uncle Henry. It was covered with blood, just as it had been the day I cleansed Billy.

I climbed from Jenny's still body and wiped the blood onto the front of my shirt—my dad was no longer around to beat me—and folded the blade into the handle. I pulled up my shorts and dropped the knife into my front pocket. Standing above Jenny, I examined her.

New life ran through me, energizing me. I had just been given another glimpse into what life as a member of the God race would be like. I stared at what once was living and now was dead, all determined by my actions. Like God dropping someone from a heart attack, I had chosen when Jenny would leave this world and enter the next.

I gazed upon Jenny's mostly nude body and my penis suddenly came to life, rising to the occasion, becoming a tent pole for my shorts. Just as it had happened with Angie. I dropped my shorts, grabbed my penis, and began stroking, staring at the dead girl lying between my feet. Out of nowhere the story of Onan flashed through my mind. He had been commanded to blow his load inside his dead brother's wife, giving her a child. But instead, he decided to pull out and "spilled his seed on the ground." He disobeyed God's order and God struck him down. I stroked harder, faster, and was soon overcome by the moment. My legs almost buckled as I sprayed my seed on her. And on the ground. After catching my breath, I looked skyward. "Go ahead. Strike me down."

I stood there, Jenny lying dead, covered in my semen, and dared the Gods to do something about it. But I knew They wouldn't. Because I was getting stronger. Strong like Them. Becoming one of Them.

I pulled up my shorts and crawled from the hole. I looked around and saw no one. I jogged back to the car. I took several deep breaths and told myself to relax. I wouldn't be a very good driver if I didn't. When I climbed into the car, I was careful not to get blood on the seats. Didn't want to listen to Carla's bitching. I scanned the road in either direction, saw no other vehicles, and headed back to town.

I drove straight home, filled up the kitchen sink with a mix of bleach and water, and stripped. I dropped my clothes into the mix and let them soak while I showered. After putting on clean clothes, I returned to the sink, drained and cleaned it thoroughly, and stuffed the clothes into a plastic bag. I carried the bag outside to the trash can.

Time to inspect the Subaru. The seats were okay. Blood from my hands coated the steering wheel and some drops had hit the floor mat, but that was easily cleaned.

Afterward, I headed to the local greenhouse. A great big rose bush in the front yard would sure look good. And it would be a nice surprise for Carla, too. She was always telling me we needed to do something to beautify the yard.

The Punisher

I'M SO SICK AND tired of people trying to tell me how evil I am. I'm the one strapped down to the fucking confinement chair while they stand over me, weapon in hand, evil oozing from their glare, dripping from their every pore. Each of them, individually and as a population, is Satan. Fuel in the fires of hell. They are the ones who give evil reason to thrive. Their actions strengthen the legion of the damned.

Evil is real. And it is stronger now than ever before. Because the governor's Criminal Zoo breeds it. Encourages it. Nurtures it. Turns it back onto the world. If mankind ever had a chance at redemption, that chance died the day the Zoo opened its doors. Right along with society's soul. Civilization—yeah, that's a fucking joke. Nothing civil about it. Man is far crueler than any animal. Far more brutal than any beast. Animals kill for food, to protect their offspring, their mates. Man kills for fun. But he takes it beyond just the act of killing. Man adds in pain and suffering so the killing is more enjoyable. Those who come here, come to hurt me, I know they'd kill me if they had the chance. My suffering is not enough. They want me to suffer. And then die.

They can't kill me, however, because the Zoo *protects* me. Yeah, I like that. Protects me. Because if they kill me, the Zoo can't sell any more tickets to see me. For I'm the star. A main attraction in the most horrifying show on Earth. Step right up, see the Three Monkeys Killer right before your very eyes!

But I know something they don't want me to know. I know I frighten them. I scare them. I give them nightmares. That's why they call *me* the monster. That's why they tie me down, cut on me, try to keep me in my place.

Because of my awareness of a God race, they punish me. Because I know of my full potential, my ability to one day join this race of Gods, they hurt me, dehumanize me. They, the sick fucks who visit me, the L2s who come in with their broken record stories of sorrow, want to believe I'm the cause of evil in the world. But I'm not the cause. I'm the cure.

God said it best. "I am." Well, now I'm saying it. I am the punisher. I am the cleanser. I am the righter of wrongs. I am the one who removes soiled flesh and its accompanying sin. I am the one who takes dirty souls and sends them into the afterlife clean, pure, and new. *I* am.

They want to label me. Serial killer. They can't grasp the concept of who I really am. What I really am. What I am becoming. So I sit in this fucking hell today, tomorrow, next week, next month, waiting for them to come and hurt me. Waiting for them to try to break me. But they won't break me. They can't break me. Because one day I will be a God. And when that happens, I will visit iniquity on them all.

A Glass of Tea with the Sheriff

CARLA WAS ASLEEP WHEN the dark green sedan pulled into the driveway. I must admit I was kind of surprised— about the visit, not about Carla sleeping. Surprised, but not completely unprepared.

I was tending my rose bush, clipping off wilting leaves, watering it, and making sure it would always be a befitting monument to a fun-loving spirit who was once called Jenny.

A man of average height, slightly heavy, climbed from his car and pulled off his sunglasses. "A hot one today, isn't it?" he asked as he approached.

"Sure is." I nodded.

The man's face was deeply tanned and a bit wrinkled from many years in the Texas sun. He was clean-shaven, and he wore his black-and-gray-speckled hair short and proper. He sported a light-colored pair of slacks, white button-up shirt, and a bolo tie with a tiny rattlesnake head encased in the clear acrylic center. I'd seen the bolo ties for sale here and there throughout my life and I'd always wanted one. I never would have worn it; I just thought the snake head was cool. But not cool enough to pay thirty to fifty bucks, depending on the store.

The man's sleeves were rolled up, like he was a real working-class man. But I knew better. When you lived your whole life in

Clemensville, you knew who everybody was, especially Sheriff Melvin Murphy. It was, after all, his third term in office.

"Say, you wouldn't happen to have a few minutes to spare, would you?" Sheriff Murphy asked as he folded his sunglasses and stuck them in his left breast pocket. From his right pocket he pulled out a pair of round spectacles and slid them on his face.

"I suppose I could spare a few minutes." I wiped sweat from my brow with a gloved hand. "Let's get out of the sun. How about a glass of iced tea?"

"That'd be great, thank you. By the way, I'm Melvin Murphy." He held out his right hand.

"Yeah, I know who you are." I pulled off my gardening gloves and dropped them to the ground. I wiped my sweaty hands on my T-shirt and accepted his handshake. "I'm Samuel. Samuel Bradbury." His grip was firm, almost uncomfortable. I released my hand; he held a second longer and then did the same. I led him into the house.

"Have a seat," I said, gesturing to the couch. I moved to the kitchen and poured two glasses of tea. Sheriff Murphy accepted one with a smile and a nod. I hadn't necessarily planned on having a glass of tea with the sheriff today, but I suppose now was as good a time as any to get this talk over with. I knew he was coming eventually. Because I'm smarter than him. I'll always be a step ahead.

"I'm visiting all the residences in the area and was wondering if maybe you had seen this girl recently." The sheriff pulled a picture from his shirt pocket and held it out. "Her name's Jennifer Nelson. She goes by Jenny."

I took the picture from the sheriff. His spectacles couldn't hide the focus of his eyes—my exposed forearms. I looked at the girl. She was as beautiful in print as she was in real life. "I sure have."

The sheriff took a sip of his tea, lowered his glass, and leaned forward like he was excited by my news. "When was the last time you saw her?"

"Just yesterday."

"Really? That's weird."

"Why?"

"Because that's when she disappeared."

"Oh, yeah?"

"Yeah," he said. "Her parents said she never made it home from school. As you can imagine, they're worried clean out of their minds right now."

"I'll bet." I nodded.

"She goes to school just a block down the street. You live between her school and her house."

"Yeah, I know. She told me."

"So you've talked to her, then?" The sheriff's eyes opened a little wider.

"Sure. She usually walks by when I'm working in the yard. Must be just getting out of school, because it's usually in the mid-afternoon. She says hi to me all the time."

"Did you talk to her yesterday?"

"Yeah."

"No kidding?" He pulled his spectacles off. "What'd you talk about?"

"I was pulling weeds when she walked by. We didn't talk more than a few seconds. She said she was in a hurry. She had to meet someone."

"She tell you that?" He used the front of his shirt to clean his glasses.

"Yeah."

"She say who?"

"Nope—just that she was supposed to meet someone."

"A boy someone or a girl someone?"

"Don't know for sure. But I'm figuring it was a boy."

"Why?"

"Because she was acting all excited."

"Excited? In what way?" He replaced his glasses.

"You know, that look you get when something exciting is about to happen with someone special. You could see it in her eyes, on her face."

"You're pretty perceptive, it sounds like."

"Yeah, I kind of have a gift. I usually know what people are feeling even before they tell me."

"What else did you notice?"

"Nothing, really. Like I said, we only spoke briefly."

"You have a wife? A girlfriend? Anyone else living here?"

"I have a Carla. She's a wife. By definition only."

"She see the girl?"

"No, she was at work."

"She here now?" Sheriff Murphy looked around the living room.

"Yeah, she's sleeping."

The sheriff glanced at his watch. "Really?"

"Yeah, she usually works the graveyard. But yesterday she had to pull a double. So she's catching up today."

"So she worked yesterday during the day?"

"Yeah, I just said that."

"And then she worked the night shift?"

"That's why they call it a double shift."

"Long day."

"I know, huh. I told her the same thing."

"So yesterday you were by yourself? All day and into the night?"

"Yeah," I said, never turning my gaze away.

"Must have been lonely. Any neighbors out doing yard work or washing their car or anything at the time you talked to Jenny?"

"Don't know. I was busy with my own yard."

"I see. So anyway, Sam, you wouldn't—"

"Samuel," I interjected. "If my father had wanted me called 'Sam,' he wouldn't have put the 'u-e-l' on the end."

"Yes, of course... So anyway, *Samuel*, you wouldn't happen to know anything about her disappearance, would you?"

"Nope."

"That's too bad." He stared at my arms again. "You got some pretty good scratches there."

"I sure do."

"You mind me asking what happened?"

"Not at all."

The sheriff stared at me, seemed to be willing the words out of my mouth. I said nothing. After a long moment, he shrugged. "So what happened?"

"I got pretty scratched up while planting the rose bush in the front yard. The one I was working on when you showed up. I've never planted one before. Thorns were a lot sharper than I'd imagined. Damn thing got me good, didn't it?"

"Sure did. How about that scratch by your eye?"

"Same thing. The bush."

"Really? Sounds like that bush really gave you a whooping."

"I know. I wasn't paying attention and bent down to trim some leaves from the bottom, and I leaned right into one of the branches. Lucky it didn't put my eye out."

"No kidding."

"It's awfully pretty, though. Wouldn't you say?"

"The bush?"

"Yeah, the bush."

"It certainly is. Mrs. Murphy's been on me to do some beautifications to our front yard. But I hear rose bushes require a little more attention than other plants to thrive. What's the secret?"

"Got me." I shrugged. "I just trim it and water it."

"Really? Nothing special, huh? Maybe I just heard wrong. So where'd you get it?"

"Down at Martin's greenhouse."

"When was that?" The sheriff's brow lifted.

"Yesterday."

"Same day as the conversation with Jenny?"

"Yeah."

"You had a busy day."

I didn't respond.

"About what time was it that you got the bush?"

"Must have been shortly after I saw Jenny. I was putting some water to the lawn and that's when I got the idea. I wanted to surprise Carla with it, so I had to get it into the ground before she got her break between shifts."

"And what time was that?"

"That I planted the rose bush? Or that she got a break?"

"Both," the sheriff said, and then he took a small sip of his tea.

"I'd say around four o'clock on the first, and not until real late on the second."

"That's interesting."

"What, that Carla got off real late?"

"No, that Jenny disappeared right about that same time."

"Boy, I sure hope you find her. She seems like a nice kid."

"From what I'm told, she's a terrific kid. A parent's dream. Anything else you can tell me?"

"Nope. Now you know as much as I know."

The sheriff watched me for several seconds. "Well then, I better be getting a move on." He rose from the couch. "More people to see, more questions to ask. I'll take this to the sink," he

said, grasping the glass of tea. Before I could respond, he moved
to the kitchen and dumped the tea down the sink drain. "My
goodness, Samuel—your sink shines prettier than the diamond
in my wife's wedding ring. Not a spot on it. Do I smell the faint
hint of bleach?"

"I help with the house chores so Carla doesn't have to do all
the work."

"Yeah, my wife's always on me about chores, too." He turned
from the sink and walked toward the front door. "You don't mind
if I stop in now and again just to keep you updated on things,
do you?"

"I'd be disappointed if you didn't, Sheriff."

Sheriff Murphy opened the door; I followed him out. He
pulled the spectacles from his face, placed them in his right
pocket, and from his left dug out the sunglasses. He slid them on
and climbed into his car, looking in the direction of the rose bush.
"She's a leaner."

"Huh?"

"Your rose bush…she's leaning a bit to the left."

"Oh, that. Yeah, my first attempt."

"So, your wife like it?" Sheriff Murphy asked.

"She said it was crooked."

The sheriff nodded. He grabbed a card off the dashboard and
held it out. "Feel free to give me a call down at the station if you
should remember anything else that might be important, okay?"

"I certainly will," I said, reaching for the card.

He didn't move, his eyes hiding behind the sunglasses.

"Do you need something else, Sheriff?" I held his stare.

He shook his head. "Nope. I've taken up too much of your
time already. You have a good day, Sam."

"Samuel."

"Yeah, of course." He nodded and drove away.

I shoved the card into my pocket. Why the hell couldn't anyone ever get my name right? I could only attribute it to laziness. Oh well—more important things to worry about. I wasn't going to have anyone poking fun at my rose bush because it wasn't straight. I grabbed my gloves and went for the shovel.

One Of Them Epileptics

CARLA ONCE BROUGHT UP the subject of having a child. I thought she was teasing. I laughed and told her we would actually need to have sex to produce a kid. She didn't laugh at my joke. After realizing she was serious, I put the kibosh on that right away. I told her the world was not kid-friendly and if we had one we would just be putting another innocent soul in harm's way. I also told her that a kid would take a lot of time and money that we didn't have. And finally, I pointed out that she couldn't even take care of a dog. How was she going to take care of a kid? I believe it was that last argument that silenced her.

Obviously Carla's pregnant friend, Irene, was more persuasive with her husband. Even though she was already having complications with her pregnancy, she insisted on having the baby. I told Carla the whole thing was a bad idea and it would come back to haunt her one day.

I liked Irene but, honestly, I had my worries about her. I saw the way she looked at me. Her eyes clearly revealed the sin in her heart; she had adulterous thoughts about me. About us. At first, I tried to pretend the looks meant something less harmful—like maybe she just thought I was a great guy. But after a while, I couldn't deny the truth any longer. She desired me.

I gave a hell of a lot of thought to the subject of how to handle that situation. I didn't necessarily want to punish her. But since the time of Eve, people have sinned. And because of those sins, people faced the vengeance of their Gods. That was just the way life worked—all you had to do was read the Bible for proof of that. So why should Irene be any different? And seeing as how I was working on joining the God race, and punishment was the Gods' big thing, my hands were tied. It wouldn't be easy, though.

Irene was always nice to me. One of the few people who were. I wondered how the Gods handled the dilemma of punishing their favorite children. Interesting how the Bible never covered that little topic. But whether they struggled or not, the fact remained that bad things happened to good people, so the acts of punishment must have been justified. Yes, of course it was justified, because only through punishment was the soul cleansed. So in the grand scale of things, even though the human mind deemed it severe, the Gods actually healed the souls of the sinners through their acts of punishment. They were definitely a very wise race.

The day before Jenny's body was discovered, I dropped Carla off at work—I needed the car so I could grab some more employment apps—and parked a block down from the convenience mart. When Irene left for the day, I followed her home. She lived about five miles east of town, in the middle of nowhere. Her husband, Al, had business in Dallas for the next couple of days. This information had been relayed to me by Carla.

Irene turned into her driveway and I pulled in behind her.

"Samuel, what are you doing here?" She had a confused look on her face as she climbed from her car and saw me walking up the driveway. It wasn't hard to interpret; she was nervous because of her unexpressed feelings. Irene was a married woman with a baby on the way, and it must have scared her to think of me the way she did. She obviously didn't trust herself, especially with her husband out of town. It kind of made me mad, thinking Irene would jeopardize birthing her child through a canal contaminated with the sin of adultery. I hadn't gone out there to give her a lecture on right from wrong, however, so I held my tongue.

"Carla said Al was in Dallas. I just wanted to make sure you made it home safely," I said, and then smiled.

"That's very nice of you. Thank you." She returned my smile and then shifted toward the front door. "As you can see, I made it. Drive safely on your way back and tell Carla hey for me." She unlocked the door and opened it.

I'm not stupid. She wouldn't have opened it so blatantly wide with me standing there had she not wanted me to come in. I took her up on her invitation and followed her into the house.

"What? Samuel, what are you doing?"

Her feelings for me were obviously stronger than I thought. She looked downright frightened—like something was going to happen between us, something she would regret later—as I entered her living room. She had nothing to fear; I wouldn't let that happen.

"Don't be so nervous, Irene. Geez, I'm just your company picnic three-legged partner, remember?"

"I have a lot to get done, and Al's supposed to be back any time now."

It was probably hard for her to go against her feelings, the feelings that told her to ask me to stay. She obviously wanted me to catch her in her lie.

"You have anything cold to drink?" I asked.

"I'm not sure what you're doing, Samuel, but you really need to leave, okay? Al will be here any moment. And I'm telling you right now, he'd be more than a little mad to find you here."

I moved toward her. "I don't think so, Irene. You're not a very good liar. Carla already told me Al won't be back for several days."

She backed away, unsure of her ability to control herself if I should touch her, her sexual desires probably pushing at their boundaries. I reached for her, but she spun away. *Good job, girl. Fight the desire.* She moved into the kitchen and darted for the phone sitting on the countertop. I moved quickly, not wanting her to make the mistake of calling somebody. In her nervous state, she must not have been thinking about how she would explain why she had invited me in.

"Irene, you can relax. I'm not here because I want something illicit to happen between us."

"Then why are you here?" She backed against the countertop. Her hands swept the area around her. I wasn't sure exactly what she was looking for, but the pan she grabbed just made her look ridiculous.

"Seriously, Irene? What are you going to do, smack me over the head with a frying pan?" A fleeting thought of Brutus passed through my mind. "Put it down."

She shook her head. "Samuel, you're scaring me. Please leave."

"I will, but I have to do something before I go."

"No, Samuel, you don't have to do anything. I'm not kidding. You need to leave right now." She raised the pan over her head like it was a battle ax.

"Do you know how silly you look with that pan over your head?" I moved toward her. "Put it down." I'm pretty sure I looked a lot tougher when I had the pan raised over my head, ready to turn out the lights on Carla's mutt.

"Don't come any closer, Samuel—I'm warning you. Get out of my house or I swear to God I'll crack your head wide open!"

Her words were big, but the fear behind them was even bigger. Was she that terrified of her feelings for me? "You really shouldn't use the Lord's name in vain." I didn't have time to explain that there was actually a race of them.

"Please, Samuel, please leave," she whimpered.

"Okay, okay." I held up my hand and took a step back. "I'm sorry I scared you. I'll leave now." I felt bad about her inner struggle. She was definitely caught in a serious conflict. I took another step back, ready to ease her turmoil.

Irene slowly lowered the pan, but did not set it down.

"Now, let's just calm down," I said, suddenly stepping forward and reaching for her. She swung the pan and I ducked out of the way just in time. "Jesus, Irene! Are you crazy! That could've really hurt!"

Her eyes grew wide and she threw the pan. Her aim was terrible. It crashed into the counter behind me. She tried to run past me. I reached out, caught her by the hair, and pulled. Her feet shot into the air and her head snapped backward. She landed hard on the linoleum floor, flat on her back. She fought to take in air. I shook my head. *Just be thankful you don't have asthma.*

I bent down, leaning on one knee next to her and looking into her scared eyes. "You've got to relax, Irene." I helped her into a seated position. "Now seriously, you're way too uptight. Take in deep breaths. Slow and easy. Just breathe, okay?"

She caught her breath and immediately put it to use with wasted words. "Please don't hurt me or my baby."

"This has nothing to do with your baby. It's about you. It's about consequences. About sin. You have sinned. The Seventh Commandment: *thou shalt not commit adultery.* You've broken that one."

"I don't know what you're talking about. I haven't committed adultery with anyone!"

"Maybe not physically, but you have committed it in your mind and in your heart. And sin in the heart is sin in the spirit. Irene, you've contaminated your soul."

"You're crazy! Please, Samuel, please leave me alone!"

"Are you going to sit there and tell me you haven't had immoral thoughts about me? About us?"

"What?" she asked in a high-pitched voice. "Have you lost your mind?"

"Hey, that's enough, okay? No more lies. I see the way you look at me. The way you've always looked at me. I'm a smart guy, Irene. You don't have to say the words. And you know what, if I weren't married, I definitely would've taken you up on your offer. But I didn't because I have standards and morals. Something you apparently don't have. And now, because of that, you have to be punished."

"I never offered you anything. I'm happily married. Samuel, I love my husband. Please don't hurt me!"

I dropped to my ass, sat directly behind her, my legs straddling hers, and pulled her up against me, my chest to her back. I wrapped my arms around her and felt her warmth in my embrace. It was nice, except for her shaking. But I understood. To be so close to someone you're not supposed to be close to. To touch them but not get to feel them, it would be hard.

"Please, Samuel," she sobbed.

"Shhhh, it's going to be all right." I gently caressed the side of her face. Her skin was soft. But she didn't relax. Instead, she pushed my arms away and tried to jump up. I threw an arm tightly around her neck and pulled her back. I reached into the pocket of my shorts and pulled out my Uncle Henry. During the many years of possessing the pocketknife, I had practiced opening it with one hand just in case of an emergency, like if I was attacked by a gang of drugged-up Hell's Angels. With my left arm wrapped around Irene's neck, my right hand snapped the blade into the open position. The steel reflected the light from the kitchen ceiling.

Irene must have seen the knife, because she started screaming for all she was worth. I was forced to move my hand over her mouth.

"Irene, you have to be punished," I said, resigned. "And believe me, these aren't just empty words when I say this is going to hurt me more than you."

She wasn't listening. She only screamed louder. And then she bit my hand, really hard. I yanked it away, losing a small chunk of flesh.

"Owww!" I screamed, just before pummeling her on the top of her head with my fist.

She had a damn thick skull. Either that or her adrenaline was jacked through the roof due to all the excitement, because she didn't even seem to notice the blow. It did hurt my hand, though. I guess so far I was right—it was hurting me more than her.

"Don't do this! Oh God, Samuel, please don't do this!"

She was only making everything more difficult. I was working a lot harder than I wanted to, not to mention quite possibly at risk of infection because of her bite. Didn't she know how dirty the human mouth was? My hand bled from her teeth marks. I would have to treat it with rubbing alcohol when this was over, just to be safe. I moved out from behind her and shoved her backward, to the floor. She lay flat, looking up at me as I straddled her, pinning her to the floor, her arms by her sides. Her eyes became impossibly wide.

"Irene, you need to be very careful, now. You don't want to make me angry, okay?" I found my words suddenly funny and I almost started to laugh as I thought about an old TV series, *The Incredible Hulk* with Bill Bixby. *You wouldn't like me angry.*

"Please, Samuel...please don't hurt me. I never did anything to you."

"I know."

"Then let me go, okay? I won't tell anyone about this. I won't even tell anyone you were here. I promise. Just go away and we'll forget this ever happened, okay?"

"Don't worry. I will as soon as I'm done." I gave her a comforting smile and then I plunged the Uncle Henry into her right eye.

Her scream sliced through the kitchen. If she had any fine crystal glasses in the cabinet, I'd bet they all shattered. Her arms escaped me and her hands shot to her face, frantically grabbing for the knife. Before she could get hold of the blade, I yanked it out. It actually made a weird sucking sound. The whole thing was pretty interesting. I wondered why we never dissected an eye in high school biology.

"Irene, you can't sin against God and not expect to face the consequences. You've got to be smarter than that. Everyone pays the price sooner or later."

She tried kicking her legs; her arms flailed, trying to strike anything within reach. She found her mark several times, hitting me in the face and on the shoulders. I stabbed the knife into her left eye.

I didn't think I stuck it deep enough to hit her brain, but her entire body suddenly went into violent spasms. So I don't know, maybe I did. Bloody foam sprayed from her mouth, snot ran from her nose, and a mix of blood and slimy goo flowed from both eyes. I could smell the goo. Smelled like rotten chicken. I didn't remember Billy's eyes stinking. Maybe they did, but I was just too caught up in the moment to notice. Or maybe I did hit Irene's brain and that's what stunk so bad. I quickly removed her eyes. Her ears went next. I followed by cutting out her tongue.

Irene's whole body went into crazy spasms, like she was having a seizure or something. I wondered if she was one of them epileptics. I remember having one of them in our junior high. What was her name? I can't remember, but she really creeped me out. Watching her flop around on the floor one day in class was gross.

Irene tried again to climb out from under me. I was surprised by how much strength she still possessed, especially with all the blood she had lost. It took a long time for her to quit thrashing around. Finally, she went limp.

I exhaled loudly, relaxed a little, and looked around. The kitchen was a terrible mess, like a giant water balloon had been dropped from the ceiling. Only filled with blood instead of water.

Another good pair of clothes ruined. As my dad would have noted, clothes don't grow on trees.

The first thing I did was pull off my shoes and then strip completely naked. I dropped my clothes into her kitchen sink, pushed in the sink plug, and filled the basin with cold water. I found a bottle of bleach in the cabinet and poured some into the water. Next, I grabbed the dishtowel that was wrapped through the refrigerator door handle and wiped my body, especially my feet, until they were clean. I dropped the towel on Irene's body.

I found what I was looking for in the hallway closet: bed sheets. I grabbed two and headed back to the kitchen, careful to avoid all the blood. After laying the sheets next to Irene, I lifted her onto them. Man, she must have put on some serious pounds since becoming pregnant. And she sure as hell couldn't blame it all on the baby. I wondered if Al had a problem with that. I rolled her up in the sheets, hoisted her into the air, and carried her out the back door as if she were my new bride. Now getting a full appreciation for her weight, I definitely would've told her to slow down on the pickles and ice cream.

Wearing nothing but my birthday suit, I crossed the yard, hoping not to step on any stickers because those damn things really hurt. I headed out to the field behind her house and laid her body in a patch of weeds. So there I was, standing buck naked with the sun hovering just above the horizon. I looked around and saw nothing but flatness for miles. I had nothing to worry about. As a matter of fact, I enjoyed the freedom from my clothing, existing as Adam and Eve had in the sacred Garden of Eden.

I unrolled the bed sheets from around Irene and then undressed her, placing her clothes in a neat little pile next to her. I stood above her naked body, viewing her swollen breasts and even more swollen belly. The late evening sun felt good on my back and probably would've felt good to Irene. Too bad she was dead. I studied her body, appreciating her beauty. She was way prettier than Carla.

The dark mound between her legs brought about the familiar tickle in my stomach. I grabbed myself, stroked myself. And just as I had with Jenny, I sprayed my seed on Irene. I looked skyward. Nothing. No punishment coming my way.

My heart pounded and I breathed heavily. I wanted to stay and stare at Irene, now covered with blood *and* my semen, but it was time to go. I stared a moment longer, and then turned from her, now heading for the shed in the backyard. I found a shovel. I also found a pair of work boots caked in dried mud. Irene's husband had much bigger feet than I did, but the boots did the trick. I had to admit, I must've looked pretty silly digging in that field, naked except for an oversized pair of muddy boots.

The hole I dug ended up being only a few feet deep and not quite long enough. I had to fold Irene's body into a fetal position. I stuffed her in, stomping on her a couple of times to make sure she would fit, but I didn't bury her just yet. I had some cleaning up to do first.

I went back into the yard, kicked off the boots, and returned to the kitchen. I squeezed as much water as possible from my clothes and examined them. The bloodstains weren't completely gone, but they had faded to a brownish color. I found Irene's dryer in the utility room. While my clothes dried, I spent more than an hour cleaning the kitchen with bleach and rags. I swabbed the floor, the cabinets and countertops, the walls, and even a few places on the ceiling. When I finished, I put the rags into a plastic trash bag and carried it to the backyard. I put the boots on again and headed for the makeshift grave. I stuffed Irene's clothes and the sheets into the trash bag, dropped the bag in with Irene, and stomped it flat against her. Then I grabbed the shovel.

After Irene was completely covered, I trampled the mound several times, packing it down until it was solid. I pulled a few weeds from the surrounding area and dropped them haphazardly over the grave. Blood coated the weeds where I had set the body, so I filled a five-gallon bucket—also from the shed—with water from the backyard spigot. I splashed the weeds, returned the bucket, shovel, and boots to where I had found them, and headed back to the house. I wondered why anyone would kill someone for no good reason. It took way too much work to cover everything up.

Once inside, I pulled my clothes from the dryer, got dressed, and gave the house a quick walkthrough. Everything looked pretty good, so I headed for the car. The grave would eventually be discovered after Irene's husband reported her missing, but I almost laughed as I thought about him trying to explain his boot prints everywhere.

I pulled out of Irene's driveway and headed back to town. I contemplated the death process for a living baby inside a corpse. Did it suffocate? Or did it starve to death? How long would it live? I had no idea; we never discussed that in high school biology.

On the way back to the house, I began to shake with excitement. I had chosen when Irene's life would end. I'm pretty sure I made the same decision for her baby. Weren't those choices a God made? And if I was making God-like choices, wasn't I becoming more like a God, one act at a time?

A Person Of Interest

I WILL NEVER FORGET THE look of hatred in Sheriff Murphy's eyes the night he knocked on my door with the news that they had found the body of young Jennifer Nelson. It was the day after I had visited Irene.

Carla was working and I was getting ready for bed. I had no desire for company, but the sheriff didn't ask to be invited in. He pushed me out of the way.

"Sit down, *Sam*," he said. "We need to talk."

"If my father had wanted—"

"Shut up and listen! And I said *sit down!*"

"Hey, you don't have to be so rude."

He grabbed me by the shoulder and pushed me to the couch. His grip was powerful, reminded me of my dad's.

"You know, you can't just come in here and—"

"We found Jenny today."

"Oh, thank God. Is she okay?" I looked up from the couch. He stood directly over me.

The sheriff's top lip pulled up, an animal-like snarl. I wondered if his yellowed teeth bothered him when he looked into a mirror. "No, she's not okay. She's not okay at all! She's dead!"

"Oh, no." I shook my head. "I'm so sorry to hear that."

"Really?"

"Listen, Sheriff, I don't know what you—"

"And now, guess what."

"Come on, it's late. I really don't care to play guessing games."

"We have a husband out of town that can't get hold of his pregnant wife." The sheriff glared at me. "Apparently she's turned up missing."

"Excuse me, Sheriff, but either she's turned up *or* she's missing. She can't be both."

Sheriff Murphy's eyes narrowed. He took on the look of a tiger ready to pounce. "If you think this is a good time to be funny, you are sadly mistaken. I'm inches away from beating the shit out of you."

"Hey, you can't—"

"And if we throw in the human remains that were found not far from here, things look pretty bad. Got any ideas about what's happening in my town?"

Oh, so now you own the whole town?

"My job, Sam," the sheriff said, not waiting for a response, "is to protect the people of this community."

"Sheriff, I don't—"

"But I'm not doing a very good job of that right now, am I?" He glared at me.

He wasn't going to let me finish anything I said, so I didn't bother.

"I have a daughter. So I'm sure you can understand when I say finding the mutilated—" He stopped himself. "Finding the body of a dead girl upsets me more than you can imagine. I'm sick, absolutely sick to my stomach about this. This is my town. These people expect me to protect them."

"I can imagine how upset you must be."

"Oh, yeah? Can you, really?" He paused only a moment. "Here's the deal, Sam. I think you're a strange fellow. As a matter of fact, I really don't like you much, not much at all. You leave a bad taste in my mouth, like I just chewed on a chunk of shit. My gut is telling me to lock your ass up right this second. Only I don't have anything to go on just yet."

"You are being extremely rude, Sheriff. I didn't do anything to deserve this kind of treatment."

"You admitted to seeing Jenny, to talking to her, the day she disappeared. You were the last person to see her alive. And you're off on your time frame from that day."

"What do you mean?"

"You said you planted the rose bush at around four, remember?"

"Yeah?"

"Turns out you didn't even buy it until almost five thirty. Receipt tape from the nursery."

"Okay, I guess I remembered the time wrong. So sue me."

"What did you do between three fifteen, which would have been about the time Jenny walked home from school, and five thirty, when you bought the bush?"

"Probably chores around the house. Is that a crime?"

"No, but murder is. As soon as I get the lab results back... Oh yeah, did I happen to mention she had flesh underneath her fingernails? I'm going to pursue this like a starving pit bull in search of fresh meat. If the trail leads back to you in any way whatsoever, may the Lord have mercy on your soul. I will not rest until I chew you up and shit you out!"

"How dare you threaten me!" I jumped to my feet, wanting the sheriff to know he had definitely crossed a line. "You have no idea who you're talking to!"

"Is that so?" The sheriff gave me an odd look. "Why don't you tell me, then?"

"I know things about the spirit world that you could never understand or comprehend. I'm becoming something you could never even imagine."

The sheriff stepped toward me, brought his face close to mine, almost touching. "Really? Well then, maybe each Sunday morning, instead of wasting my time listening to the pastor, I should be coming here for lessons."

"Don't mock me." I gave him a stern look.

He didn't flinch. "If I didn't have to follow the rules of the badge that this community has entrusted me with, I would get to the bottom of this right now." He raised his hands, like he was about to grab me. "I would take you apart, piece by stinking shitty piece, until you told me what happened the day Jenny disappeared."

Was he actually shaking?

"So let me leave you with this," he said, now poking me hard in the chest. "I believe you are a sick son of a bitch and I can't wait to have you locked up in my jail. And when that happens, I swear to God, Samuel fucking Bradbury, no one will be able to save your hide. No one!"

I backed away. I wasn't scared; I just didn't like someone touching me, invading my personal space. "'Thou shalt not take the name of the Lord thy God in vain.'"

"What?"

"The Third Commandment. That's the second time you broke it."

"Oh, yeah? Well, how about this one: 'thou shalt not kill.' You do remember that one, don't you?"

"The Sixth Commandment. Yes, I know it well. I know them all well. Now, get out of my house, Sheriff."

"A little FYI…you're now what we call a 'person of interest,' Sam. But only because I don't have enough evidence yet to make you a bona fide suspect. I will, though. Yep, I certainly will. So I'll be back soon—real soon, my friend."

My friend. He spoke the words as if they were coated in vinegar. I steeled my nerves. "You are an uninvited guest in my home. Now get out."

He stared hard at me a moment and then moved toward the door. Just before he let himself out, he turned back. "We'll be keeping an eye on you, so stay close."

After calming down, I walked through the house, deciding if there was anything I really needed to take with me when I left.

Twisted Metal and Shards of Glass

A s I sit in the Criminal Zoo, I look back at certain times of my life, examining some of my decisions and how they led to ending up here. My dad had beaten into my head—literally—the word "consequences." "Samuel, good decisions end in good consequences. Bad decisions end in bad consequences. Which kind do you think you should make?"

One decision I still question was, did I awaken that morning so many years ago with any intentions of hurting my father? I mean *really* hurting him.

My dad had a doctor's appointment in Midland. He suffered from an enlarged prostate and it was playing hell on his ability to take a piss. Just another excuse for him to act like an asshole. He had asked me to drive him because he couldn't find his glasses. Without them, he couldn't see worth a damn, or so he said. If it had been me who lost my glasses, and if I wasn't almost twenty-three years old, he would've busted my ass.

I told him I had other plans. I really didn't, but I had no desire to spend time alone with him, time spent being told how worthless I was. He wasn't having any of my bullshit and he did the whole guilt trip thing until I finally agreed. So I drove him to Midland, but I wasn't happy about it.

I sat in the waiting room at the doctor's office while he disappeared with the nurse. I wondered if she stayed in the examining room while the doctor stuck his finger up my dad's ass. I hoped she did, and I hoped she laughed, because my father had a thing about people laughing at him. It enraged him. I hoped the doctor stuck his finger so far up my dad's ass that it came out his mouth. And I hoped my dad squealed like a stuck pig, the nurse laughing the whole time.

After about twenty minutes, my dad returned to the waiting room. I examined his eyes to see if he had the look of a man who had just been ass-banged while a grown woman laughed. If it happened, he wasn't giving me anything.

"Come on, let's get the hell out of here," he said.

"How'd it go?" I held hope that it had been traumatizing.

"I visited a damned ass doctor! How do you think it went?"

Maybe the trip was worthwhile after all.

Dad had to pick up a prescription from the hospital pharmacy and then we headed back to Clemensville. He had complained the entire trip to Midland, whether about my driving, the state of the government, or his inability to take a "Goddamned piss." I couldn't stand to listen to it all the way home, so out of desire to shut him up—as opposed to having meaningful conversation—I brought up my new goal.

"I'm going to make a movie."

I regretted it immediately after the words hit the air.

"*You're* going to make a movie?" His words dripped with acid.

"Yeah," I defended. "I'm going to make a movie."

"About what? What could you possibly make a movie about?"

Having an abusive asshole for a father. "My childhood."

He stared at me, his nose wrinkled. "You're kidding, right?"

"No, I'm not kidding. What's the problem with me making a movie?"

"What the hell do you know about making movies? What, you think you just go out there and *make* a movie? You think just

anyone can do it?" He laughed. "You making a movie? That's
funny as hell!"

I gripped the steering wheel hard. How could I have been
so stupid? "People make movies all the time. They had to
start somewhere."

"Uh-huh," he grunted. "So your movie is going to be about
mowing lawns? A real edge-of-your-seat film!"

"No, my movie is not about me as a landscaper. It's about me
growing up in Clemensville."

"Riveting!" He laughed.

Why did I even bring this up? What was I thinking?

"Hey, I've got a great idea for you! You could make a movie
about the time you killed your cousin."

My head whipped around, my eyes no longer on the road.
"That wasn't my fault. Jeremy should've been paying attention."

"Yeah, he just fell off that ol' haystack all by himself, right?"

"As a matter of fact, he did. And I sure as hell wasn't the one
who left a pitchfork on the ground, either."

"That's the damnedest thing of it, Samuel. No one else seems
to recollect leaving that pitchfork there."

"So? That doesn't mean I did it."

"Of course not. I'm sure that pitchfork just up and walked
itself to the haystack."

"I didn't do it!" I returned my eyes to the road and said
nothing. I suddenly had no desire to talk to my father. Ever again.

"Make a movie…" my dad mumbled. "You couldn't make a
movie if your life depended on it."

"You know what, Dad, whether you believe in me or
not doesn't matter. I know I can get my movie discovered by
Hollywood, and then I'd finally get the hell out of this stupid little
town. And when I do, I'm never coming back. So you can just sit

in your dumpy old house and wish you hadn't been such a jerk to me all these years."

My dad slapped me hard across the face. "I don't care how old you are, you will not talk to me that way! Do you understand?"

I stared straight ahead, gritting my teeth so hard my jaw muscles cramped.

"Boy, I asked you a question." Out of the corner of my eye, I could see him staring at me. He repeated the question, inserting a pause between each word. "Do...you...understand?"

"I understand." Tears welled in my eyes like I was nine again. No. I would not cry in front of my dad as an adult.

We drove in silence for quite a while before he asked, "So, what's your hard-on with Clemensville?"

Was he kidding? Clemensville offered only stagnation, living life day to day as a plumber, a store clerk, a county employee, or a struggling landscaper. It offered life without dreams, no hope of a future filled with adventure. I envisioned being a famous moviemaker and being interviewed on a talk show, maybe even *The Tonight Show*. I would accept all the praise for my work with a big fat smile. I would tell funny stories, laugh with the audience, and talk about my upcoming film due for release. And when asked about my childhood and where I came from, I would reply, "You know, I live only in the present. As far as I'm concerned, I'm from Hollywood, always have been and always will be."

"You can daydream all you want." My dad's words pulled me from my *Tonight Show* appearance. "But truth is, you mow people's lawns. I did that, too. When I was ten."

The busiest intersection in town was at the north end, where Broadway intersected 349th. Broadway ran east and west, connecting Clemensville to farms and ranches outside of town. The intersection was an indicator of just how small our little corner of the world was. It was one of the few with actual traffic lights; all others were controlled by stop signs. If you were traveling north or south, you met a flashing yellow light. If you were traveling east or west, a flashing red light.

I noticed the farm truck rumbling down the road long before it got to the intersection. It moved toward us, coming from my right, at a speed obviously exceeding the limit. My dad wasn't paying attention. And even if he had been, he couldn't see without his glasses. He had moved on to the next topic: how the Dallas Cowboys had become a bunch of lazy bums and how the entire NFL was headed down the drain. A subject I had no interest in.

I kept an eye on the truck, its speed staying steady as it hurtled in our direction. My foot almost lifted off the gas pedal. But instead of slowing down, I sped up.

"You know," my dad said, "it's bullshit the price they charge for game tickets nowadays. It's because of how much they pay all those Goddamned, spoiled millionaire babies on the field. It makes it impossible for a regular guy to go to a game. If I were a team owner, I would get all the other owners together and we would agree on a set amount to pay the players."

I didn't respond.

"I would pay only so much for a lineman. Those fat asses don't deserve much. And don't even get me started on what I think a punter or placekicker should make. I would pay just so much for a running back. Of course the quarterback gets paid the most, but not the ridiculous amounts they're getting paid now. Not even half of that. Maybe a fourth of it. If every team did it, it's not like the players could walk off."

I watched the truck. It bounced toward the intersection. I looked to my dad. He was shaking his head, mouth turned in a frown. I gauged my speed. I sped up a little more, not exceeding the speed limit by too much.

"Spoiled babies," my dad grumbled, looking straight ahead. "And what's up with all the celebrating in the end zone? What happened to guys like Walter Payton, the guys who would quietly kick your ass by scoring three or four touchdowns on you and then simply hand the ball over to the ref? I shouldn't even watch anymore."

The truck wasn't slowing down. My hands began to tremble.

My dad turned to me. "I suppose you'd just go out there and make a movie so you'd have enough money to pay those babies, huh?"

I looked past him, at the truck barreling towards us.

"Maybe I'll become a golf fan," he said, and then laughed. "Now there's some real athletes! Plaid short pants and all. Dressed just like clowns."

The intersection was maybe a hundred and fifty yards in front of us. I looked straight ahead, but out of the corner of my eye I could see the truck. It hadn't slowed any. Our light flashed yellow. Its light flashed red.

My dad finally noticed I had accelerated. "Hey there, Dale Earnhardt, aren't you going a little fast?"

One hundred yards.

"If you get a ticket, I'm not paying for it. You can use your lawn mowing money." He laughed.

Fifty yards.

"Don't worry, Dad," I said. "I got it covered."

"Samuel, you couldn't cover the cost of a candy bar."

Twenty-five yards.

I looked at my dad, smiled, and then squeezed my eyes shut.

"What the hell are you doing? Jesus Christ, Sam—"

He didn't have time to get through the 'u-e-l' before the world exploded into twisted metal and shards of glass.

Lucky Ticket

WHEN I WOKE, I didn't know where I was. The room was dark and the bed didn't feel like my own. Curtains draped across a window to my right were closed against the light of day, which still found a way to seep around the fabric. I tried to sit up, but a bolt of pain exploded from my head and ran down the length of my body. I tried to turn my head but couldn't. I reached up to my neck and found a soft, stiff collar there. Another brace, plastic—not soft at all—covered my torso.

My face stung like somebody had jammed me headfirst into a hornet's nest. I reached up and felt the bandage wrapped around my head. After a moment, I dropped my hands to my sides and explored the edges of the bed. My right hand brushed across a hard plastic handle with a button in the middle. I pushed it. The upper half of the bed rose, causing me excruciating pain. I released the button. My left hand found a bedside table and something resembling a remote control for a TV. It was attached by a cord to something else—maybe the wall? There was a single button on the apparatus. I carefully pressed it, ready to pull away if the bed started moving again. Nothing happened.

The door swung open and harsh lighting outlined a curvy female figure in the doorway. She took a step into the room. "Yes, Mr. Bradbury?"

Another flash of pain shot through my head. I closed my eyes against it and willed it to go away.

"Mr. Bradbury? The button? You pushed the call button," the full-figured lady said.

I opened my eyes and she pointed to the table beside the bed.

"Where am I?" I asked.

She took another step toward me. "You're in Midland Regional, Mr. Bradbury. You're going to be okay." She fixed a smile on her face.

"What happened?"

"You were involved in an accident."

An accident? What kind of—wait...the truck! The truck hit us!

"Where's my dad?"

She paused, like she didn't know what to say. Her smile fell from her face. "I'm going to get the doctor. He can tell you everything." Before I could ask another question, she turned and exited the room.

A moment later, a thin man with even thinner dark hair entered. He wore a tie, a white lab coat, and a stethoscope around his neck, just like in the movies. "Mr. Bradbury, I'm Dr. Jensen."

"Hey, Doc." I tried to wave a hand, but my arm felt too heavy.

"Mind if I turn the lights on?"

"I don't care."

The doctor flipped the switch and the light tore through my eyes like burning spears.

"Turn 'em off!"

"Sorry," he said. "Head's still hurting pretty bad, huh?" He flipped the switch again.

"Yeah. Can I get something for it?"

"You bet." He turned to the nurse, nodded, and she stepped out of the room. He dragged a chair beside the bed and sat down, taking a deep breath. "Mr. Bradbury, I'm afraid I have some very bad news for you."

I said nothing.

He paused a moment before saying, "Samuel, your father was killed in the accident three days ago."

"Three days ago? I've been in here for three days?" *Shit! How the hell am I going to pay for three days in here?*

"Yes, but did you hear me? Your father was killed."

I searched for words, but nothing came to me. I gave the doc a blank stare.

"I understand this must be a horrible shock for you. Please know that we are here to help you in any way we can." The doctor reached out, took my hand.

His hand was soft, not rough with calluses like my father's when he slapped me.

"How did he die?" I had to speak the words softly so they didn't assault my pounding head.

"Samuel, the truck slammed into his door. He took the majority of the impact. What do you remember about the accident?"

"It wasn't my fault, right?"

"No, you had the right of way. The truck had the flashing red light, but it didn't stop."

"So my dad's really dead?"

"I'm so sorry for your loss, Samuel."

I wondered how Sheila had taken the news. "Where's my sister?"

"She came in shortly after you arrived. She's been in and out since."

"Where is she now?"

"I saw her maybe half an hour ago. She was headed outside to get some fresh air. Said she'd be back soon. Shall I send someone to find her?"

"So what exactly happened?"

"You mean with the accident?"

"Yeah, with the accident."

"You were hit by a farm truck."

"I mean, what happened to my dad?"

"Samuel, I just told you. The truck struck his side full force. He didn't have a chance."

"Was he killed instantly, or did he live for a little while, suffering?"

"Thankfully, he was killed instantly. No suffering."

I sighed. The doctor gave me a compassionate squeeze of the hand. If my head hadn't hurt so much I would've laughed at his gesture.

"You didn't see the truck coming?" the doctor asked.

"Obviously not, or I would've hit the brakes."

"The driver was drunk. He ran the intersection."

"Where is he?"

"Where he belongs. In jail. I'm quite certain he'll be facing the most serious charges."

So it ended like that for my dad—the victim of a drunk driver. Yet I survived. The Gods were watching out for me.

I wondered how much money I was going to get when I sued the drunk bastard who hit us. Somebody was going to pay for my three days in here, and it sure as hell wasn't going to be me. Maybe this was my lucky ticket out of here. Maybe my next stop would be Hollywood.

The Arm of God

THE LAWSUIT PRODUCED NOTHING. Not a damn thing. The piece of shit farmer wasn't merely an out-of-control drunk; he was also a big-time loser. His car insurance coverage had lapsed, his farm was in foreclosure, and his ex-wife—who had left him a couple of months before the accident—had cleaned out the meager remains of their savings. When questioned during the legal proceedings why he was drinking the day of the accident, he blamed it on the "bitch who took everything."

It didn't take long to figure out that my dad hadn't been any better off. He had no life insurance, the second mortgage on his house equaled the value of the property, and his life savings, including the sale of all his belongings, was about four thousand dollars. Sheila and I split the money, which left me with a whopping two grand to get to Hollywood.

If I ever wanted to get out of Clemensville for good, I would need more than that. I would need to think big. Think bold. So I took a road trip to Las Vegas to get the hell out of town and maybe, just maybe, double my money. Or even triple it. Six grand? I'd have enough cash to cruise to Hollywood and rent a little apartment. Then I could start on my movie.

I'd never gambled before, but how hard could it be? Call out a number and color, pull a lever, or add your cards up to twenty-one. I'd heard of people winning hundreds of thousands in Vegas, even millions. I'd never been there, but I figured winning a few thousand dollars certainly wasn't asking for too much. It wasn't like it was going to break any of the casinos.

In hindsight, my plan was flawed from the start. My car broke down on the way there, and it cost me $300 to get it fixed—not counting the ninety-five bucks to tow it. Gas, motels, and meals added up to more than I thought they would. And I had no idea there were so many ways to lose money in Vegas. In a matter of two days, I barely had enough to get home.

Due to heavy road construction on I-40, I took I-15 out of Vegas and headed north before I cut back onto a two-lane highway that crossed northern Arizona and into New Mexico. Had I realized how many curves and twists there were in that road, I never would've taken it. I would've stuck to the interstate and waited out the construction.

I had just passed through Shiprock, New Mexico—a shitty little town known only for a popular landmass not far away. The sun was coming up. I had been driving all night long and was having trouble keeping my eyelids up. I really wanted to get home. I probably shouldn't have been doing eighty-five on that narrow road.

Without realizing it, I had drifted off to the side. By the time I saw the woman, it was too late. She was standing beside her car, the driver's side door open and the hood up. She was looking down and had a phone pressed against her ear. I slammed on the brakes and tried to swerve—honestly. I slid sideways and missed the lady's car, barely. But she wasn't as lucky. I took her out with the passenger side of my car.

I skidded to a stop maybe a hundred or so yards past her car. My heart was in my throat. I threw the car into reverse and backed to where the woman had been standing. I jumped out and searched for her. A pair of flip-flops lay by the side of the road, but the lady wasn't in them. Where the hell was she? Maybe she was still alive. Then I saw her cell phone lying in the dirt. I picked it up and put it to my ear.

"Allie!" a frantic male voice screamed through the phone. "What happened? Allie! Are you there? Are you all right? Allie!"

"Oh, man," I muttered. "Suck me sideways."

This wasn't good. Not good at all. *Just my damned luck.* I dropped the phone to the ground and stomped on it.

I turned around, trying to locate the woman.

Two bare feet stuck out of some tall grass several yards away. They weren't even bloody; maybe she was just a little banged up. I ran to her. For being knocked right out of her flip-flops, she really didn't look all that bad. Her face was pretty broken up, but that was about it for outward appearances.

I had been speeding recklessly. Not just a little, but a lot. If she was dead, and I was to get caught, there'd be no way I'd get out of this one. According to the TV police dramas I watched now and again, I'd probably be facing vehicular manslaughter. I didn't have any money for a lawyer. And everybody knew the hacks the courts appointed didn't care whether they got you off or not. They still got paid.

"Shit," I said, shaking my head. I kicked her foot. "Hey, lady, are you all right?" She didn't respond, so I kicked her harder. "Lady, wake up!"

Nothing.

Son of a bitch! Why does shit like this always happen to me?

Suddenly I received a message. A message from higher up. Call it an inspiration, or maybe enlightenment. Whatever it was, it had to be from Him. Or Them? This hadn't been an accident. Way too big a coincidence. The lady just happened to be standing in the road? The exact stretch of road where I just happened to be driving, at the exact same time? Okay, yeah she was actually standing on the *side* of the road, but still…just a chance encounter? I didn't think so. I looked down at her. Tilted my head.

"So what'd you do?"

She didn't answer.

"Must've been bad, for this to happen and all. They sent me, the arm of God, to serve punishment. Swift and just."

Still no comment.

"Let me guess: cheated on your husband, right? Adultery. That's a bad one. Eternal tortures of Hell, lady. It's just not worth it. Was that him on the phone? The boyfriend?" I paused. "You can't hide your sins from the Gods, honey. They know. And they sent me." It all made sense. The road construction. My choice to take this alternate route. All part of the divine plan. They had directed me.

They had given me a test and I passed with flying colors. The adulteress was punished. Cool.

It did leave a bit of an inconvenient mess on my end, though. I looked skyward. "Hey, how about a little help on the cleanup, you know?"

The Heavens didn't part, a giant broom didn't speed earthward and sweep everything up. I stared for a moment more.

"Fine. I'll take care of it myself."

She had been talking to someone on her cell phone. The boyfriend? Or hell, could've been the husband. He had probably just found a note that she was leaving him and wanted to know what the hell was going on. That's what women did right before they left you. A note.

I kicked the woman's leg. "You deserved this, bitch. He didn't do anything to you. Just loved you with his whole heart. And you left him. Like the bitch you are."

I needed to get moving. Whoever was on the phone was probably now calling the cops. I didn't have much time. I scooped the woman into my arms. As I lifted, she bent in the wrong direction in several places, including her neck. Now I knew why she wasn't responding.

I carried her to my car, dropped her to the ground, and popped the trunk. I took off all her clothes. Shorts, shirt, bra, panties. I don't know why I did that. I just did. I stared at her naked body. It was nice. Really nice. I would've had sex with her if she'd asked. But she never would've asked. Girls that looked like her thought they were too good for me. Or they wanted money.

"Not so high and mighty now, are you, princess?" I asked.

I knew I was pressing my luck, timewise, so I picked her up and threw her in my trunk. I grabbed her clothes and shoved them under my car seat. I would get rid of them later.

I ran to her open car door and saw her purse in the front seat. I climbed in, grabbed her purse—*with cash?*—and her insurance and registration papers from the glove compartment. I wiped off the glove box with my shirt. I wasn't leaving any fingerprints. I jumped out of her car and looked down the road each way. No traffic. I set the woman's stuff on the top of her car, pulled the Uncle Henry from my pocket, and mutilated the vehicle identification number on her dashboard.

I pushed her car door closed with my knee, slammed the hood down with my elbows, and grabbed her stuff. I went back to my car to examine any damage done to it. There was a small dent in the passenger side door and some blood running down the paint. But that was it. With the bottom of my shirt, I wiped the paint clean.

The screwdriver in my glove box was the next order of business. I took off her license plates, careful not to touch the car, and dropped them next to the lady in my trunk. And then I got the hell out of there.

I figured the farther away I was before the locals had a positive ID on the car, the better my chances of avoiding getting caught. I just hoped she hadn't been able to tell her husband where she was before I hit her.

I drove—jacked up on monster-sized cups of coffee and caffeine pills—the rest of the way home, never being stopped once. I went the speed limit the whole way.

I arrived in Clemensville later that afternoon. The first thing I did was set my alarm for three the next morning, and then I slept.

I burned her clothes in a trash barrel. Getting rid of the body was almost as easy. There were a lot of sinkholes just outside of town. A body could be dumped in one of them and not get noticed for a long time.

A Confused Look

NEVER DID MAKE MY movie. After my dad died, and my divinely inspired but costly trip to Vegas, I continued working my landscaping business and barely kept the bills paid. The Gods should've reimbursed me for doing Their work out on that desolate stretch of highway. Would it have killed them to throw a few hands of blackjack my way?

When I married Carla, I put the movie dream away for good. I didn't want to be told I was nothing but a dreamer, to get my head out of the clouds and my feet on the ground. But if I had made it, I know it would've been a blockbuster and my life would've taken a great big turn for the better.

It took me a while to let go, but I finally came to terms with my reality. Maybe I wasn't going to be a famous moviemaker, but I sure as hell didn't plan to spend the rest of my life in Clemensville, either.

And then a guy and his stupid dog finally came across the woman's skeleton left in the sinkhole so long ago. The news crews showed up and everyone got paranoid.

Everything just kind of went to hell from there. The sheriff ended up finding Jenny's body. Irene's husband reported his wife missing. Her whereabouts were soon to be discovered. So, twenty-four hours after Sheriff Murphy's second visit to my house, I returned the favor.

He lived in the ritzy west end of town, in an area I couldn't afford. His residence was made public the last time he was up for re-election, when his opponent made a big deal about his "high-society living and forgetting about the common people." The mudslinging was heavy and the challenger talked about Clemensville needing a man who was "one of the people." A man who lived like everybody else, not in an expensive house that most others couldn't afford. But it obviously bothered the sheriff's opponent more than it bothered everyone else, because Melvin Murphy was re-elected by a pretty fair margin. He explained that because of his job, and his wife's as an elementary school principal, they lived a blessed life. He said working hard and enjoying the benefits of their labor was not a sin, nor did it separate him from those whom he vowed to protect. He lived the American dream and would do whatever it took to ensure that others could live it too.

When the time came to repay Sheriff Murphy's visit, I volunteered to drop Carla off at work. She had worked the night shift last night, and after Irene didn't show up for work, she had to work Irene's shift again today. She got in a few hours of sleep and then went right back to work. Carla bitched, but I saw it as a great opportunity for her to make a little more money. She was always complaining that we didn't have enough. Women—they need to learn to make up their minds.

Carla assumed Irene must have had another doctor's appointment in Midland and didn't bother telling anyone. She called Irene inconsiderate. I told her not to be so quick to judge. "Irene was kind of forgetful," I said. "Probably just a simple mistake."

Carla stared at me, her head tilted. "What do you mean *was*? *Was* kind of forgetful?"

"Was. Is. All the same." I quickly changed the subject. "I need the car to pick up some more apps."

"Oh, bullshit. Don't give me that nonsense," she responded, shaking her head. "For all the ones you've supposedly filled out, you sure as hell aren't getting any phone calls."

I looked at her, hurt in my eyes. "I just thought I could spend a few extra minutes with you on the way to work. I haven't seen you much the last few days. Plus, I thought it would be nice if I picked you up in the morning. You could tell me about your night, that's all."

"Yeah, right. Just don't be late," she answered.

"I won't, honey."

I went home and watched TV for a couple of hours. When the clock in the living room struck nine, I figured it was as good a time as any to pay the sheriff and his family a visit. My suitcase packed, I climbed into the car and drove to the man's house, my headlights boring a tunnel through the darkness. I didn't really have a plan, but I knew that whatever happened, my time in Clemensville had come to an end. Everything was probably going to work out just fine, though, seeing as how I was well on my way to becoming a member of the God race.

I parked in front of the Murphy residence and steeled my nerves. After a moment, I climbed from the car and stared at the house. I remembered something a buddy of mine, Paul, once said. "You know, Sam, if someone wanted to fuck with you, I mean *really* fuck with you, there's not a damn thing you could do about it."

I guess he wasn't actually that good of a buddy. I met him back in the Texas Jack's days, and saw him around once in a while. Come to think about it, he was always fucking with me.

It was time for me to test Paul's theory on the Murphy family.

I stood on the curb in front of the sheriff's house for a moment—looked at my watch—and then made an important decision. It was late, but not too late. I would simply walk up to the front door and knock. The sheriff would assume that if someone wanted to rob his home or hurt his family, that person certainly wouldn't park right in front of the house, stand on the front porch, and alert the family to his presence by knocking. I pulled out my Uncle Henry from the front pocket of my khaki shorts, snapped open the blade, and carefully inserted it into my back pocket—handle exposed. Then I knocked on Sheriff Murphy's door.

A few seconds later, the door partially opened, its movement halted by a thick gold chain. At first, I wanted to drive the heel of my hand into the door, splintering the chain and the lock from the doorframe like I had seen done in the movies. But what if I wasn't strong enough to break through and all I did was hurt my hand or my wrist? That certainly would've given the sheriff reason to question my visit. Not to mention being really embarrassing.

The sheriff peeked around the door, his eyes registering surprise. Then they turned mean. "Sam, what in the hell are you doing here?" He wore a pair of sleep pants and a T-shirt. A black handgun hung at his side, gripped in his right hand.

The gun gave me momentary pause, but it was too late to turn around. "I've been thinking about what you said the other day. I have some information about Jenny that might help you out."

Sheriff Murphy's eyes narrowed. "What do you know?"

"Can I come in?" I asked.

The sheriff stared at me suspiciously.

"I'm unarmed and you are a veteran police officer. I don't really think I present much of a threat. Do you?" *Blind him with his own ego.*

He thought about that a moment and then said, "You know what? You're absolutely right. You don't present a damn bit of threat to me." He closed the door. I heard the chain lock slide from its track. The door opened and the sheriff stood, framed by its archway. He didn't raise the handgun, but he made no show of putting it away. "So now you have information about Jenny, huh?"

"Yeah, I think I do."

"Okay, what it is?"

"Can I come in? It's kind of cool out tonight."

He gave me a hard stare and then brought the gun level to my forehead. "Sam, do you realize that right now I can legally shoot you as an intruder, for no reason at all?"

"Yeah." I swallowed hard.

"Do you also realize I think you're a sick bastard and would have no qualms whatsoever about pulling the trigger?"

Only one way out of this. Forward. "Do you want the information or not?"

"Yeah, but I just want you to realize that any stupid stunt will get you killed. Do you understand?"

"Yeah, I got it." *Stay calm.*

"Okay, come on in." The sheriff backed away from the door, giving me room to enter but never taking his eyes off me.

I stepped through the doorway, exhaled, and forced myself to relax. I occupied my mind momentarily with the beauty of his home. Hardwood floors, fancy light fixtures, paintings on the wall, and it was big—really big! I think I could've fit most of my house in his living room.

"Who's here, Daddy?"

A little girl walked into the room. I was instantly overcome by her youthful beauty. She wore a pink nightgown and matching pink slippers. She had long blond hair, the prettiest blue eyes in the world, and skin that looked every bit as smooth as my mom's. Maybe she was four.

Sheriff Murphy turned his head. "Honey, get back to bed."

With the sheriff focused on his daughter, I snatched the Uncle Henry from my pocket, stepped into him, and plunged the blade into the side of his neck. The knife drove in all the way to the handle.

The sheriff screamed and dropped his gun. He whirled around, but not before I yanked the knife free. I stabbed him in the chest as he lunged at me. He landed on his knees with a loud *thud*, his hands flying to the knife. I pulled the Uncle Henry out of him before he could get a hold of it. That's when his little girl found her lungs. She pierced the air with a shrill scream. I moved toward her and the sheriff grabbed my leg with one hand. With his other, he reached for his gun. I kicked the sheriff in the face with everything I had. His hand fell from my leg and he tumbled backward.

Mrs. Murphy ran into the room, her light blue nightgown flowing and her face frozen in terror. She looked at me, turned her eyes to the floor—to her husband—and screamed.

Too much screaming!

I grabbed the gun from the floor and spun toward the shrieking lady. She jumped in front of the little girl and put her hands up defensively.

"Please don't hurt us," she pleaded, tears flowing down her cheeks.

I had no way of seeing the blow. The sheriff's fist caught me on the side of the head and knocked me to the floor. I hit hard, the gun flying from my grip. Sheriff Murphy dove for it. But I was already on the ground. I grabbed the gun, rolled to my back, and pulled the trigger. A small hole opened in the upper left side of the sheriff's forehead. He flew backward. For a moment, he sat there staring at me as if he wasn't completely convinced this whole thing was happening. Blood bubbled from the new wound in his head. He wore such a confused look, it was almost funny. Okay it wasn't *almost* funny. It *was* funny. Then he toppled over.

The woman screamed again.

"Enough with the screaming!" I turned toward her and fired; her entire nose collapsed inward. The woman dropped to the floor, revealing the frightened little girl standing behind her. The child's mouth opened. I was sure more damned screaming was coming. I ran to her, threw my hand over her mouth. "No more screaming!"

She stared at me with eyes as big as golf balls, not making a sound. The screams in the house, not to mention the gunshots, had no doubt alerted the neighborhood. I stuck the gun in the waistband of my pants, hoisted the kid into the air, and headed for the front door. The little brat bit me before I took two steps. I jerked my hand away and struck her with an open hand. At least I didn't have calluses like my dad.

"Don't do that again!" I covered her mouth, this time hard enough that she couldn't bite me.

I stepped over Sheriff Murphy's body and was amazed at the amount of blood that had already pooled beneath his head. But then again, I'd heard head wounds tend to bleed a lot. The sheriff's eyes were still open.

I moved quickly to the door, carried his daughter down the driveway to the car, and placed her in the backseat. That's when I heard the sirens. They were faint, but getting louder.

I had driven a little more than two blocks when a patrol cruiser flew past me. I was doing the posted twenty-five miles an hour, looking straight ahead, as if I knew nothing of what had just transpired behind me. I continued to the nearest gas station.

I pulled up to the pumps, climbed from the car, and locked the doors. I watched the girl through the car window as I filled the car with gas. She lay curled up motionless on the backseat. I topped off the car's tank and headed into the store for a carton of chocolate milk, a box of Pop Tarts—strawberry, my favorite—a box of NoDoz. The clean-cut young man working the cash register smiled. That was before he found out I had no money and no means of paying for my gas. I pulled the gun from my pants and shot him where I thought his heart probably was. His smile disappeared as he fell over backward.

The Gods spoke to me again. *Good job*, They said inside my head. They wanted the kid dead. Man, I was surrounded by sinners.

It was time to leave Clemensville forever. But first, I had a quick job to do. Couldn't very well haul a four-year-old kid around with me. Although she was pretty damn cute.

My Little Angel

NEVER LOOKED BACK AS I drove away. The stinking little town of Clemensville would be nothing more than a bad memory.

I wish I could've kept the girl. Psalms 127:3: "Children are a gift from the Lord; they are a reward from Him." She could have been my reward. A witness to my transformation. A spirit proclaiming my greatness. But in the end, I couldn't realistically travel while taking care of a child.

I pulled over on a desolate stretch of road, climbed into the backseat, and gently caressed her hair. She cried in my arms. I comforted her as best I could. But time ran out and I had to get moving.

"You truly are a gift from God," I told her. I smiled. I wanted her to understand I knew the truth of her existence. I ran the back of my hand ever so gently over her cheek. So soft. So pure. Surely straight from Heaven. "My little angel," I said, pulling out my Uncle Henry.

Tears escaped her terrified eyes, ran down her cheeks.

"Don't be scared, honey. A new life awaits you."

The Way Everything Works

A FTER RIDDING MYSELF OF the girl, I drove the hour and a half to my sister's place in Monahans. How she could live in that crappy little town, I never understood. But I had nowhere else to go. Plus, I really needed to get cleaned up.

"JESUS, SAMUEL, IT'S TWO in the morning." Sheila stood in the doorway, rubbing her eyes. She wore a cotton T-shirt and a pair of pink boxer briefs. Her hair—sometimes blonde, other times brown, once even red; tonight back to brown—shot in all directions like Medusa's snakes, angry at being awakened.

"Hi, Sis. Glad to see you, too."

She must have finally gotten the sleep rubbed from her eyes, because a look of bewilderment flashed across her face. "Holy shit, Samuel, is that blood?"

"I guess it is."

"What the hell happened?"

We stood on the front porch of her trailer, the exposed light bulb shining down on me. The unit sat on a corner lot in a trailer park on the south side of town. A streetlamp fastened to a telephone pole illuminated much of the property.

"Can I come in? I need a place to stay for the night. I think I might've gotten myself into some trouble." Killing the gas station attendant was a bad decision. They would have me on camera. *Bad decisions end in bad consequences.*

"Some trouble? What trouble? What happened? Why are you covered in blood? Where's Carla? Is she all right?"

"Sheila, please." I held up my hand. "You'll get all your answers, but first I really need to get cleaned up. You don't happen to have any clothes here that'd fit me, do you?"

"No, I don't think so."

The look in her eyes told me she was afraid of me. "Why are you looking at me like that?"

"Samuel, I don't think—"

"I said, 'why are you looking at me like that?'"

"Oh, I don't know...maybe because you're standing on my doorstep in the middle of the night covered in blood!"

"Hey, I know showing up here like this is a bit of a shock, but I can explain. I have some things, very important things, I need to tell you. But first, I've got to get out of these clothes." I pushed past her and entered the trailer. "You'll understand everything soon, okay?"

She followed me in; I pulled the door closed behind her and pushed in the lock on the doorknob. "Just relax on the couch for a minute. I'll explain everything, okay?" I headed for the bathroom and closed the door.

I pulled off my shirt and bent over the sink to splash cold water over my face and onto my hair, then went to work with a white washcloth hanging on a towel rod. Sheila would be mad about the washcloth, but she'd get over it. I turned the cold water to hot and washed my face, chest, arms, and stomach. The warm water felt good. I was about to slide out of my jeans when I thought I heard Sheila talking in the living room.

"Hey, who you talking to?" I asked, pushing the bathroom door open.

She flinched and hit a button on her cell phone. "Huh?"

"Sheila, who'd you just call?" My heart beat faster.

She stared blankly at me.

"Oh man, Sheila, please tell me you didn't just do something stupid. You didn't, right?" I moved toward her. "Who did you call?" *Stay calm,* I told myself. *My sister wouldn't do anything to hurt me.* I put my arm around her; she trembled. "Come sit with me."

I walked her to the couch and sat her down. *Relax. Be calm. Talk to her.* I sat next to her.

"I told you I would give you all the answers you wanted. Now, if you've called someone you shouldn't have, I won't be able to tell you the things I need to tell you."

"You're scaring me."

I pulled her close. "Hey, I love you. Don't be scared. You're my sis, remember? My own flesh and blood."

She pushed me away. "Why are you all bloody? Did you do something to Carla?"

"No, unfortunately she's fine," I said. "Actually, better than fine. But this isn't about her. There's something I need to tell you. Something really amazing has happened, is still happening, in my life. Something very, very important."

"What's happened?"

"First, tell me who you called."

"No one. I was about to call a friend, but I changed my mind."

"I thought I heard you talking. You wouldn't be lying to me, would you?"

"No. I promise."

"Good." I exhaled in relief. "I've come to awareness."

"Awareness? Awareness of what?"

"Actually, I'm surprised it's taken me this long to get it, seeing as how I've studied the scriptures all my life. And I'm surprised more people don't get it."

"I have no idea what you're talking about."

"I know; that's the problem. We don't pay close enough attention. We're all too absorbed in the chaos of our everyday lives to really understand the way everything works."

"Samuel, it's late. Maybe you should—"

"It says it in the Book of Genesis. It was right there in black and white, right in front of my nose the whole time."

"What was?"

"*Our* image. Make man like *Us*." Why was my sister looking at me so strangely? "Don't you get it? God.... But not just the *one*, I'm talking about *all* of Them."

"All of them? All of who?"

"Gods, Sheila. Gods."

"Jesus, Samuel, you're not making any sense whatsoever."

"Don't you get it? I'm talking about the realization, the understanding, that we all can become Gods."

She slowly shook her head from side to side. "Samuel, I really think—"

I pressed my finger to her lips. "It's already started."

I had hoped that she, being my sister, would understand better than anyone what I was trying to tell her, what I was revealing. Apparently she didn't. The strange look—perhaps confusion, dismay, doubt—returned to her face. She tried to stand up. I grabbed her wrist and pulled her back down.

"Let me go! I don't know what kind of trouble you've gotten yourself into, and I'm sorry if you have, but I want you to leave, now!"

"Come on, Sheila, it's me, Samuel. Your baby brother. You can't kick me out."

She looked at me like she didn't know me, as if all our years of growing up together had suddenly evaporated.

"Why are you acting like this? I came here to tell you—" The crunch of gravel outside and the sound of a car motor stopped me midsentence. "Oh, no. Tell me you didn't call someone over." She stared at me.

"Jesus, Sheila, who'd you call?" *Shit!* I didn't want this to go bad.

"Chad."

"Who the hell's Chad?"

"He's my friend. I told you to leave. Samuel, I gave you a chance." Tears welled in her eyes.

"Oh God, Sheila. Oh my fucking God." Disappointment cut through me.

"I'm sorry." Her eyes filled and tears ran down her cheeks. "You scared me. I didn't know what else to do. If you haven't done anything wrong, I'll just tell him I was worried about you, that's all."

"How could you do this? I'm your own brother, for Christ's sake." I jumped from the couch, placed my hand on the bulge created by the Uncle Henry in my pocket, and headed for the window. I pulled the curtains aside and my heart missed a beat. I watched as a police officer climbed from his cruiser. "A cop? Chad's a Goddamned cop?"

"He's my friend."

"You're fucking him, aren't you? You little whore, you're fucking a cop!"

"No, Samuel, we're just friends."

"Right, that's why he drops everything to come over here in the middle of the night. Shit—Sheila, you have no idea what you have done!" I moved to her, grabbed her by the shoulders. "And just as Judas did to Jesus, you have done to me. You can't let him in. Tell him to go away!"

"I'm sorry," she cried. "I'm so sorry."

The sound of footsteps on the porch penetrated the door. The doorknob rattled.

Cast It Out

THE ABRUPT POUNDING ON the front door made me jump. A muffled voice followed. "Hey, Sheila, it's Chad. Let me in."

"Tell him everything's fine," I whispered. My heart raced. "Tell him to go away."

Sheila whimpered. "Don't hurt me, Samuel. I didn't do anything to you."

I released one of her arms and pulled the Uncle Henry from my pocket. I snapped it open with one hand. Dried blood clung to the blade. I pushed the knife against her throat. "Tell him everything's fine!"

I hated the look I saw in her eyes. It wasn't supposed to go like this. Always in the past, I was the one who took her fears away. I was the one who checked under her bed for monsters. I was the one who opened the closet door, ready to pummel the boogeyman. I was the one who intercepted our father's rage, often taking a beating so Sheila wouldn't have to. Now, my sister was terrified, and her terror came not from our father, but from me.

The man's voice penetrated the door again, louder this time. "Sheila, open the door!"

My heart slammed against my chest. "I'm not kidding, Sheila! Tell him you're fine! Tell him to go away!" I pushed harder on the blade.

"Samuel, please don't hurt me," she pleaded.

"Sheila," the man called through the door. "I'm coming in."

I grabbed my sister by her hair and she cried out. I pushed the blade against her flesh until a thin stream of red appeared. "Tell him to go away!"

"Everything's fine, Chad! I'm fine!" She was terribly unconvincing.

There was a pause and then a massive slam against the door. It almost caved in.

I released Sheila, jumped to my feet, and darted to the door. "I have a gun!" I did. But I stupidly left it in the car. Chad didn't know that, though. "If you try to come in, I swear to God I'll kill her!" I screamed in my most menacing voice.

I ran to my sister, grabbed her arm, and yanked her down the hall. I threw her into the bedroom, closed and locked the door behind us, and pushed her down onto her bed.

Do as God does enough times and become as He is. As They are.

"I don't have much time!" I shouted, holding her down. "But I have to do something. It's not something I necessarily want to do, but something I *have* to do."

"No! Samuel, let go." Tears streamed from her eyes. "Don't do this."

I shook my head and climbed on top of her. "Don't cry, honey."

"Let go of me!"

She tried to push me away. I held her tightly and moved to kiss her on the cheek. The sting of her slap caught me off guard. Without even thinking about it, I punched her. "Oh, Sheila, I'm so sorry! I didn't mean to do that."

She screamed. Blood ran from both nostrils and streamed down either side of her face. "Samuel, stop!"

I forced her arms out to each side and put a knee on top of each arm, pinning them down.

I grabbed her jaw and pried her mouth open. Making a fist with my left hand, I wedged it into her mouth. She bit down hard; pain shot through my hand and up my arm. But I couldn't let the pain stop me. I pushed my hand to the left side of her mouth and flexed my fist as hard as I could. I shoved it downward, opening her mouth even further. Her jaw cracked and seemed to separate at the hinges. She screamed louder than ever. I pulled my hand free and was stunned by what I saw. Her eyes were wide with terror as she struggled in what I could only assume was an attempt to close her gaping mouth. But it wouldn't close. It was frozen wide open. She screamed again and again.

The entire trailer shuddered. Chad had busted through the front door. I was out of time.

Do it. Do it now. Become as God is, now.

I grabbed her tongue. "Sheila, while you have existed in this unholy world, you have sinned. Because of the things you have said, your soul is contaminated. From the tiniest white lie as a kid to the hurtful lies told as an adult, you have soiled your soul." I held the Uncle Henry in my right hand and stabbed it into her tongue.

She tried to scream, but because of my grip on her tongue and the knife blade, her attempt was only a gurgle.

"And even worse," I continued, "you've probably taken men into your mouth and allowed them to spray their seed upon your tongue. Your disgusting actions come with dire consequences."

The bedroom door rattled.

I turned to the door and screamed, "If you come through that door, I'll pull the trigger! I swear to God I'll blow her fucking head off!"

I returned to my sister and sliced through her tongue, amazed every time by how muscular the tissue was. I threw it to the floor and continued the ritual.

"Sheila, through your ears you have been subjected to evil. You have listened to things a pure spirit should never hear. Men have whispered filth into your soul." I pushed her head against the bed and, with great effort, sliced off her left ear. She jerked violently.

"Sheila!" Chad screamed from outside the door.

Sheila tried to squirm out from under me. Blood poured from her head and mouth.

"Hold still!" I commanded.

I cranked her head to the other side. Despite her fighting, her right ear came off a little easier. I moved on.

"In the book of Mark, Chapter 9, Verse 47, we are told, 'If thine eye cause thee to stumble, cast it out.' Because of the immoral things you have watched, the evils to which you have borne witness, you have stumbled. Your soul has been defiled, stained, and contaminated. But I can give you true and eternal freedom from the sins your eyes have witnessed. I can cast them out."

She kicked in desperation, tried to free her arms.

"You have watched as men undressed before you, with fornication on their mind. By your own choice, you have watched your body be violated, allowed things to be done to you which desecrate the soul."

I removed her left eye. And then her right.

Sheila thrashed from side to side. Blood splattered me, her, the bed, the walls, the floor, everywhere. It took all my strength to hold her down. I really had no idea my sister was so strong. I wondered if she'd been working out.

The bedroom door exploded. Chad charged in, his service revolver leading the way. His eyes grew instantly wide, his mouth dropped open. I suppose it did look pretty bad.

"Oh my God!" he yelled.

"Do you see what you've done?" I screamed at Chad. "Because of your filthy lust for my sister, I had to take these actions. You did this. I hope you're happy, you fucking bastard."

Sheila again tried to scream. And again, nothing but gurgling and blood frothing in her mouth. She thrashed underneath me. The thunderous discharge of the gun startled me. A hole suddenly appeared in the wall just to my left.

"Hey, wait a minute!" I clenched the Uncle Henry in my right hand, held up my left hand directly before me and looked at the cop, bewildered. He fired again. I heard another hole punch into the wall. But this time, it sounded like it was directly behind me. I looked at my hand and was confused by the blood that now ran from the hole in the middle of it. I looked down and saw a matching hole in the right side of my chest. Blood ran down my stomach. My eyes darted back to the cop. He stood with his feet spread; he briefly swayed, and his gun trembled in his hands.

"Just wait one Goddamned minute!" I screamed.

Chad squeezed the trigger again. Another explosion. My head was driven backward. And then there was only blackness.

The Beginning of the Nightmare

I SPENT OVER THREE WEEKS in the hospital recovering from the bullet that passed completely through my chest—after putting a hole through my hand—and another that struck me just above my left eye. That bastard didn't have any reason to shoot me twice. I was no threat to him. He had a gun and I had a tiny little pocketknife. Police brutality at its worst. Had I not been well on my way to Godhood, his disregard for what's right and what's wrong could've gotten me killed. But he did it to impress my sister, I know he did. And I was certainly going to bring that to the attention of the judge when my day in court came.

The doctor said it was a miracle I was alive. He said my head was turned just enough that the bullet penetrated the frontal bone of my skull at a slight angle, altering its trajectory and sending it into my sinus cavity. It then smashed sideways into a second wall of bone, fragmenting before it could enter my brain. He said the first bullet missed my heart by millimeters. Angles and millimeters—whatever. A budding member of the God race could be hurt during the whole "God-making" process, but obviously I couldn't be killed. And after the transition was completed…well, just watch out, world, because my vengeance would spill forth.

Immediately after my recovery, I was moved to the Midland County Detention Center, where I remained during my trial for seven counts of murder and one count of attempted murder. It wasn't fair that they counted Irene's unborn baby as a murder victim. I never even touched the kid. And attempted murder? I wasn't trying to kill my own sister. Why the hell would I do that?

I spent the entire time in isolation. I was allowed to go out to the yard and get some exercise for one hour a day, but all the other inmates had to return to their cells first. Apparently they all wanted a piece of me because I was a child killer—as if the savages in the detention center had morals and values. And the jailers were no better. To them I was a cop killer. I was the most hated prisoner in the whole jail.

My initial court appearance happened through video hookup. I was assigned a public defender, a woman, but she didn't last long; I don't even remember her name. After only a week of working on my defense, she asked to be removed from the case. She was obviously intimidated by my intelligence. So the state assigned me a new defender, this time a man. His name was Robert Michaels.

I'm still not convinced Bob gave my defense his all. He seemed like a smart enough guy, but it was almost like he didn't trust me, like he kept expecting me to attack him if he turned his back. And he seemed conflicted, like he was possibly going against his own convictions. I was even compelled to remind him at one point, "Bob, you're a lawyer. You don't have convictions, remember?"

Had his response not been so annoying, it would've been comical. "Samuel," he said, "I have more conviction in one fingernail than you'll ever have."

He was full of shit. No one had more conviction than I did. He sat in his fancy suit and tie, staring across the table, looking down on me like I wasn't smart enough to understand what kind of trouble I was in. He took notes while we talked, but I knew he never really planned on working for me. I'm sure each night he went home to his spoiled little wife and spoiled kids, watched TV, and probably fell asleep in his recliner to a brainless reality show. He probably didn't give my loss of freedom a second thought. If I was really a cold-blooded killer, I would've killed him right there.

Regardless of our differences, however, he was at least professional enough to stay with me through the trial, which turned out to be a complete mockery of the legal system. I was told they were going to film the proceedings for TV. It pissed me off that they didn't ask my permission, and even worse, they never offered me any money.

On the first day, half a dozen deputies escorted me from my jail cell—via the back door to bypass any media—to a waiting black van with heavily tinted windows. I asked the deputy at my side if they got the vehicle from a Secret Service garage sale. He was clearly born without a sense of humor.

My hands were shackled to a heavy and extremely uncomfortable chain wrapped around my waist. My feet were also shackled; another chain connected the one around my waist to the one around my feet. I told them that the chains were hurting me, but they didn't care. My pain apparently didn't matter anymore.

My movement was more shuffling than anything else, my stride limited to twelve inches. I wore a heavy bulletproof vest over a donated dress shirt and tie. I didn't really believe I needed the vest, but they didn't give me a choice.

I was stunned to see the chaos when we pulled up to the courthouse. The front steps were packed with news crews and photographers. *All this for me?* We drove past the melee and pulled up to the back of the building. When the van came to a stop, we were alone, but it didn't take long for a throng of reporters—they came out of nowhere—to converge on us. The mob overwhelmed us as the cops escorted me from the vehicle.

People pushed and shoved for a better vantage point. Dozens of cameras were crammed into my face and flashes went off like machine gun fire. The deputies did their best to push everyone back, but there were just too many people crowding in on us.

A jacket was thrown over my head. The officers flanking me each grabbed an elbow, without regard for how hard they squeezed, and pulled me forward. I had great difficulty moving my feet fast enough to keep up. Someone shoved me in the back, again with complete disregard for my comfort. I fell forward, my hands still chained to my waist.

The deputies at my sides must have been as surprised by my fall as I was, because no one caught me. I landed on the pavement, face first. The pain was horrifying, like someone had just smashed my face in with a frying pan. Now I knew what Brutus must have felt.

Suddenly, hands were all over me. Where were they when I was crashing to the ground? They yanked me up and carried me into the building. They hurried me down a hallway, into a back room, and then slammed me into a chair as if the frenzy had been my fault. As with my dad, I tried to control the tears. I didn't want to give those assholes the satisfaction of seeing me cry. Even so, tears ran down my cheeks, mixing with the blood pouring from my nose and mouth and dripping onto my pants.

"Jesus H. Christ," one of the deputies shouted. "We can't take him into the courtroom looking like this."

I looked at the man. "You shouldn't take the Lord's name in vain. I'm—"

"Shut up!" the deputy exclaimed.

I was just about to tell him he didn't have to be so rude when Bob, the subpar public defender, entered the room.

"What in the hell? What did you guys do to him?" He looked at me, his nose and forehead crinkled, and then to a deputy.

"The clumsy bastard fell down outside," the deputy said. "I think he was trying to make a break for it."

"You liar," I screamed. "You—"

"He's lucky we didn't shoot his sorry ass." The deputy stared at me. "Maybe next time he won't try to run."

"You sure are tough when I'm wrapped in chains," I said, returning his stare. "Let me out of them and let's see what happens."

The deputy leaned in. "I can't think of one thing in the whole wide world I would like more than going a few rounds with you, ass-fuck. But fortunately for you, I can't."

"Enough already," Bob said. "The judge will need to be notified. My client needs to be cleaned up and given medical attention and a clean set of clothes."

My jaw began to quiver. My mouth filled with saliva and blood. "I think I'm going to be sick."

"Yeah, that's just what we need," the officer closest to me said. "Get this piece of shit to the bathroom before he pukes all over everything."

A cop jerked me to my feet and shoved me forward, this time gripping the back of my Kevlar vest. We exited the room, crossed the hallway, and moved toward a bathroom. I didn't make it. All the excitement, along with my pain and the sorry excuse for food served in the jail that morning, pushed me over the edge. I threw up all over myself and the deputy in front of me.

"Motherfucker," the deputy cursed. He spun around with his hand raised, ready to punch me. "You puked on me, you stupid bastard."

Another officer grabbed his arm. "Aaron, are you crazy? You can't hit him!"

"Why the fuck not? He puked on me! Besides, he's a piece of shit and we all know it!"

"So? We don't get to hit every piece of shit we meet. Otherwise I would've already laid the warped bastard out. Now, relax."

"He's a cop killer."

"I know. And if we could take him out, I'd be the first to put a bullet between his eyes."

"You guys already tried that. And I'm still here."

The officer let go of Deputy Aaron's arm and turned to me. He leaned real close. "Just give me a reason."

Aaron lowered his hand and laughed. "They're going to sentence you to the Confinement Center. And then you know what happens? After you lose your mind in there, they send you to the Criminal Zoo. And once you get in there, you're fucked. Torture city, baby."

Both cops glared at me and then shoved me into the bathroom. They cleaned me up with little effort and returned me to the room from which I had just come.

Bob shook his head. "My God, this is an absolute nightmare."

Unfortunately, it was only the beginning of the nightmare. If I had wanted a fair trial, I was in the wrong courtroom and the wrong town. And because of the national media coverage, maybe even the wrong country.

The judge granted me a one-day delay and ordered me back to jail so they could clean me up. Afterward, they escorted me to my cell. And during the whole process, not one single person said they were sorry.

A Mockery

B OB HAD WARNED ME that my sister would be the star witness for the prosecution. I didn't believe him. She wouldn't testify against me; I was her baby brother.

I was wrong.

The first time Sheila walked into the courtroom, escorted by two sheriff deputies, I knew something was wrong. Her movements were rigid. The way she walked, her mannerism, and the harsh expression on her face. It just didn't feel right.

She wore a light blue summer dress, revealing how much weight she had lost. It wasn't that she was ever fat, but she certainly was never that thin before. She didn't look healthy. Her hair was bleached blonde and shorter than before, but it still covered whatever kept her sunglasses pulled against her face. Maybe she had her ears reconstructed. Deputies led her to a chair directly behind the prosecution's table and then the officers moved to each side of the courtroom and took up their posts.

I turned in my seat and looked at the crowd behind me. It was standing room only. Everyone was here because of me. It was actually kind of cool.

OVER THE NEXT FEW WEEKS, the prosecution called all kinds of people to the stand. Some I knew, like an old boss, a former coworker, several of my neighbors, and then my wife. When

Carla took the stand, her eyes told me everything. I had changed her life. For the better. She was grateful. I smiled. She smiled back. On the stand, she frustrated the prosecution. She was friendly to the defense. *Atta girl, Carla,* I thought.

Other than Carla, most of the witnesses they called didn't even know me. They were either doctors or some kind of experts on this or that, talking about the fatal injuries inflicted on my victims. It was easy to see those witnesses were there simply for shock value, their only job being to scare the jury into a guilty verdict. I saw right through their ploy. I hoped the jury did too.

And then the prosecution called their second-to-last witness.

"Your Honor," the prosecutor began, "we would like to call to the stand Ms. Sheila Bradbury."

"Proceed."

The prosecutor turned to my sister. Suddenly the volume of his voice increased dramatically. "Ms. Bradbury, could you please come forward!"

She rose from her chair and was escorted to the stand. The trial became a mockery from that moment on.

The prosecutor turned to the jury and shouted, "For the record, ladies and gentlemen of the jury, Ms. Bradbury's hearing has been seriously impaired due to Samuel's attack."

"Your Honor, I object!" Bob jumped to his feet. I was surprised he had the balls to even bring up an objection before the judge. "The prosecution is implanting the notion that the details of the attack on Ms. Bradbury have already been established, when in fact they have not. That is the whole purpose of these proceedings, is it not?"

"Objection sustained," the judge responded. Bob returned to his seat as the judge continued, facing the prosecutor. "The prosecution's last remark will be stricken from the record. The need to inform the court of Ms. Bradbury's impairments is understandable. However, you must do so without leading the jury to prematurely assign guilt."

The prosecutor faced the judge. "Yes, sir." He turned back to the jury. "Because of the injuries Ms. Bradbury sustained during her attack, I must speak loudly, almost yell, if she is to hear me. She suffered tremendous hearing loss, almost total loss, due to equilateral eardrum damage sustained in the knife attack, as divulged by our expert medical witnesses. And she will only be answering questions phrased in yes or no format, since her tongue was also viciously cut out."

Bob climbed back to his feet. "Your Honor, again I must object. The prosecution is not only exploiting Ms. Bradbury's physical conditions to initiate sympathy for the witness, but he is also attempting to influence the emotions of the jury by using such adjectives as *viciously*."

"That's an adverb. Overruled. The prosecution is simply bringing awareness to the jury as to why his voice is elevated and why all his inquiries will be introduced in a basic yes or no format. And I think we can all agree the jury is well aware of the brutality involved in the attack on Ms. Bradbury, regardless of who carried it out. The prosecution may continue."

Bob shook his head and returned to his seat.

Sheila was dressed more formally than during any of the previous days. She wore dark slacks, a white blouse, and a dark blazer. I wondered who picked out her clothes, making sure she matched. I could do it. I could be the one to get her dressed each day, to make sure she looked as beautiful as possible. As a matter of fact, I should be the one to do it. I was still her brother, after all. We were family.

She had removed the sunglasses and, despite her eyelids kind of caving into her empty sockets, she still looked like my

big sister. I wanted to tell her that everything would be fine if
everyone would just leave us alone.

Things weren't fine, though. Everything just kept getting
worse. My sister's answers to the many horrible and extremely
unfair questions asked by the prosecuting attorney swayed the
courtroom. He referred to me as a "malevolent aberration of
mankind." I didn't know exactly what that meant, but I wasn't
whatever he called me. I was a soul rising from the mediocrity of
mankind through spiritual enlightenment.

I turned toward the crowd behind me, as I did each day,
and was pleased by the attendance. Full house. And I began to
understand. I was not a celebrity. These were not my fans. I was
a budding God, and these were my followers.

Bob questioned Sheila after the prosecution finished. It didn't
go well. He stumbled with his questions, continually having to
rephrase them so she could answer yes or no. He got flustered.
Watching him up there was like watching a car crash in slow
motion. He was supposed to ask her things that would help me,
but he obviously didn't remember that.

It didn't help that Sheila put on a *poor me* act for the jury. I
had seen it before. She did it all the time as a kid. She wouldn't
answer a lot of Bob's questions, pointing to where her tongue
used to be. The judge instructed Bob to rephrase his questions
again and again.

Sheila was helped down from the stand and led to the
aisle. I reached for her as she passed, but one of the deputies
rudely shoved my hand away. He glared at me, daring me to do
something about it.

Finally, the last witness was called. Chad, the piece-of-shit cop
from my sister's trailer, took the stand. Yeah, the same guy who
had tried to murder me. Why wasn't he on trial for attempted

murder? He was also fucking my sister. Wasn't that a conflict of interest?

Chad took his seat, his eyes locked onto mine. Suddenly every little detail of that night flooded back. Chad bursting into Sheila's room and his look of disbelief, immediately erased by the twist of hatred. He hated me without even knowing me. He didn't know what was going on, had no awareness of the spiritual act I was engaged in. And yet, he hated me. He raised his gun and pulled the trigger for no reason at all.

I held his gaze in the courtroom. Ultimately, when I took my place beside the other Gods, the cop before me would wander without hope through eternal damnation. I would make sure his suffering was great.

Chad told his side of the story and I could tell the jury bought it. Despite my continued insistence, Bob never did bring up the fact that the asshole was fucking Sheila. Bob had told me the most difficult aspect of the trial would be how we approached my defense, since the *innocent by reason of insanity* plea had been abolished by the State of Texas shortly after the Violent Criminal Human Zoo Act was passed. Apparently too many people— people who really meant to hurt others—had been getting off with that defense. With a better option available, the "you're not guilty, you're just crazy" philosophy no longer cut it.

After the prosecution finished all their bullshit, Bob got his turn. It was time for him to step up and become the star, the hero who saved the day. But he didn't. He called very few witnesses, mostly experts who didn't know me for shit, and none of them did me a damn bit of good. The prosecution objected to a lot, the judge sustained most of the objections, and Bob fizzled right before my eyes. It was obvious he was overwhelmed. He rested his case after only five days.

All the testimonies were heard, mine not being one of them—even though I told Bob I thought I should take the stand. Closing arguments were given, and the case was turned over to the jury. They deliberated for less than a day.

Guilty on all counts.

After the verdict was read, the judge turned to me. "Mr. Bradbury, you have been found guilty by a jury of your peers. You will be immediately remanded to the authorities of the great State of Texas. Sentencing will take place directly after Violent Criminal Human Zoo criteria is examined. If you are eligible, I will recommend death in the Confinement Center, with Criminal Zoo option intact."

The judge said it with about as much emotion as if he was assigning me a junior high homeroom.

Death in the Confinement Center

THE VIOLENT CRIMINAL HUMAN ZOO Act states that the "Death in the Confinement Center" sentence cannot be imposed by a single man—meaning the asshole who called himself a judge couldn't enforce his not-so-hidden agenda of screwing me over without a little help. Yeah, he could "recommend it," but he couldn't mandate it. So said my shitty lawyer.

Once a person is found guilty of a violent crime resulting in the torture or death of another person, a checklist of conditions is reviewed by the judge before the Confinement Center "with Zoo option intact" sentence can be considered. It means you will never see freedom again. Ever. Other than death, there's only one way out. The Zoo. And I heard the Zoo was worse than death.

If the crime does not meet all the requirements of the sentence, the judge must impose traditional prison sentencing. If the crime does fit the criteria of the Confinement Center sentence, it is introduced during the sentencing phase. Once it is introduced as an option, the sentencing jurisdiction automatically reverts back to the jury. It is written in the law that "only through the unanimous vote by a jury of one's peers shall the accused be condemned to death in the Confinement Center."

I was never given the opportunity to examine the checklist, because the judge was not required to go over the list in front of me. Bob did tell me later, however, that one of the main points on the checklist was "absolute and indisputable DNA evidence." He told me that because of DNA exonerations in the past, forensic science was front and foremost during the Zoo consideration. So what if my DNA was found at the crime scenes? It didn't prove my actions were done with criminal intent. I don't remember God ever being put on the stand for murder. But none of that was considered, and my actions apparently fulfilled all the requirements. The whole thing was bullshit and the judge knew it.

The day after the jury found me guilty, the judge returned sentencing jurisdiction to them. My jailer informed me of this information with a twisted smile. Two days later, I was hauled back to the courtroom to face the jury's decision.

"Mr. Bradbury, please rise and face the jury," the judge commanded.

I stood and looked defiantly around the courtroom. Everyone stared at me. Except Sheila. She sat silently in the front row, her head bowed, her hands folded in her lap.

"Has the jury come to a decision?" The judge stared at the foreman.

The man rose to his feet. He held a large envelope in his right hand. "Yes, Your Honor, we have."

The judge paused for dramatic effect. I squeezed my hands into fists and clenched my teeth. My heart raced. I looked at Sheila. She sat forward, her head tilted in the direction of the voices.

"Proceed," the judge finally said.

"Your Honor, after careful and prudent deliberation, we the jury," the foreman cleared his throat, "sentence Mr. Samuel Bradbury to death in the Confinement Center, with the Criminal Zoo option intact."

A wave of electricity burst through the courtroom. Sudden chatter erupted everywhere. My legs buckled and I dropped into my chair. *How could this be?* Two deputies came to me, grabbed me by both arms, and pulled me back to my feet.

"Order! I will have order in my courtroom!" the judge commanded with a strike of his gavel. The room became quiet.

"Mr. Foreman," the judge said, looking at the man. "In accordance to the law, the Confinement Center can only be sentenced with a unanimous vote. Do you have the unanimous vote required for this sentence?"

"Yes, Your Honor, we have a unanimous vote. As required by law, the vote was taken, documented in writing, and sealed in this envelope." He held up his right hand.

"Bailiff, the envelope, please," the judge said.

I stood, flanked on both sides by the officers, and watched everything unfold in a state of shock. The world had suddenly taken a horrible, surreal turn.

The bailiff passed the envelope to the judge. He opened it, scanned it briefly, and then looked at me. "Mr. Bradbury, the vote is indeed unanimous. Therefore, the court rules that you shall die in the Confinement Center. If you wish, you are afforded the right to choose the Criminal Zoo as an option. Mr. Bradbury, I must add, I have toured both facilities. May God have mercy on your soul." He looked at the deputies. "Please escort Mr. Bradbury out of my courtroom."

I stared at my sister. "Sheila, tell them! Tell them the mistake they're making! Tell them who I am! What I am becoming!" I tried to pull free, tried to go to her, but the deputies held me firmly.

Sheila turned in my direction, her face expressionless. She rose from her chair and felt her way toward me. She almost tripped over several pairs of feet as she moved toward my voice. People gently helped her along. The deputies' grip on my arms became vise-like as she approached. I tried to reach for her but was restrained.

"Tell them the truth, Sheila. Don't be swayed by the ignorance in this courtroom. Don't let them judge me like this."

She stood directly in front of me, reached up to touch my cheek, her face void of all emotion. Her sudden slap—stinging, hard like my dad's—caught me by surprise. Then she turned and walked away.

"Sheila, no!"

The deputies forced me toward the back door.

"No! Let go!" I screamed.

The officers dragged me from the courtroom and down the corridor, my head spinning. This was not how soon-to-be-Gods were supposed to be treated.

The deputies shoved me through the back doors and into the waiting van. They climbed in beside me and the door slammed shut.

"Holy shit, that's the first time I've ever seen anyone actually get Death by Confinement Center!" one of the deputies said, looking at his partner. He turned to me. "Or you get to choose the Criminal Zoo. Fuck me, think about it! Sitting around waiting for death to take you away, or choosing to be tortured just to get out. Can you imagine that shit? I wouldn't want to be you, pal." A smile followed his words.

"Fuck you," I said.

"No, my friend," the deputy responded, shaking his head, "you're the one who's fucked."

Terrifying at Every Turn

HONESTLY CANNOT DECIDE WHICH hell is worse. The four-walled enclosure that keeps me prisoner measures seven feet by twelve feet. Spacious compared to the Confinement Center. One wall is made almost entirely of thick, clear acrylic. It's called the "viewing wall." Behind the wall, visitors with Level 1 clearance—merely observers—gather to watch what takes place. I get to see people. I get to hear them. They talk to me. I talk back if I want. But the ones who come into my enclosure, Level 2s, seek only one thing. My pain.

The L1s stand behind the protection of the acrylic, viewing me as if I were an animal in the Denver Zoo. They visit with each other, their mouths moving fast and their hands gesturing excitedly, while I am tortured.

A door exists at the right end of the viewing wall. It's standard width, but only half the height of a normal door, and it has a damn serious locking system with several backup mechanisms. I'm told that it's short like that so I can be shot through the head as I dip beneath the frame while trying to escape. The design, according to my keeper, came from the ancient Anasazi tribes of the southwest. Makes sense to me, I suppose. In those days, if someone you didn't know or didn't like stuck his head into your dwelling, you could put an arrow right through his brainpan.

The corridors outside the enclosures are wide enough for a ton of visitors. Pressure pads line the hallway floors; motion detectors line the walls; cameras run the length of the ceilings; heat sensors are everywhere; sound is monitored and recorded in every room; laser beams sweep through the air twenty inches above the floor. The net result of this security: anybody can be detected anywhere in the facility at any time.

Along with the viewing wall and its dwarf door, the cell has three other walls; my keeper told me they are a foot thick. Because of the wall thickness, the screams of other inmates cannot be heard. I guess that is one thing to be thankful for. The enclosure's walls are covered with a six-inch foam pad and laminated with smooth white vinyl. Non-textured white linoleum covers the floor, also with a foam pad beneath.

I questioned the reason for foam padding everywhere. My keeper said one of the original inmates of the Zoo had tried to commit suicide by lowering his head, sprinting the length of the room, and ramming into the far wall—not padded at that time. He survived the attempt, sustaining brain and spinal cord injuries, but was turned into a drooling retard—paralyzed from the neck down. After being in here, I see his act as a success.

Like the Confinement Center, there are no clocks in the Zoo. No calendars. No specific days or dates. We do not celebrate Christmas. There is no Thanksgiving, no Easter, no Halloween. I think I might have had a birthday, but I'm not entirely sure.

In the Confinement Center, I had a claustrophobic reaction to the absence of all time. I felt as if I were being suffocated by a total time vacuum. It's hard to explain unless you've felt it, but it was unsettling to the core of my being. It brought horrible awareness that my life wasn't mine anymore. It doesn't get any better in the Zoo.

I have since come to accept a timeless world, terrifying at every turn. Besides, I have far more pressing issues to worry about—like the small drain plumbed into the middle of the room, directly beneath the confinement chair. The drain sits about an inch lower than the rest of the gradually sloping floor. At first, I didn't appreciate the design. Now, I know all too well its purpose: easy cleaning with a hose.

An acrylic bubble hangs from the ceiling in the corner of the room closest to the door. The bubble houses a video camera. My keeper informed me on my first day that real-time video runs to a secured control room twenty-four hours a day. If anything should go wrong, the control room officer sounds the alarm and the Regulators are scrambled. I have tried to jump up and smash the bubble, but I can't even crack it.

Every room is wired to pick up even the slightest of sounds. Every noise, every conversation is recorded and kept on audio file for the full twelve-month period of Zoo incarceration. If I fart, it's going to be documented for all to hear. The assholes in the control room can also address me if they want through a tiny speaker installed right beside the camera bubble. But they never talk to me, which is fine. I don't want to listen to their bullshit.

An impact-resistant plastic toilet is anchored to the back wall. I'd heard that before this place was the Criminal Zoo, the toilet—along with the sink and bed frame—had been made from molded cement. The cement fixtures were removed for the same reason the walls were padded; another inmate had escaped the Zoo, via death, by repeatedly bashing his head against the cement sink corner. He apparently ruptured a large blood vessel in his brain and died before they could do anything about it. Good for him.

I know the toilet is impact resistant because I've kicked it as hard as I could many times, resulting in nothing more than splashing the half-empty bowl of water. There is no lever to flush it with, only a button to push. I guess they don't want to chance me breaking anything off the toilet to use as a weapon. The toilet comes with a sensor that automatically shuts off water flow if it is plugged in any way.

I can't take a shit in front of people. Now, I'm behind a glass wall on display all day long. Sometimes it is almost impossible to hold it, but I go to the bathroom only after the lights are turned off. I lie to myself, tell myself it's even too dark for the camera with infrared capabilities to see anything. The female inmates deal with the same humiliating setup, though I'm told there are only three in here. One microwaved her baby, one decapitated her child—throwing the body away and hiding the head under her bed—and the last one raped, murdered, and dismembered a young girl. My keeper told me this last woman kept the girl's teeth and made a bracelet out of them. *And they call me a monster?*

A tiny sink, also shatterproof plastic, is anchored beside the toilet. A pressed button emits cold water only. Sensors shut the water off when the sink is filled halfway to the top; no more water is available until the sink is completely empty again.

We are allowed a tiny tube of toothpaste, but not a toothbrush, as it could be sharpened into a shank. When I can't stand the rancid taste in my mouth any longer, I eat the toothpaste.

There aren't any showers in the enclosures. No mirrors, either. We don't get combs or brushes, but that's not a problem seeing as how we don't have any hair. We are taken to the cleaning facilities every week. We are stripped of all clothing, secured into a confinement chair, and then our heads—male or female—are shaved. The men's faces are shaved, our fingernails and toenails clipped, and our bodies hosed down. Like in our sinks, the water is always cold.

My bed is nothing more than a thin mattress on a hard plastic frame anchored against a side wall. But at least I have a bed. Not the floor, like back in the Confinement Center. We don't get bed sheets. We might strangle ourselves. They want us to stay alive. So we can be tortured. By people who pay a bunch of money.

The only other piece of furniture in the cell is the confinement chair. Its sole purpose is for my restraint while enduring a visitor with Level 2 clearance.

The room is kept at a non-varying temperature. If I had to guess, I'd say maybe seventy degrees. We are given a fresh pair of underwear every day. Every three days we are given a fresh white T-shirt and a pair of orange, Zoo-issue pants. Unless, of course, you have a Level 2 visit. In that case, fresh clothing is issued as you exit the infirmary Repair Shack.

It didn't take long for me to understand the white T-shirts. Blood shows up well on them, giving the L2s more satisfaction and the L1s more to get excited about.

We are fed twice a day, just like dogs. Breakfast is served a short time before visiting hours begin. Dinner is served right after they end. If you just had an L2, however, eating is the last thing you're thinking about. Breakfast consists of lumpy oatmeal, just like my dad used to make, quite often cold, and a glass of water. Dinner is usually a small, burned hamburger patty on a bed of sticky white rice. I don't believe it's real meat. It is served with a side of fruit and vegetables. With that meal, we also get a glass of milk. Because of the injuries I've sustained to my tongue, I haven't been able to eat the traditional dinner for a while. I can get soup down most of the time, though.

Shortly after I arrived at the Criminal Zoo, I went on a hunger strike, quickly realizing that starving to death was a better option than living here. I should've just stayed in the fucking Confinement Center. There, they would've let me die. Problem solved. But here I am an attraction. I am a draw. I bring in money. So death is no longer an option.

After my third day without food, my arms and legs were strapped into the confinement chair and a doctor forced a feeding tube—reminded me of an aquarium air hose—into my nostril and threaded it down to my stomach. No one gave me any sedatives. The tube was forced to curve down my throat, past the gag reflex. I fought the restraints, wanting nothing more than to rip the tube from my nose. I thought I was going to choke to death. I panicked and my entire body jerked against the harnesses. I tried to scream, but because of the tube it sounded more like I was gargling with tomato paste. If it had been possible, I would have cried, puked, yelled, and pulled the tube out all at once. But none of it was possible. The zookeeper held my head still and told me if I screamed again he would light me up with his Zap-stick. Finally, the tube reached my stomach, and some kind of liquid food was pumped into me. My keeper smiled and then squeezed harder, giving me a headache. He said, "We can do this every day if you like, One-Zero-One-Three."

Remember, I'm a number. Not a name.

"I've got nothing better to do," the keeper added.

Death through starvation would not be an option.

After the force-feeding, they ripped the tube from my nose and laughed as my eyes filled with tears. I coughed until my face was bright red. I had a sore throat for several days.

I wish it were only sore throats that plague me now.

The Same Stupid Questions

"**S**o, CZ One-Zero-One-Three, what makes you do it?" the zookeeper asks. "What makes you want to mutilate people?"

He's a new one. All the new ones stare at me the same way, like I am something unexplainable. And they all ask the same stupid questions, perhaps believing there should be an explanation for everything. *How could you? Why would you? Do you feel sorry for what you've done?* Yet no one ever asks me, *How are you holding up in here? Is there anything you need? Anything I can do for you?*

I am restrained in the confinement chair, enduring the horror that is the wait for another L2. To be strapped down and awaiting yet another sick bastard who will cause me great suffering is a nightmare beyond description. My heart pounds; I grow sweaty, nauseated, lightheaded.

Today, the leather straps are a lot tighter than normal, painfully so, around my wrists and ankles. Even the strap around my waist is uncomfortable, hindering my breathing.

"You put the straps on too tight," I say with a struggle.

"Yeah?" the keeper says. "Tough shit."

His words confirm that he is just another asshole, like everyone else who works in this hell on earth. It must be one of the job requirements. And to make matters worse, on this day I'm wearing something new. The keeper placed a stupid-looking leather helmet on my head, informing me that it is actually fashioned after a skydiving helmet, but with a modification. There is a buckle attached to the back of the helmet. Once the chinstrap of the helmet is secure around my jaw, the back of my head is pushed against the chair and the helmet is buckled into a newly installed strap. I had noticed the strap after returning from a hygiene day, but had no idea of its purpose. The strap is pulled tight and my head is secured to the chair.

I am never given a schedule of visits. Each morning I wake up and wonder if I will make it through the day without my blood being spilled. Each night that follows a visitor-less day, I try to get some sleep, pushing from my mind the awareness that no visit today simply doubles my chances of a visit tomorrow. I exist in terror—every hour, every minute, every second of every day in terror.

When the keeper enters my enclosure during visiting hours with his Zap-stick aimed in my direction, I know an L2 is coming. I am strapped into the chair and the keeper kills time by analyzing me, trying to make sense of my universe by asking his stupid questions. Bile rises into my throat as I await my torturer.

The Level 2 visitor must first go over the rules of the visit, sign multiple liability-release forms, and get fitted for the stupid Zoo jumpsuit, usually taking what would seem to be about fifteen to twenty minutes. Or I don't know, maybe it's only five minutes. I know what's coming, yet there's nothing I can do about it.

"The straps are cutting off my circulation," I say to the keeper. "They really hurt."

"Answer my question and maybe I'll loosen them," he replies. "Why do you do it?"

"Loosen the straps."

One at a time, he loosens each restraint a single hole. "Okay, now answer my question. Why do you do it?"

"Do what?"

"Ruthlessly murder people, like a savage animal."

"I don't murder people."

"Yeah you do. Otherwise all of your victims wouldn't be dead and you wouldn't be in here."

"Even if I told you why I did what I did, you wouldn't understand."

"Why, because I'm not crazy as a loon?" The keeper stares at me.

"No, because you don't know what I know."

"I know you're a warped, motherfucking psychopath."

"You're not spiritually evolved enough to talk about this with me."

"'Spiritually evolved enough?' Oh, so it's a God thing, right? Let me guess—God told you to do it." He laughs. "Isn't that what all the psycho crazy fucks say? 'God told me to do it'?"

"No. God didn't tell me to do anything. He can't make me do anything. If anything, the *Gods* probably didn't want me doing what I was doing. I probably scared Them. Maybe They weren't ready for another one."

"'Another one?' Another what?"

"God."

"What in the hell are you talking about?" the keeper demands.

"I was shot in the chest and the head at point-blank range. I should have been killed. But I didn't die. Why not?"

"You know what they say…cockroaches will be the only creatures still crawling after Armageddon."

"I was becoming one of Them."

"Becoming a cockroach? I got news for you, pal, you're already there."

"No, asshole. The Gods. I was becoming one of Them and They must not have wanted it to happen. Maybe They were scared I would get stronger than Them. Maybe that's why I'm in here. To stop my spiritual growth."

"Jesus, you're even crazier than I thought."

"Believe what you want. I don't care."

"Yeah, no shit. You don't care about anything, especially human life. Be thankful I'm not carrying a gun right now. Because if I were, I'd go ahead and test your whole 'becoming a God' theory. I'll bet if I fired off a round or two into your forehead, you'd prove to be extremely mortal." The keeper smiles. "But I don't have a gun, so you just sit tight until your L2 comes in here and fucks you up a little bit. I'll just have to be satisfied with daydreaming about how much fun it'd be to put a hole in your head."

"You're the asshole who doesn't care about human life. You're in here talking about shooting people in the head."

"Hey, fuckface," the keeper says. "You deserve this. That's the difference between you and me. I wouldn't do it to innocent people. Just shit-eating cockroaches like you."

"Put your little Zap-stick down and let me out of this chair. Face me like a man. Then let's see how tough you are."

"Are you kidding me?" The keeper laughs. "You're awfully small to be talking all big like that. I'd squash you like the fucking bug you are."

"All I hear are words."

"Oh, believe me, little man, if I could get away with it, I'd show you just how far from a God you really are. They should have finished your sick ass off the night you were caught at your sister's house."

"Yeah? Well, if they had finished me off then, I wouldn't be in here and you'd be a security guard at Walmart."

He hits me, opened handed across the face. Tears form in my eyes, but I will not cry. I'm done with that. I have only one means of survival in here. And that's to become tougher than everyone else. The keepers, the L1s, the L2s, all of them. To become the toughest bastard they've ever seen.

A Special Visitor

THE HORROR STARTS ALL over again. The Level 2 visitor ducks beneath the doorway and enters the room. He stands up and moves toward me. Despite his stupid jumpsuit, I recognize him immediately. I watched him on a talk show once.

He looks at me and smiles. "Hello, Exhibit CZ One-Zero-One-Three. My name's—"

"Suck me sideways. I know who you are. You're the governor. The asshole who came up with Criminal Zoo. The creator of a dark shit stain on society."

Governor McIntyre stops, tilts his head, and then says, "'Suck me sideways?' 'Shit stain?' Colorful. I'm already glad I came."

I stare at him. "So glad I could entertain you."

"And you would be Samuel Bradbury, the infamous Three Monkeys Killer, right before my eyes. I've read all about you."

"I know who I am." *He called me Samuel.* "Why did you just call me Samuel?"

The keeper, eyes narrowed, stares at the governor. "Sir, I thought we were instructed to—"

"I'm the creator, right?" Governor McIntyre interrupts. "I can call you Samuel if I like. I know your story inside and out. I have access to all the exhibits' paperwork and documents. All the files. Name, age, spouse, children, place of birth, family members. Everything."

"Isn't that an invasion of my privacy?"

"Privacy?" the governor echoes. "Sorry, Samuel. You have no privacy. You're the Three Monkeys Killer. The star attraction of the Criminal Zoo."

"I hate when people call me that. It's ridiculous."

"You think so? I think it's kind of clever. *See no evil, speak no evil, hear no evil?* Wasn't that your signature method of killing? But tell me, Samuel, did you kill everyone that way? Or was there one who died in a different manner?"

"I have no idea what you're talking about," I respond.

The governor looks at the keeper standing in the corner and asks, "Can I get a chair?"

"Sure, Governor," the keeper says. He turns and spends several seconds unlocking the door he had just locked. He sticks his head and arm through the opening and pulls a chair from the hallway. He closes the door, resets the multiple locks, and slides the chair to the governor.

Multiple L1s gather outside the viewing wall. It always happens when I have a visitor. But this is a special visitor. There will be an even bigger crowd that usual.

Governor McIntyre takes a seat, leans back, and crosses one leg over the other. His hands, free of surgical gloves, come to rest on his lap.

"Where are your gloves?" I ask.

"Don't need any."

I stare at him. "I watched you on TV. This place, this fucking hell, it's all because of you."

"Actually, it's the creation of a frustrated nation. A country tired of being preyed upon by sociopathic killers such as yourself. I merely came up with the idea and moved it forward. So it's more because of you—you and your kind—that this place exists."

"Bullshit."

"You didn't have to come here, Samuel. You chose to, remember?"

My name. It feels so good to hear my name.

"Yeah, right—like that was any kind of choice. You're sick. Making people choose between losing their mind while they die in a white nightmare, or coming here and getting tortured by complete strangers. That's warped, man."

"Hey, 'white nightmare'...I like that. Perhaps you've just renamed the Confinement Center. Anyway, I simply came up with a solution to a longstanding problem: what to do with people like you."

"Are you here to hurt me?" I ask.

"I make it a point to personally meet every exhibit. Takes a while to get to everyone, but here I am."

I stare at him, saying nothing.

The governor drops his leg to the floor, then leans forward. "No, I'm not here to hurt you. There are enough people out there who'll do it for me. I'm here to understand you."

"Why is it that everyone wants to *understand* me? Like there's a prize in it if you figure me out."

"Don't be flattered," the governor replies. "I visit in depth with all the exhibits."

"Quit calling me that. We're not exhibits. We're humans."

"No, you are not human. You left humanity behind when you murdered innocent people. Tell me about your victims."

"There are no *victims*. I didn't do anything wrong."

"Do you remember them? Each of them?"

"Look, Governor, I'm not sure what you're going for, but I'm no riddle to solve."

"Did you look them in the eyes before you killed them? Did you see fear? Was that what turned you on?"

"What are you getting at?"

"Who was your first? Do you remember?"

"Hey, you're the guy with the files. You tell me."

The governor stares at me. Almost like he's staring through me. Says nothing.

"I'm not supposed to be here. This is a mistake," I inform him.

"Really? A mistake?"

"Yeah, really."

"We have an explicit and comprehensive checklist to make sure we don't make such mistakes when sentencing someone to the 'white nightmare,' as you call it, and then to the Zoo." The governor pauses a moment, then asks, "Did you know that one in every twenty-five people is a sociopath?"

"What does that have to do with anything?"

"That's four percent of our population. Around fourteen million Americans. I thought maybe if I visited with you, you could help me. Show me what makes you tick. You know, like why you're hardwired so differently from the rest of us."

"You will never understand me. Nobody will. You can't understand what I was becoming before I was put in here."

"Sure sounds like a riddle to me."

"Not a riddle. A transformation."

"Ah, yes, I read that during interviews you stated you were becoming a God. So what's stopping you now?"

"Do you know how to become a God?"

"Tell me."

"Simple. Do as a God does enough times and become as a God is."

"That's it?"

"What else would there be?"

"I don't know, I guess I was expecting there'd be some kind of powerful, heavenly intervention or something." The governor looks disappointed. "At least a magic spell."

"If you make fun of me, I'm not going to talk anymore."

"So you can't finish becoming a God because you can't do as a God does anymore?"

"I can't even do as a man does." I glare at him.

"I want to know about you. About how you became a monster. About your victims. About why they're now dead. Help me understand."

"I'm not a monster. Besides, I thought your files told you all about me."

"They tell me stats. Not how your mind works. Help me, and maybe I can help you."

"Help me?" I ask with skepticism. "How can you help me?"

"I can help you get out of here."

"You just called me a monster."

"Who knows—perhaps even the heart of a monster can be changed."

The keeper stares hard at the governor. "Sir, are you kidding?"

"Keeper, mind your own business," Governor McIntyre advises.

I nod. "You should want to help me get out of here, because if it weren't for you, I wouldn't even be in here. None of us would."

"See, that's where you're wrong. *You* are the reason you're in here. Your actions have placed you here, not mine. But how about this: there may be a way to get you out."

I stare at him, trying to decide if he means it. "Why would you help me?"

"When I first envisioned this place, I was angry. Incredibly so. I had just lost my wife, and I wanted the blood of the person who caused me such horrible pain. But that was years ago. I still believe each of us must be held accountable for our actions, but now I seek something more valuable than revenge. I seek understanding. I want to truly understand why some people wouldn't hurt a fly and others think nothing of slaying their neighbor. If we know our enemy *before* he becomes our enemy, we can better protect ourselves from him. If we can identify those four percenters, we can better protect ourselves against them."

"And you think I'm one of those 'four percenters'?"

"Absolutely."

"Then once again, why would you want to help me get out?"

"Don't get me wrong," the governor says. "I still very much believe in the need for this place. Violent crime has fallen dramatically since the Criminal Zoo's inception. Now people have a little more at risk if they are caught. But I have come to the awareness that perhaps we need more than just this place. I'm willing to listen if you're willing to talk. You have nothing to lose."

"You would help get me out of here…like set me free?"

"Set you free?" The governor laughs. "Good Heavens, Samuel, of course not. But I could possibly help you get into a regular prison, where you'd at least be treated like a human. As a matter of fact, better than that. I hear the exhibits that make it out of here are Gods in prison. There's your chance to become the God you always wanted to be."

I look at him and then past him, to the viewing wall. The crowd of L1s is large. Bigger than I've seen in a long time. For once, I'm not the one everybody is here to see.

"Samuel, help me understand the mind of a sociopath and I'll do everything I can to make it worth your while. Perhaps by offering you release from the Zoo, I can save thousands, if not hundreds of thousands of people, from being preyed upon in the future. And when I say I'd help you get out of here, I am deadly serious."

"'Deadly serious?' Wow." Maybe it's time to tell someone everything. "Let me out of the straps and get this stupid helmet off me. And then I'll talk."

The governor looks over to the keeper.

"Sorry, Governor McIntyre, but that's against Zoo policy," the man says, shaking his head. "The exhibit must remain in the confinement chair, restrained, during the L2 visit."

"I take full responsibility for whatever happens," the governor replies.

"Sir, are you crazy?" The keeper looks dismayed. "This man is a serial killer. He mutilates people just because he has nothing better to do. What makes you believe he won't come after you?"

"Because he doesn't want to be in here anymore. Besides, you'll be right behind me, and you have a Zap-stick. If he makes a move in my direction, hit him with it."

My keeper stares. "You're not really going to try to help this sick bastard get out of here, right?"

"That's not your concern. What is your concern is doing as you are asked."

"My concern is my job. If something goes wrong, I'm fired."

The governor turns to the ceiling camera. "I, Governor Jon McIntyre, hereby request that exhibit CZ One-Zero-One-Three be released from his restraints." He turns back to the keeper. "There, it's official. Now please release Mr. Samuel Bradbury."

I am released of all straps. Unbound, free to move. Free to attack. Free to show the governor how I feel about his fucking Zoo. But I wouldn't get far. The keeper would be on me in seconds, Zap-stick jammed into my head. Not worth it. Besides, Governor McIntyre has just offered me something no one else can. He offered me hope. So I tell him my story—being a kid, Mom leaving, living with my dad, all the way to now, an exhibit in the Zoo.

Upon wrapping up my memoir, the governor looks at me, shaking his head. "My goodness, Samuel. That is a tale of woe if I've ever heard one."

"Yeah," I say. "You should've been there."

In an Unexpected Direction

A NEW DAY, A NEW L2. But now things are different. I have renewed hope in my heart. The governor's visit changed everything. He's now in my corner. I told him everything he wanted to know and he promised to make good on his offer to help. I want out. Not after a year. I want out right now. I have no idea how long I have been in here, but every day is hell. Seems like years.

I am strapped into my confinement chair, my new L2 glaring at me. He is a big man, even bigger than my keeper. The Zoo knife looks tiny in his giant mitt. The look in his eyes terrifies me. All the other L2s look at me with hatred. I can identify with hatred. There is a sick familiarity, not comfort by any means, but a recognition accompanying that stare. But not this huge man. No, instead he looks at me with nothingness. There is only blackness in his eyes, void of all emotion. I don't like it. I have no idea what hides behind the blackness.

The L2 goes in an unexpected direction before my keeper can jump in. The man doesn't go for my face like all the others, but for my left hand. In the blink of an eye, he stabs the knife straight into the middle knuckle of my pointer finger. The blade goes all the way through my finger, through the knuckle, and into the chair. I scream.

"Hey!" the keeper yells. "You can't do that!" He moves to the L2. But the huge man is fast. He punches the keeper in the head before the Zap-stick becomes an issue. The keeper goes down in a heap. The L2 turns back to me. Still only blackness in his eyes. No excitement. No rage. Nothing

"Help!" I scream. "Help me!"

The piercing alarm suddenly drowns out my cries. Its shrieking confirms that the control room is aware of an L2 gone rogue. The Regulators will be dispatched. The man finishes what he started. He cuts off my pointer finger at the middle joint. I scream and scream, try to scream the pain away. The alarm is undeterred by my howl.

The L2 quickly moves to the next finger. Cuts off my middle finger with unbelievable power and speed. The little pocket knife was never intended to be used to amputate body parts, an offense that's strictly prohibited. Then the giant takes off my ring finger. Stabs straight into the joint, twists, separates the bones, and slashes. Like he's done this before. Three fingers gone. Only my pinky and my thumb left.

The enclosure door swings open. The man turns to face the Regulators, their guns and Zap-sticks held at the ready. The L2 stands tall. Smiles. Drops the knife. I watch, as if from a dream.

"Okay, okay, fellas—you got me," the L2 says. He raises his hands. "No need for weapons."

Without warning, a Regulator lunges forward and hits the man in the chest with a blast from the Zap-stick. I watch the man fall in slow motion, wonder if this all really just happened. The excruciating pain in my left hand confirms it in the moment before I waver, surrendering to the darkness that often takes me away from these L2 visits.

Blackness, like the man's eyes, starts at the very edges of my vision and quickly closes out the light. Time for me to go away, at least for a little while.

I CLIMB FROM THE DARK ABYSS. I am in the Repair Shack. My right wrist is handcuffed to the metal bed railing and my left hand feels like it's in a hamburger grinder. What is left of the hand is heavily bandaged. A renewed surge of pain brings nausea with it. I turn my head and vomit on the bed linen.

"Hey!" An attendant runs into the room. I've seen him before. He's an asshole. "You stupid fuck, don't do that. Now I have to clean that shit up."

"My hand..." The words feel as if they are sandpaper against the lining of my throat. "My hand hurts really bad."

"Fuck, I'll bet," the attendant says. "Dude, that shit had to hurt. Having your fingers cut off by a pocketknife, one at a time? Ouch!" He laughs.

The pain is overwhelming, a fire burning throughout my entire soul. "Please help me..."

The attendant says something, but his words are lost as I drift back into the abyss.

We Are Human Beings

AWAKEN TO THE VOICES of others and to the powerful antiseptic smell of the room. The painful throbbing coming from the remains of my left hand immediately reminds me where I am. I look down and examine their bandage job. Shitty at best. A psycho fucking L2 cuts my fingers off, and these guys bandage me up like they don't give a shit. Probably had to get home to dinner.

My right wrist is still handcuffed to the metal railing of the bed—standard practice. I look around and confirm that I am not alone in the Repair Shack. Several other beds are filled with inmates, also chained to their frames.

When we're out on the floor, we're not allowed contact. It is rare that we even see each other. We are in lockdown twenty-four hours a day, interacting only with our keepers and our L2s. We are allowed out of our enclosures for Repair Shack time and for hygiene days. We do not get physical fitness time, nor do we get any reprieve from our own minds. In the Repair Shack, and *only* in the Repair Shack, the rules are relaxed slightly. Here, we are treated as close to human as we will ever be.

We are given low-grade pain medication for serious injuries; we are given antibiotics for infections; we are allowed to rest. But most importantly, we are allowed to visit while our bodies heal. It is during this time that I learn about others who share my hell.

I look to my right. A man lies in bed, moaning. I can see his arms, shoulders, and head. The rest of him is covered by a white sheet. Both arms are wrapped in gauze from the wrists almost to his armpits. He bears burn scars over most of his shoulders, and just about all of his face. His injuries tell me everything. He is an arsonist and his last job must have gone terribly wrong.

Perhaps I can take my mind off of my own pain if he tells me about his. "Hey, buddy," I call out. "What happened to you?"

He moans but doesn't look over.

"Hey, pyro, why are you in here?"

His head turns, his empty gaze falls on me. He says nothing.

I need interaction with someone other than an L2, so I push for conversation. "We never get to talk except in here. What's your story?"

He stares at me. It is hard to look into his grotesquely scarred face, but that's exactly what I do.

After a pause, he speaks. "I started a fire."

"No shit. All I have to do is look at you to see that. And?" I wait for more, but he turns his head, looks up at the ceiling. "A fire doesn't get you sent here. Who died?"

"In California. Forest fire."

"Yeah?"

He turns back. "A day after I started it, a fire crew was overrun by the blaze. Two men and a woman were killed."

"That's bad, but I still don't see how that got you sentenced here. A jury unanimously voted death by Confinement Center for that?"

"The fire crew was trying to save a man and his ten-year-old, handicapped son, who were camping at the time. They got trapped in the fire. The fire crew covered the boy and his dad with one of those space-age fireproof blankets. They didn't have time to cover themselves. They died heroes. The boy died a few days later. Apparently he was pretty cooked. Like a turkey in an oven. I think that's what got the jury."

I nod. "A cooked handicapped kid...yeah, that'd do it."

He looks at me, his eyes vacant.

"Why'd you do it?"

He just stares.

Blocking my own pain, I encourage him to continue. "Maybe it'd make you feel better if you talk about it while you can. It makes me feel better to listen." Actually, my hand hurts like hell and his sorry story probably won't make it feel any better, but it will give me something else to think about.

"My arms hurt so fucking bad I can hardly take it!" he shouts all at once. "Give me something. Fuck!"

An attendant enters the room. "Settle down, One-Two-Five-Seven. Stop whining like a little bitch. What do you need?"

CZ1257. Not a name. Not a man. An animal. An exhibit.

"My arms hurt. Please give me something for them."

The attendant turns from the burned man and walks to a cabinet immediately above a sink. He fishes a key from his pocket, inserts it into the keyhole just below the cabinet handle, and pulls open the door. He retrieves a small plastic container from within the cabinet. He then fills a small paper cup with water and returns to the man. He taps out a pill. "Here, take this."

The firestarter takes the pill.

"Can I have one?" Actually I want more like twenty, but I'd start with one.

The attendant walks to my bed, taps a pill out for me.

"Can I get some water, please?"

He returns to the sink, fills another cup, and moves beside my bed. He holds the cup just above my mouth. "Open up."

I do as I'm told and he drops the pill onto my tongue.

"Nice tongue. Great scar pattern," the attendant says. "Makes you look tough." He smiles like he just said something funny. He pours a little water into my mouth.

The attendant throws the cups into a trash receptacle in the corner. He locks everything up and heads back to his desk on the other side of the doorway.

I turn back to the man lying next to me. "So why'd you do it?"

The inmate looks at me. "I was a part-time firefighter for the forest service. It had been an unusually quiet fire season and I was broke. I needed the money."

"You started a fire to go back to work?"

"Yeah."

"And you didn't intend to kill anybody?"

"Absolutely not. I'm not a murderer. I told them that at the trial!" Tears flow down his charred cheeks. "I don't belong here. I didn't mean to kill anybody. It was an accident." He smacks his bandaged arm against the bed rail, follows that with a scream.

"Come on, guys, give me a break." The attendant's voice reaches us from the other room. "I'm working on a crossword puzzle in here."

I look at the inmate's arms, at his shoulders and face. "Were you burned fighting fires? Or is all that from being in here?"

"I never got burned once on the job. Every one of my injuries is from this fucking place. My L-twos all come in with a lighter. It's the same every time. A little black lighter with 'Criminal Zoo' printed down the side in white. And they torture me with it. It hurts bad. Every time, real bad." His tears escalate into an all-out wail.

"All those burns from just a lighter?"

"They hold the flame against my skin. In their eyes, I see hatred. They don't even know me, but they hate me. I never did anything to them. Why do they hate me?"

"Because they're animals. Why else would they come here?"

"When I had hair on my arms, it caught on fire. I can still smell it. Every time I close my eyes I smell it. It makes me sick just thinking about it. Now, there's no hair left. They drag the flame up and down my skin. The smell of my burning flesh makes me sick every time. I scream, but they don't stop. They never stop. Not until my keeper makes them." He stops talking and wipes his eyes. He looks at me. "What happened to your hand?"

I look down at it, and then back to him. "Rogue L-two. Cut off my fingers."

"No shit? Hey, were you the one the alarm sounded for?"

"Yeah. Regulators were dispatched and everything."

"They get the guy?"

"Oh, yeah. Zapped his ass unconscious."

The firestarter nods. "So what happened to your ears? They're pretty fucked up."

"My L-twos come in with a pocket knife. Same design as your lighter—black knife, white logo of the Zoo down the side. That's what the asshole used to cut off my fingers. Usually they cut on my ears, scar 'em up pretty bad."

"And the scars around your eyes? Why there?"

"They cut around them, around the safety goggles. Hell, they'd cut my eyes completely out if the keeper would let them. And look at what else they do." I stick out my tongue.

"Your tongue looks like shit."

"Thanks."

His face suddenly scrunches up. "Wait a minute. Eyes, ears, tongue…holy shit. You're that one guy, aren't you?"

"Oh God, don't say it."

"The Three Monkeys Killer, right? You're him, aren't you?"

"It makes me sick when people call me that."

"Yeah, man—I heard all about you. My keeper told me you were here. My God, I can't believe the shit you did!"

"Wait…what? What are you talking about? You're in here for the same reasons I am."

"Bullshit! I accidentally killed a few people. But you…you're a fucking psychopath, man. You cut the eyes and tongue out of your victims. You cut their fucking ears off, man. You maim and kill."

"Hey, buddy, I've got a news flash for you. You murdered four people just so you could earn a paycheck. If anyone's a psychopath, it's you."

"That's some serious bullshit and you know it! You're the fucking psycho!"

The attendant stomps into the room. "Enough with the arguing. You sound like a couple of third-graders. If I hear any more yelling, I'm going to recommend that both of you are put back on display."

The attendant knows, and I'm sure he knows we know, that he doesn't have the authority to do that. Only the staff doctors can authorize an inmate's return to display. He gives us a hard stare and then leaves the room. I try again with the pyro.

"Listen, whether we like it or not, we're in here together. We have enough enemies from the outside. Let's not create enemies on the inside, too. What's your name?"

"I'm CZ One-Two-Five-Seven."

"No, not the bullshit number they gave you. Your name. What's your real name?"

"Does it really matter?" the man asks.

"Yeah, it matters. Our keepers and our visitors may have forgotten that we're still human, maybe even the whole world has, but we haven't. Our time in the Repair Shack is the only time we get to remember that we are not animals, that we are human beings. If even for a minute, let's remind each other of that. My name is Samuel. Samuel Bradbury."

The firestarter stares at me, his face softening. "My name's Gary. Gary Metters."

"So where you from, Gary Metters?"

"Sacramento," he says. "That life, my freedom, it seems so long ago..." He trails off, his tears returning.

"Gary from Sacramento, I'm Samuel from Clemensville, Texas."

"Yeah, I know. I've heard all about you."

"Hey, don't believe everything you hear," I say with a forced laugh, trying to ignore my throbbing hand.

Gary sighs. "I don't know if I can do it. I don't know if I can make it a year."

"Sure you can. We'll be kings in prison. One year in hell and then we're the badasses on the block!"

"I got no idea how long I've been in. Already feels like two years. How about you?"

"No clue," I respond. "I used to count the days by each light cycle. Lights on, lights off—one day, you know? But after a while, I lost track. No way of recording it. So hell, it's gotta be...oh, I don't know...maybe seven or eight months now? Feels like forever. Or shit, it could only be four months. I just don't know. But I know I'm tough enough to get out of this fucking shit hole."

"Time stands still in here," Gary says.

"Why'd you push the button?" I ask.

"Because I lost my mind. I seriously went crazy in there. I got claustrophobic as shit. I couldn't take the silence anymore."

"Me too. I started thinking I was disappearing, slowly being erased. I couldn't take it. And now here we are."

"So that means we're going to Heaven when we die, right? Because we've already been to Hell."

"That's the way I see it. But even if we don't, Hell will be a breeze compared to this place."

Failure to Thrive

FEEL LIKE SHIT. I'M burning up. And then I'm ice cold. And then burning up again. I am given medicine but I don't know what kind. They tell me my hand, or what's left of it, is infected. And the infection is possibly in my blood. "Sepsis," the Repair Shack doctor tells me, sounding concerned. I'm sure he's worried that I won't get my full twelve months of torture.

In my sickened state, all I can think about is my vulnerability. That asshole could've easily killed me. I realize any one of my L2s could kill me before the keeper could stop them. I shudder, not just because of the fever.

Gary the pyro attempts to carry on a conversation from his bed, but I'm unable to follow. After more antibiotics, my fever breaks and I awake in a pool of sweat. The linens are changed by a grumbling attendant while I stand naked, shivering and handcuffed to my bed. The only time I am released from the metal railing is when I have to go to the bathroom. And I do that as infrequently as possible, seeing as how "going to the bathroom" means nothing more than doing my business under watchful eyes in a toilet plumbed into a closet—minus the door—at the far end of the Repair Shack.

The meals served here are the same as those served in the enclosures. I stick to soup.

I'm learning what amputees mean when they say *phantom pains*. I feel pins and needles sticking into the ghostly remnants of my hand. I wake up in the middle of the night, my missing fingers itching and stinging to the point that I can't take it any longer. I am given more pain medication and told to go back to sleep.

The firestarter is returned to display before I am. When the keeper comes for Gary, shackling his feet and hands and helping him from the bed, he crumples to the floor and weeps. "On your feet, One-Two-Five-Seven!" They pick him up and he grabs the railing of his bed and screams for them to leave him alone. They rip his hands free and drag him, kicking and screaming, from the Repair Shack.

My father once said, "Samuel, we are given no cross that we cannot bear." And then he slapped me hard across the face. I fought back the tears. "There, see? I hit you because I wanted you to see you could handle it," he explained. "It hurt, but you handled it." He slapped me again. Harder. "See, there you go. Handling it. Just like Christ could handle His cross." My father *was* my cross.

Now, I have an entirely new and far heavier cross to bear. I have tried to be strong. I wanted to prove my worthiness to sit among the Gods. But it has become too much. My father was wrong; we are given crosses that are unbearable. I can't carry mine any longer. God and His race have abandoned me. Because of this, I have grown extremely confused. I hate God—single or plural. I hate all of mankind. And I hate this place most of all.

After an undeterminable amount of time, the doctor enters the Repair Shack, removes all the bandaging from my hand, and examines it. "Good news, One-Zero-One-Three. The infection is gone." With a smile, he proclaims, "I knew we could beat it. The hand has healed nicely, and now, my friend, you are healthy enough to be returned to your enclosure." The smile stays on his face. I get the feeling that I'm somehow supposed to be grateful, like he's waiting for a "thank you." I stare at him, emotionless. He nods and leaves the room. Moments later, my keeper comes for me; the shackles are put on and I am uncuffed from the bed. The keeper leads me from the infirmary, down the corridor, and into my enclosure. I think of Jesus as He was led to the hilltop. I know His suffering all too well. *No cross you can't bear*, says my dad.

Fuck off, Dad.

I SIT IN MY enclosure, unable to sleep. The lights have been turned off for the night. As usual, I had a large crowd of L1 visitors, but that was it. As nice as that is, it only increases my chances of having an L2 tomorrow. I tried to put on a brave front in the Repair Shack, to impress Gary the firestarter, give him hope. But it was just an act.

This last episode with my psycho L2 really took the wind out of my sails. Along with three fingers. The only thing keeping me going is Jon's offer to help. If he can pull some strings and get me out of here, I can tough it out for a little while longer. One day at a time. I truly wonder how long I would be able to take this existence filled only with pain and suffering. With Jon, there is hope. Without him, there is none.

I have not had spiritual growth since before coming here. In fact, my spirit has withered and weakened. Before this place, I was close to Godhood. Now, I am as far from it as any spirit has ever been. I wonder if the Gods are laughing at me. Laughing because they stopped me. Relieved because they know the potential I once had.

My destiny has been stolen. I now exist, yet I do not. This isn't any better than the Confinement Center. I shouldn't have pushed the damn button. Feeling pain isn't better than feeling nothing at all. Pain fucking hurts. That's all it fucking does. Doesn't make me feel alive. Only hurts! I don't want to hurt anymore. I don't want people cutting me up anymore. That son of a bitch cut off my fingers. Took parts of my body from me without even asking. Jesus, talk about being violated. I can't do another fucking visit like that one. So this is it: either Jon gets me out of here, or I get me out of here. Jon's way, I go to prison. My way, I go to the afterlife.

Yesterday, in the Repair Shack, I ate my last meal. I am now officially on a hunger strike. If they want to keep me alive, they will have to do it with the feeding tube. Time to force Jon's hand. I'm not staying in here anymore.

I read in a newspaper once about a baby dying from a "failure to thrive." At the time, I had no idea what that meant. Now I do. I will make no effort whatsoever at living.

Sick Bastards

ANOTHER L2, ANOTHER VISIT to the Repair Shack. More fucking pain. So tired of it. Where is the governor? He hasn't been back to see me since his offer to help.

Today my Repair Shack bunkmate—recovering from a badly broken arm—is a self-described "recluse" who lived on a farm twenty minutes outside of Lincoln, Nebraska. His ticket to hell was punched when he kidnapped a twelve-year-old girl as she left a convenience store. He told me how he kept Amy—that was her name—imprisoned in his basement for more than three years with a dog chain, a spiked leather collar, and a padlock. He also told me he had fathered two children with her. He spoke with a hint of pride as he told me he had delivered both children—one boy and one girl—without any help whatsoever.

"How come she didn't just take the collar off when you weren't there?" I ask.

"Couldn't. I had it padlocked to her neck. The only thing that could take it off was the key in my pocket. But that girl sure had spirit. She worked on it every damn day. I swear to God I had to buy a new collar every other month. And those damn things were thick, too! I have no idea how, seeing as how I kept her nails clipped, but she managed to dig into the leather and tear it to the point that I had to replace it. Gotta give her credit for effort. Fingertips was always bloody, you know? Had to be pretty sore."

I have nothing to say. I hate this man. He is a monster. But I need to hear his voice. Someone talking, not trying to hurt me.

"Yep, everything was going along just fine," the recluse from Nebraska says, "until one night when Amy complained of a real bad gut ache. She had been feeling her oats a little earlier that day so I had to knock her around a little. You know, put her back in her place."

I seriously don't want to hear this, but I desperately need the interaction.

"She wasn't doing as told, you know, so I gave her a few solid kicks to the gut while she lay on the floor, crying. The next morning she was pretty pale and didn't really move around a lot. I tried to get her to eat some breakfast, cooked her up some eggs and toast, but she wasn't hungry. Of course I was concerned with her well-being, but what was I supposed to do, you know? It's not like I could just run her down to the doctor's office."

"So what'd you do?"

"What the hell do you think I did? I tried my damnedest to nurse her back to health. I unchained her, bathed her, brushed her hair, hoping it would help her feel better. I offered her food each day, but she only got worse. Her color got worse, got all grey on me, and she kind of went into a comatose state."

"Yeah? And then what'd you do?"

"Nothing I could do. She died down there in the basement."

"So you raised the kids until you got caught?"

"Hell no, I didn't raise no bastard kids! Can you imagine those little retards running all over the place, breaking everything and making a mess?"

He gives me no time for a response.

"Well I certainly can, and I wasn't having none of that shit! So after delivering each one, I held them underwater in the bathtub. After they was dead, I chopped them up with my hatchet. I dumped the parts into a plastic bag and then took the bags to the county landfill, because I didn't think it was all that sanitary having body parts buried all over my place. Besides, I had a dog. He would've just dug everything up."

"I had a dog once." If only I could go back to the days of Brutus. "Mine was a great big ol' Saint Bernard named Cujo. Yeah, you guessed it, Stephen King fan. So anyway, I didn't want Cujo digging up my yard, you know?"

"So how did you get caught?"

"Stupid luck. Just like Amy's kids, I disposed of Amy's body at the landfill. A month later, a baby goes missing from his crib. The mom swore the boy had been kidnapped, but she'd been having a party and using drugs the night the kid disappeared. Turns out she was a known meth head. The cops didn't believe her story so they ended up taking cadaver dogs down to the landfill, thinking maybe the woman threw her kid away. They never found the boy, but they sure as shit found my little Amy. One thing led to another, and next thing I knew, the cops was knocking on my door. I guess Amy died of internal bleeding—that's what they said during the trial. I'm surprised they could tell, 'cause I cut her up pretty good, you know?"

With nothing whatsoever to add to this conversation, I remain silent.

The recluse doesn't seem to care. "Yeah, the bleeding probably had something to do with the steel-toed boots I was wearing when I kicked her. If I could've done it all over again, I would've just kicked her with tennis shoes on."

I do not belong in here with these sick bastards. I don't want to listen to him anymore. "I'm tired. I'm going to take a nap."

IT'S DARK WHEN I awaken to voices. I hear them wheel in a gurney. I know the sound well. The keepers are whispering, which is strange because they don't usually give a damn about interrupting our sleep. The squeaky wheels of the bed go silent and the voices fade as they move into the next room.

The putrid smell of spoiled chicken invades the room. At first I think it's my imagination. But it gets stronger and I realize it's real. Did my bunkmate, the recluse, release a fart from the deepest regions of his bowels?

"Hey, buddy, that's not cool," I say.

There is no response.

Along with the scent of spoiled meat, there is an odd sweetness, like a fruit basket left to ferment. I am confused. I have never smelled anything like it.

"Hello?" I call into the blackness.

"Be quiet!" a voice calls from the other room.

"Hey, listen, there's something pretty rotten in here. You should come and check it out."

"If I come in there, it'll be to crack you upside the head. Now shut the fuck up and go to sleep."

And then I hear movement coming from the direction of the smell. Someone shifting on the gurney to my right. "Hello?" I repeat.

There is no answer. Just the smell. The more I take it in, the worse it gets. It's starting to make me sick.

"Hey, I think I'm going to puke in here."

"If I have to come in there and clean up any messes, I swear to God I'll crack your skull open like a fucking walnut. Now go back to sleep!"

I breathe through my mouth as best I can. I can almost taste the smell. I tell myself it isn't as bad as I'm making it out to be. I close my eyes in hope of a visit from the sandman. But I wonder if that'll happen. The stench next to me might just turn him around in his tracks.

What the hell did they bring in?

A Whole New Level of Horror

NOT MUCH SHOCKS ME anymore. Not after being in here. But when I wake up—the room now fully lit—and roll my head to the right, to where the smell comes from, my heart almost stops.

Only a couple of feet away, a man lies on his gurney completely nude. His red skin—not pinkish, like he fell asleep while sun tanning, but blistering, like he fell asleep lying on the sun—is covered head to toe with festering sores and open lesions. Yellowish pus leaks from his wounds, oozing onto the sheet beneath him. And he has no hair. Not on his head, his crotch, his arms or legs, not even on his eyebrows.

His right arm, like mine, is handcuffed to a side rail. He's on his back, his eyes open and unblinking, staring at the ceiling. His chest rises and falls with each breath.

I shut my eyes briefly and then open them again, expecting they are playing a trick on me. They're not.

For lack of anything better, I say, "Hey, buddy, you don't look so good."

His head rolls toward me and his eyes, red like the rest of him, meet mine. His stare says it all: he is already dead, he just hasn't realized it yet.

"My God, what the hell happened to you?" I ask.

No response.

I stare at him a moment before calling out to the attendant manning the desk in the next room. "Yo, this guy looks bad. Really bad. I think he needs help."

"Hey, One-Zero-One-Three, you just worry about yourself," a voice returns.

"What's going on?" the recluse from Nebraska asks, awakening. I turn to him as he rises up on an elbow and looks past me. "Oh my God. What the hell happened to that guy?"

"I know. He looks terrible, huh?"

"Geez, pal, you look like shit," the recluse says, his eyes locked on the new guy.

The spoiled chicken pretending to be a man doesn't respond. He simply stares.

"Come on, have a heart!" I yell into the next room. "Get this guy out of here. He stinks to high heaven."

A chair scrapes against the floor, as if someone is pushing themselves back from a desk, and then the attendant enters the room. He is the stocky, bald albino—one of the more cruel Repair Shack staff members. "You fuck-nuts are getting on my nerves."

"Come on, you can't seriously leave him in here," I plead. The living dead man is really freaking me out. "What the hell happened to him?"

"That's RS Twenty-Nine. Ask him yourself. He's a little drugged up right now, though. So I don't know how much you'll get out of him." Albino laughs.

"RS? What's that? Why not CZ like the rest of us?"

"Sorry, pal, classified. I could tell ya, but then I'd hafta kill ya." The attendant laughs.

I look at the thing called RS 29, wishing whoever had cooked him would've finished him off.

"Hey, Twenty-Nine!" Albino yells. "You with us?"

RS 29 stares from somewhere behind the line dividing alive and not alive.

"I think he's comatose," the recluse says.

"Well, let's just see." Albino pulls a pair of surgical gloves from the Kleenex-like dispenser next to the sink. He slides them on and approaches RS 29's feet. With some pretty serious force, he smacks the bottom of the thing's right foot.

A little bit of life flashes into RS 29's eyes and he jerks his foot away.

"Nope, he's fine." Albino pulls off the gloves and slides them into the orange bio-waste receptacle fastened to the wall. "Stinks like shit, don't he? But he's alive."

"What's with the smell?" I ask.

"I guess that's what happens when your skin starts dying right off your body. We tried to rinse him, but it just flushed more skin off. Got too messy. And that's all I know, so don't make me come back in here." Albino turns and walks from the room.

I direct my gaze to the heap of spoiled flesh and ask, "What the hell did they do to you?"

RS 29 looks at me for a moment; his eyes once again show little life. "Doc." His voice is weak.

"'Doc?' Who's Doc?" I turn to the recluse. "You know who Doc is?"

"Which one? There's a lot of 'em in here," Mr. Nebraska answers.

"Doc gives the shots," the spoiled chicken says.

"What shots?" I turn back to RS 29.

"For the lab rat."

"'Lab rat?' What the hell does that mean?"

"Me. I'm the lab rat." RS 29's eyes, red almost to point of bleeding, show he's now tracking me.

"'Lab rat,' like they're doing some kind of research on you?"

"Yeah."

RS...Research Subject! "Holy shit. Are you saying you look like that because they're experimenting on you?" This is a whole new level of horror.

"Yeah."

"How the hell did you end up being a lab rat?"

"I got a wife and three children. No one to take care of them now," RS 29 says. "I signed a contract. They pay my family money for my participation."

"Who pays your family?"

"Drug company."

"They give your family money if you let them test their drugs on you?"

RS 29 nods.

"How much?"

"Drug companies have lots of money. My family is taken care of."

"That's fucked up," the recluse jumps in. "I'm serious! That's some really fucked-up shit."

"What kind of drugs?" I ask.

"They don't tell me."

"You look like some seriously leftover shit," the recluse exclaims. "No, worse than that—you look like slimy-ass diarrhea. How can you stand the pain?"

"Painkillers. Keeps me pretty messed up."

"You have got to be fucking shitting me," the recluse continues. "You're seriously *letting* them do this to you?"

"Better than L-two visitors. No pain meds. If I'm lucky, they'll end up killing me."

I can't believe what I'm hearing. "You smell like you're almost there, pal."

"No shit," the recluse adds.

"So a wife and three kids? How'd you end up here, RS Twenty-Nine?" I ask, not worrying about learning his real name. He won't be around long enough to remember it.

"Got drunk at a convention, took a coworker back to my hotel. Accidentally killed her." RS 29 pauses a moment and then adds, "Didn't mean to. It got a little rough. I choked her. They say I killed her during a rape. They're lying, though. It was consensual."

"So now you let them inject experimental drugs into your system?"

"I have a family." RS 29 turns his gaze back to the ceiling. "I don't want to talk."

I lie on my bed, stunned. They're doing experiments on exhibits now?

Welcome to Auschwitz. Dr. Mengele to the Repair Shack, please.

No Reason to Continue

THE REPAIR SHACK DOCTOR examines the recluse and declares him fit to return to his enclosure. He cries when they take him away. They all cry when they go back.

Infection or no infection, healed or not, my hand still throbs. Always throbbing. And RS 29 stinks. I know I can get away from both the pain and the smell if I sink into my mind hole, so I close my eyes and go away for a while. When I awaken, I am alone.

"Where's RS Twenty-Nine" I ask the female attendant—fat, redheaded, and ugly—when she enters to change my bandages.

"Who's RS Twenty-Nine?"

"The lab rat. You know, the poor bastard you guys severely fucked up with your experimental drugs."

"I don't know anything about it." She shakes her freckled face.

"He was just in here."

"Don't know what you're talking about. Maybe you dreamed it."

"I didn't dream a fucking thing. I sure as shit didn't dream the smell. He stunk like rotten meat. You can still smell him."

"Hey, One-Zero-One-Three, I don't know what you're talking about, don't care. Let it go, okay?" The attendant finishes with my dressing and leaves the room.

I am left wondering if the redhead was right. Did RS 29 really exist? Or had I been in a pain-induced delusional state? But that smell—no way I could've dreamed that up.

I AM ONCE AGAIN GIVEN clearance to be returned to my enclosure. Lying on my bed, I stare into the darkness. Before I left the Repair Shack, they told me if I don't eat something by tomorrow, the force-feedings begin.

I have no idea how long I have been in the Zoo. A day feels like a month, a month like a year. I think maybe I'm almost through my one-year sentence. Maybe not. Maybe I'm only halfway done. Never in my life, awake or dreaming, could I have envisioned something so horrendous as my time here. It's not fair. *Life's not supposed to be fair, Samuel.*

"Shut the fuck up, Dad."

I don't deserve this. The suffering that takes place behind these walls is far worse than anything I or anyone else has ever done. No one deserves this. No one.

The governor hasn't come back. Was he just fucking with me? Just taking his cruelty to a new level? Offering me hope, only to slowly let it fade away? Wasn't it bad enough that he mentally tortured me so badly I willingly chose physical torture instead?

Fuck you, Governor Jon McIntyre.

NO GOVERNOR, NO REASON to continue. Not in here. Not one more day. My biggest desire has become my own death. Unfortunately, all means of accomplishing this have been removed. The quote "I think, therefore I am" drifts into my head. It's a bunch of bullshit. I think, but I am nothing. I am alive, yet I am not. My sole purpose for existence is for the sick indulgence of others.

The eternal tortures of hell await the fornicator. The preacher's words drift through my mind. Could this hell on earth all be due to a stupid fucking summer afternoon in a tree house with a whore named Angie? Was my whole life just punishment because of Angie? I really had trouble buying into that. The preacher didn't know jack. The tortures of hell don't mean a fucking thing compared to the tortures of the Criminal Zoo.

I have been abandoned in here. I wonder why my sister hasn't tried to contact me. Sheila could have been visiting all along. She could come as an L2, but not with intentions to hurt me. She could come and save me from suffering for at least a day. She could come in and just talk. Ask me how I'm doing, tell me how she's doing. I would've done it for her. Love is supposed to know no bounds.

Stark Raving Mad

I AM DONE. NOT IN the near future, not even tomorrow, but right now. I simply will not exist inside this place one more minute. I exhale with no intention of inhaling again. I pinch my nose closed with my right hand and I shut my mouth. I will not allow any more life-sustaining oxygen into my body.

Within a few seconds, my lungs begin to burn. I keep my nose and mouth closed as several more seconds pass. The burn in my lungs gets worse. I really want to open my mouth, but I don't. I fight for death. The burning gets almost unbearable and white dots of light begin to flash across my vision, yet I do not take another breath. The pain becomes excruciating, climbing from my chest into my throat and up to my brain. My skin begins to tingle as if tiny needles are sticking me everywhere. The outer edges of my consciousness become frayed, unravel. I want to breathe, to suck in a roomful of air, but I will not. It is time to leave the Zoo!

My mouth betrays me. It pops open, flooding air into my lungs. The burn is instantly extinguished, the needles go away, and my full awareness comes back. I pant, catch my breath, and curse my failure. I punch myself in the face as hard as I can. Pain from the blow crashes through my head, but I accomplish nothing more. I break down into uncontrollable tears.

After a few moments, I stagger to my feet, resolved to finish this here and now. I remove my Zoo-issue pants, wrap them around my neck, and begin to twist the material tighter and tighter, until all oxygen is cut off. This way, my body can't betray me. The dancing stars of light come back in full force. My head pounds with pressure, which increases each second. I twist tighter. Light erupts all around me. The needles return. Again, the outer edges of my consciousness fade. Darkness encircles my field of vision and slowly creeps inward. I twist the pants ever tighter.

And then everything is black.

I awaken lying on my back, flat on the floor. My head pounds as I look into the artificial night and wonder momentarily what happened. The pants fall from my neck as I sit up. I have no idea how long I've been out. Using more exertion than seems necessary, I slide over to the edge of my bed and lean against it.

I scream out a mix of rage, agony, and defeat.

"Nice try, One-Zero-One-Three." The smart-ass comment flows from the control room, through the little speaker in the ceiling, and into my enclosure. "Now get to bed so you can dream about another glorious day in the Zoo!"

"Fuck you."

Laughter follows.

I wonder what the weather is like outside. When I had my freedom—much like the concept of *time*—I never appreciated how one always had the weather to talk about. "Hot enough for you?" "Looks like rain." "The breeze feels good." Sayings I almost forgot existed.

The sun, or clouds, or rain, or wind was once a guaranteed part of each day. Now, my life is void of all weather. Just like the Confinement Center, the temperature inside the Zoo will always stay the same, not a degree hotter, not a degree colder. I can no longer recall what it feels like to have the wind blow through my hair. I haven't experienced the warmth of the sun on my back or the smell of a fresh spring rain for an eternity. Those experiences are nothing more than dreams.

My thoughts drift to something else once taken for granted: birds. Birds flying overhead, tweeting and cawing. Birds lined up on a power line. Birds huddled together on a tree branch, seeing who can chirp the loudest. I miss birds. Their songs. What a strange thought. I never once thought about birds before all this shit started.

Now, more than anything, I want to see a bird. A crow, sparrow, robin, it doesn't matter. Or a cat. Or, yes, even a dog. Hell, Brutus would be better than nothing. If I could do it all over again, I wouldn't kill him. Probably would even pet the damn thing.

I want to hear chirping or meowing or barking, because those noises represent normalcy. And that doesn't exist in here. No, in here all that exists are the animals known as L2s and keepers. I don't want to see them anymore. And if I can't see what I want to see, the birds and all that, then I don't want to see *anything* anymore.

The irony that it has taken me this long to think of it isn't lost. I stare into the darkness a moment longer. My heart races as I realize that when the lights were turned off earlier, it was the last time I would ever see light again. *Cast it out.* Don't look any more into the eyes of those who only want to hurt you. Whether its blackness or hatred they harbor, I don't want to see it.

I take in a deep breath and exhale slowly as I raise my right hand toward my eyes. My left hand is still bandaged and useless, will remain useless forever more. I spread my index and middle fingers apart, place one finger at each eye. "Cast it out," I mumble. Cast *them* out.

The Three Monkeys Killer is about to pull off the ultimate Three Stooges move. I plunge my fingertips into my open eyeballs.

The pain is instantly searing and sickening. I yank my fingers from my eyes and crumple to my knees. My eyes close reflexively and fluid pours out. I can't tell if it's tears or blood. My eyelids freeze shut as if to protect against any further attacks. I lean forward and vomit. I'm on my hands and knees, throwing up my guts, and the pain only gets worse. My eyes feel like they've been rinsed with battery acid.

I start running around blindly in my enclosure. Running because it's the only thing I can think to do. Trying to outrun the pain. I slam my leg into my bed, trip and land on the floor. Unconcerned about my throbbing shin, I jump back to my feet and start running again. I hit my confinement chair, topple over it, and land on my head and shoulder on the other side. The pain of the fall doesn't even touch the pain of my eyes.

"Fuck me!" I'm screaming as loud as I can. Running and screaming, like a lunatic. Stark, raving mad. I've lost my mind. I'm Van Gogh cutting off my ear. I'm—

Out of nowhere, someone tackles me. I'm slammed to the ground, landing hard on my back. My head crashes into the floor and blackness overcomes all senses.

My Blurry World

PAIN REACHES FOR ME, grips me with icy fingers, pulls at me.
I am in the dark hole in my mind and I am confused. If I
go deep enough, the pain is not supposed to find me. Yet
it does. I try to pull away, but I can't free myself from its jagged
talons. My secret place has been breached.

I open my eyes. Pain flashes through them. I quickly shut
them again. Shit, I can't go through the rest of my life with my
eyes closed. So I try again, slowly allowing my eyelids to raise.
Pain returns, but not quite as bad.

The world is blurry. Really blurry. No details at all. I see
shapes, barely. Not really colors. Just hues. Tones, from dark to
light. I try to reach for my face but can't. My arms are restrained.
My legs too. The pain in my eyes grows steadily.

"Hey!" I yell. No one comes. "Hey! Is anybody here?" I know
I'm in the Repair Shack, so someone has to be manning the desk
in the next room.

"Awake, are we?" A voice from my right. Not too far away. A
voice I know; the creator of Hell. The governor.

"My eyes. They hurt."

"Samuel, I can't even imagine," Governor McIntyre says. He
approaches. Stands next to my bed. Or at least his horribly blurry
silhouette does. "You damn near poked your eyes out, my friend.
The doc said the damage was extensive. Perforated corneas."

My memory flashes back. Holy shit, I tried to blind myself. "Governor, they really hurt. Can you give me something for the pain?"

"I wish I could, Samuel. Unfortunately, at this exact moment, there is nothing I can do for you."

"Why not?"

"Because I'm the only one here."

"Am I in the Repair Shack?"

"You are. Damn, Samuel, you did quite a number on yourself," the governor says in a tone that almost sounds impressed. "What the hell were you thinking?"

"You never came back," I yell. "You promised to help me, but you never came back."

"Hey, Samuel, you realize I am the governor of Colorado, right? It's not like I just get to hang out in the Zoo all the time. I actually have a pretty busy day job. But I'm here right now, aren't I?"

"An L-two cut my fucking fingers off! Where were you then? Fuck, it hurt."

"Yes, I heard things went a little crazy with that guy."

"A little crazy? He removed body parts. I can't take this shit anymore. I want out. Either you get me out, or I get me out."

"Sorry, Samuel. You have no means of doing that."

"I'll starve myself to death."

"Force-feeding. Works every time."

"I'm not kidding, Governor! Get me the fuck out of here like you promised!"

"I cannot lie, Samuel, you intrigue me to no end. I've never met anyone quite like you. Truth be told, I'm totally fascinated by you."

I have no response. I can only think about how bad I hurt.

"I really want to understand you. I want to understand the whys and the hows of you. I want to understand your need to have the power to decide who lives and who dies. And I want to know what would possess you to try to tear out your own eyes."

"Quit trying to understand me so much, and instead try to get me out of here."

"I am. But what I'm attempting doesn't happen overnight. I've put the process in motion, contacting the people I need to contact and getting the ball rolling. I didn't promise I'd have you out by the next day. You have to have some patience."

"Patience?" I say. "Are you fucking kidding me? You have patience when you're waiting in line to renew your driver's license. When you're buying your movie ticket. You don't have patience in here. Not when you're waiting for the next fucking knife blade to slice through you."

"Yes, I suppose. But understand, I'm working on it, okay? Just a few more days. And quit trying to mutilate yourself. Why would you do the L-twos' job for them?"

"You don't get it, Governor. I want the fuck out. Right now."

"Okay, okay. I'll see what I can do," he says. "Not to change the subject, but I haven't given up on the theory that if I can truly understand how you think, how your mind works, I can watch for it. I can teach others what to look for. I can help all of mankind. I've developed quite a national platform, you know. This place is evidence of that. Maybe I can educate the general public on warning signs to watch for, kind of like finding a serial killer before the person becomes one."

"None of you get it. I'm not a puzzle to figure out—I already told you that. You will never understand me, no matter how hard you try!" My outburst intensifies the pain.

"I'll just have to keep trying, then."

I hear footsteps. Someone else is entering my blurry world.

"Hello, Doctor," the governor says.

"Governor McIntyre, how are you, sir?" A new voice accompanies the footsteps. A new blur moves next to the Jon blur.

"Better than our friend here." Jon laughs. "Says he's pretty sore."

"CZ One-Zero-One-Three, are you hurting?" the doctor blur asks.

"Yes, I'm fucking hurting. My eyes are killing me."

"Yeah, I imagine they are. In hindsight, not a very good idea, huh?" The doctor blur moves away.

I hear a cabinet door open, a pill bottle rattle. I turn my head, try to see, but the distance turns everything into one giant blur. The door clicks closed. A moment later, the doctor blur moves back to my bed, slides a hand under my head and lifts. "Open your mouth."

I do as I'm told. Two pills hit my battered tongue. A paper cup is held to my lips. I take a drink and start coughing. Pain roars through my head.

Time to Think

SOMEONE SNEEZES. THE SNEEZE seems far away, maybe from a room at the end of a long hallway. I hear a second sneeze and realize it's perhaps only in the next room.

"Bless you," a voice says.

"Thanks." It's the governor's voice that answers.

I try to open my eyes. Pain accompanies the act. Shit, is it going to be like this every time? Slowly, my eyelids lift and the blur of the universe comes through. Still no details. Only a blurry haze.

"Can someone let me loose?"

Footsteps in the haze.

"Hey, Samuel, feeling any better?" Governor McIntyre's voice. His blur stands beside me.

"Not much. Unless having cactuses shoved in your eyeballs is feeling better."

"Is it cactuses? Or cacti?"

I turn toward the blur. "You kidding me?"

"Sorry. I've always struggled with that." I hear the scraping of a chair being pulled up. "How long do you think you've been in here?"

"In the Repair Shack?"

"No. In *here*, the Criminal Zoo. How long do you think you've been here?"

I think for a moment, trying to clear the fog from my mind. "I don't know. The Criminal Zoo phase lasts a year, so it can't be longer than that, even though it feels like it's been ten years. But honestly, I've got to be going on maybe...ten or eleven months now? Which means my time should be almost up, right?"

The governor says nothing.

"I'm right, right?"

"Samuel, you thought you had the power to decide who suffers and who doesn't," he says, not acknowledging my question. "But now you are powerless, aren't you?"

"Is my time almost up or not?"

"What did it feel like? What did it feel like when you believed you had the power to make decisions only God should make?"

"Tell me how much time I have left in here. Please."

"You know it's against the rules for me to talk about that, right?"

"You brought it up!" The bolt of pain blasting through my head tells me I shouldn't have yelled. "Please just tell me."

"When your year is up, you move on to become king of the hill in maximum-security lockup. Supposedly, they revere you Zoo exhibits. Respected as real badasses."

I want to know how long I've been in the Zoo. But my head warns me not to yell again. I sigh. "I'm begging you, show some compassion. We don't get much of that here. How much more time do I have?"

"I have a question for you," the governor says. "What did you think was going to happen? Despite what you said, doing it to become Godlike and all, you murdered innocent people and left their mutilated bodies behind."

"I told you why. We've had this discussion already."

"I know. But if that's so, then why aren't your Gods helping you now? Why do They leave you in here to suffer?"

"I don't know. I wonder that too." I let out a sigh, long and painful. "Perhaps I've made a terrible mistake."

"What?" His voice is closer, like he's leaning over me.

"While in here, I've done more thinking than in all my life. I've been forced to examine my entire existence. Time to think can have a powerful effect on a guy."

"Do tell."

"What you do to us isn't right, Governor. Not right at all." I pause a beat. "Torture is the most horrifying thing I have ever experienced. I wouldn't wish it on my worst enemy. And it has made me think. A lot. Torture is exactly what I did to people before I came here. I tortured them. And just as you have no right to torture us, I can now see I had no right to torture others."

"I thought you were *cleansing* them," the governor says.

"So did I. But after my time in the Zoo, I'm not so sure. If nothing else, this place will make you contemplate every action you've ever taken. Now I question my own actions. Was I really cleansing anybody? Or was I just mutilating them, like I get mutilated in here? It's not right. No matter what the reason, mine or yours, it's not right."

"Wow," the governor says. "I think we may have had a breakthrough."

"In church, as a boy," I say, "I learned a passage about Satan being disguised in sheep's clothing and tricking righteous people into doing unrighteous things. Maybe this happened to me. But good or bad, I followed my convictions. And if anyone truly understands this, God does. And He knows I have suffered more than any man should. When I die, I will sit by His side because I have been punished in here…in your Hell."

There is silence. The governor must be pondering my words.

"Governor, you are the only person who has treated me like a man in here. You have befriended me and I would never betray that. I will help you understand me. Please. I swear to you, while I have sinned against man, God knows the innocence in my heart. I thought I was doing what was right in the eternal sense."

The governor sighs and then says, "Two and a half months."

"Two and a half months, what? What's two and a half months?"

"That's how long you've been in here."

His words hit me like a two-by-four across the back of my head. My heart freezes in my chest. "That's impossible, Governor. That can't be." *Stay calm. He must have added wrong.*

"I'm sorry, Samuel, I really am. I'm sure it seems like a lot longer, but you still have over nine months to go."

"No. No. No!" I shake my head. My reality is bending, time grinding to a stop.

"I really am sorry," the governor repeats.

"Governor, I can't do it," I say, shaking my head. "I can't take it anymore. Not nine months, not nine days. Not nine fucking hours. You offered to help. Will you still help me? Please, Governor, please get me out of here."

The governor grabs me around my left forearm. "Samuel, listen for a second. I've contacted someone who can help you."

"Who?"

"I'm not going to say just yet. Let me keep working on it."

"Please. Whoever it is, get him in here."

"Samuel, be completely honest. No more lies. Have you really learned your lesson?"

"Yes! I swear to God I'll never hurt anyone again. There's no way I'd ever do anything to end up back in here. I swear."

The governor doesn't say anything for a long time.

"Governor, please, I'm begging you."

"You know what, my friend, call me crazy, but I believe you. You'd have to be more than just a little insane to want to come back here. Maybe you could be my ultimate success story. Maybe we can show the world that your kind can be rehabilitated after all. You could validate everything I've fought for with this place."

"I will preach against the evils of my ways until my last breath."

The governor goes silent again.

"Governor?"

"You know, I stood before Congress, faced every one of those prissy stuffed shirts, and I told them that only with this kind of punishment could we reach those who are hardwired to kill. I mean *truly* get through to them. And now, you have proven me right. You know you'll never know freedom again, right? You're headed to life in prison from here."

"I know. But in prison, I will get to stand outside. Feel the sun's warmth again. Feel the wind against my skin. Feel a drop of rain. Hear birds singing. Have interactions with other people that aren't simply about my pain, my suffering. I will become a human being again."

"Yeah, that's true. You'll be an inmate, not an exhibit. You will return to the human race." The governor pauses. "In the end, though, when you return to dust, the final judgment can come only from our maker. Whether you have earned an eternity in God's presence or you spend it in Hell will not be decided in this life, but in the next."

"Then why didn't you leave it up to God to judge us? Why create this place?"

"Because while we are on this planet, we need to be protected from those who prey upon us." Governor McIntyre sighs. "Samuel, nobody should have to experience what I went through. When I lost my wife, my heart was ripped from my chest."

"So what exactly *did* happen to her?" I ask.

Stunning Revelation

"OH, SAMUEL, IF ONLY you could've seen her. She was my day, my night. She was my everything." The governor's voice reveals that he's smiling. A smile I cannot see in the blur. "She was my fantasy. She was my reality. She was a shining light, a warmth that comforted everyone."

"What did she look like?"

"She was absolutely beautiful. Long, shimmering golden-brown hair. Brilliant green eyes. I'm not kidding, either. They were radiant. Sparkled like polished emeralds. Her name was Allison. I called her Allie."

Why did a jolt of familiarity shoot through my whole body, and why is my skin tingling?

"She'd been visiting her parents. They were the last people to see her alive. She was driving home, her car broke down, and then she vanished."

"Where did this happen?" My heart is pounding and my ears are ringing.

"The Four Corners area of New Mexico. Just outside of a little town called Shiprock."

Jesus Christ! No way!

"She was stranded on the side of the road and had just called me. She was about to tell me where she was when I heard screeching tires and her voice screaming. It was a horrifying scream, made me sick just hearing it. To this day, I lie in bed at night and hear that scream. Every damn night, that's the last thing I hear before I fall asleep. That scream will haunt me until I die."

I am dizzy from this stunning revelation. "How long ago did this happen?"

"Oh, it's been several years now. But I remember that scream like it was this morning."

This can't be! "Maybe she just ran away." The feebleness of this statement rattles through my brain.

"No," the governor says. "Someone definitely took her. Her car was found. The license plates had been removed, the VIN number had been scratched out, her insurance and registration papers were gone, and her cell phone was stomped to pieces."

I have no idea what to say. Hell, I can barely breathe.

"I called the Colorado highway patrol first, because I didn't know how close to home she was. There were no reports of any accidents, so I called New Mexico. They didn't have any reports for that area, either. But both states said they would be on the lookout for the car I described. An hour later, I received the phone call that ruined my life."

"What'd they find?"

"Just what I told you. Her car. But there were splotches of blood at the scene, on the side of the road. There were tire tracks. Imprints were taken, but nothing ever came of it."

"Any fingerprints on her car?"

"Oh, sure there were—a lot of them. Mine, hers, her parents', my parents', our kids', the mechanic's. Yes, fingerprints everywhere. But the glove box—that area had been wiped completely clean."

"So you never found out what happened?"

"Oh, I know what happened. Someone hit her, killed her, and then covered their tracks. I just don't know who. For a long time, whenever the phone rang, I prayed it would be someone with information about Allie. Someone who knew something about what happened that day. I held onto hope for years."

An odd thought strikes me. I feel cheated that I didn't get to see her eyes, if they were really as beautiful as the governor says. "That had to have been pretty hard."

"My kids asked me twenty times a day, every damn day, when their mom was coming home. What was I supposed to tell them?" The governor's words now sound as if tears have washed away the smile. "After a year of looking for her, even without a body, I had to accept the reality of it all. I finally told the kids their mom was in Heaven. We had a funeral, and we tried to begin the healing. But nothing took the pain away. Nothing even came close, until I came up with this place."

"Her body was never found?"

"If there are any remains, with modern-day DNA technology, eventually something will turn up. But here's the problem...did you know twenty-three hundred people in the United States are reported missing every single day?"

"No, I didn't."

"That's about nine hundred thousand Americans per year. The system is overloaded with data. And even if her remains are found, almost five thousand unidentified bodies are discovered every year. The last time I checked, there was a backlog of almost forty thousand bodies in various states of decomposition, waiting to be identified."

I shake my head. "I'm so sorry, Governor. But this just confirms what I'm telling you. The Criminal Zoo is your way of trying to escape your pain and your frustration. Allie was never found. Her killer was never found. So all the suffering that goes on in here is just so you can feel better. That's really terrible."

"I'm beginning to realize that. But, just like the people who pay to visit you and to harm you, I wanted revenge. I wanted to punish anyone and everyone who ever committed a violent crime. And to be completely honest, I hoped that this place would act like a giant net and someday snare the animal that killed my wife. When that day came, I'd look him in the eyes and say, *See what your actions have caused?* I'd ask him how it felt to hurt, to hurt like he's never hurt before."

Does he know? Is he just fucking with me now? Does he actually have zero intentions of helping me? What if his offer is nothing more than another way to torture me?

The governor attempts a laugh. "You know, when it's all said and done, you're right. This place, it doesn't help. I still hurt. Every day I miss her, whether the Zoo exists or not."

"All this, Governor? All this just because you wanted whoever took your wife to suffer? What about everyone else who is tortured in here? What about those of us who never even heard of you or your wife?"

"Hey, don't get all preachy on me, Samuel. Everyone in here is in here for a reason. You have to commit a horrible crime, someone has to die a terrible death, for you to end up here. So, don't try to tell me this place isn't fair. I just wish I could look the guy in the eyes, the guy who shattered my world, and say, 'Now we're even, you son of a bitch.'"

It's definitely time to change the subject. "Back to getting me out of here. Who is it that you've contacted?"

"Yeah, enough of me feeling sorry for myself. I spent years doing that. There's someone who has the authority to set you free, my friend. But you're going to have to hang tight. It's going to take a couple of days, okay?"

He sounds genuine, like he's speaking from the heart. He doesn't know. My spirit soars. "I can make it through a few more days as long as I have hope of leaving this place. And I promise you, I'll never, *ever* come back."

"I believe you, Samuel." The governor rises from his chair and says, "Well, I better get moving. As soon as I know something, you'll know it."

"Hey, I have one last question before you go."

"What's that?"

"Experimenting on human beings…isn't that going a little too far?"

The governor considers for a moment. "News travels fast around here. We instituted that phase less than three weeks ago."

"RS Twenty-Nine looked like shit."

"RS Twenty-Nine, let me think…oh, you mean Aaron. Yeah, he's a mess, isn't he?"

"He was probably one of the last people I will ever see with any detail."

"Not probably. He was. Doc said your eyes are permanently damaged."

"Thanks for that uplifting thought."

"Samuel, be assured I did some serious soul searching when the pharmaceutical companies approached me. But they convinced me and the Zoo directors of the benefits that would come from it. Imagine drugs that could cure cancer, AIDS, all the horrible diseases that afflict us. The sacrifices made by a select few could benefit millions of people."

"How do you choose who becomes a lab rat and who doesn't?"

"Not lab rats. Valuable individuals. Once they volunteer for valuable research, they themselves become valuable."

"How do you choose them?" I persist.

"A complete blood workup is run. Age, sex, genetics, and willingness to participate all weigh in. In Aaron's case, the research called for an adult Caucasian male between the ages of thirty and fifty. He was approached and given the opportunity to sign up. He could've said no."

"You should have seen him. He's going to die."

"Samuel, he's going to die either way. We all are, right? At least this way something comes from his death. Medicine will be advanced because of Aaron's sacrifice."

"Are there others?"

"This is all pretty new. I think we only have a handful of research subjects. As we develop the program, we will increase the number of volunteers and their unselfish acts will open up a whole new level of possibility. Science will leapfrog disease. And make no mistake about it, Samuel, the drug companies are very grateful. They compensate the families *extremely* well."

"Drug companies get to buy lives?"

"Only lives which would otherwise have no value."

"So now you're deciding whose life has value, and whose doesn't?"

"You guys decided that yourselves," the governor says, "when you decided to kill."

Like The Phoenix

I N THE CONFINEMENT CENTER, my world was eternally white, the
white nightmare I couldn't escape. Now my world is nothing
but haze. I can't decide which is worse.

I have no idea how long it has been since the governor's visit.
But however long it has been, however long it will be until his
next visit, I once again have hope. I guess it's only fitting that the
man who created my hell now holds the key release me from it.
I can do prison. Conversation with other human beings, which
would mean I exist—and not just for others to bury their pain
under mine.

I suppose if someone really thought about it, really
overanalyzed the whole situation, they could come to the
conclusion that it was actually *my* actions that created this hell.
But no, that doesn't really work, because there was no way I
could've known that the woman standing in the middle of the
road was the wife of a man who could, and would, accomplish so
much. And it wasn't like I tried to hit her. Jesus, just my luck...I
had to hit the one woman on the planet with a husband like
Governor Jon McIntyre.

Enough dwelling on this. It's time to think about getting the
hell out of here. It's time to think about the rest of my life.

The pain from my little eye assault has diminished to mild
discomfort. In here, mild discomfort is a good thing. Mild

discomfort means you haven't had an L2 for a while. It means your body is healing.

In less than three months I have lost a portion of my tongue, much of my left hand, my eyesight, and parts of my ears. I don't have enough body parts to last nine more months. I am still plagued by the phantom pain of my missing fingers, but it comes and goes. I can live with that. What pains me the most is the realization that I have sacrificed so much. I lost my home, my wife—actually, that's not much of a loss—my freedom and, until now, my desire to live.

I pray that my next visitor is the governor's "special" person.

I wonder who it could be. At first I think perhaps it's Sheila. But then I realize that whoever the person is, he or she must have quite a bit of authority. It can't be my sister. She wouldn't have any pull.

It's almost unbelievable to think that my life—which I had almost given up on—now harbors such hope. Hey, I can finally make my movie. It'll be about the Criminal Zoo. Now I have a story to tell.

I'm sure there are lots of people in prison who can type for me. I can tell my story, they'll type it up, and I'll put their name in the credits. Everyone will want to see what it's like in this fucking hell. I'll give them all the gory details. They'll love it. A blockbuster for sure.

And who knows…if I can get out of here, maybe I can get out of anywhere. Including whatever prison I end up in. Suddenly, I can't wait to write about my experiences. A line of scripture pops into my head: "After the suffering of his soul, he will see the light of life, and be satisfied." Satisfied would be good. But rich would be even better.

I have been given a second chance and I will not mess it up. Regardless of the good or evil I was a part of before this place, I have been reborn. Like the phoenix, I will climb from the flames of confusion and deceit, shedding death and beginning life anew. I am ready to spread my wings. It's time for me to get out of here. I have a story to tell.

A Big Deal

THE DOCTOR EXAMINES MY eyes and says they're as good as they're going to get. Time to head back to the enclosure. For the first time ever, I am ready to go back. As I am led from the Repair Shack, he says, "See you next time, One-Zero-One-Three."

No, he won't. He will not see me next time. The governor is getting me out of here. The asshole doctor won't ever see me again because I am about to be long gone.

A keeper—I think it's a keeper—leads me through the blur and back to my enclosure, soon to be nothing but a horrible memory. My spirit soars as I wonder who's going to buy my movie. Universal Pictures? Warner Brothers? Paramount? I'm not sure just yet, but I know it's going to be a big deal. How could they not want my story? The whole world will stand in line to see what happens in the Zoo.

Life's Little Joke

MY HEART BEATS RAPIDLY, matched by my breathing. I close my right hand into a fist, open it, close it again. I pace my enclosure relentlessly. I've got a good feel for where everything is so I move around without trouble. My mysterious visitor will come. My freedom will be granted. My new life will begin—life with purpose, promise, and money.

Governor McIntyre's Criminal Zoo tried to destroy me. But I rose above it, beat it, and now it's going to make me famous. And in my fame, I will be immortal. Jimi Hendrix. John Wayne. JFK. Elvis. All people whose image and spirit will live forever in the minds of the masses. And now we can add one more name to that list: Samuel Bradbury.

I LIE ON MY bed, seeing only blurred haze. Several loud clicks grab my attention. It is the all-too-familiar sound of the door locks disengaging. My heart races. Is this the visitor who will finally set me free? Is the next phase of my life, the most incredible yet, about to begin?

"CZ One-Zero-One-Three, move to the chair." The voice of my keeper.

I scramble from the bed and climb into the confinement chair. Excitement courses through my veins. I can feel it. This is not a regular L2 visit. I can feel it in my heart. This is it—*the* visit.

I listen as the keeper enters the room, his footsteps coming toward me through the haze. "I have the Zap-stick aimed directly at your head. If you make one wrong move, I will scramble your brains. Got it?"

"Yeah, I got it." I place my forearms on top of the armrest straps. He locks them down. He moves to my ankles, restraining them. He places the leather skullcap on my head. I lean my head back and he snaps it to the chair.

"Who's coming in?"

A firm hand takes hold of my left arm and tugs. It's secure. Then my right arm. Again, secure. Both legs are tested. The results are the same. I am excited, but suddenly fear is as much a factor. "Who is it?"

"The exhibit is secure," the keeper says.

More footsteps enter the room. Two blurry figures move toward me. Stand over me.

"Who's there?" I ask. Suddenly I'm hating the haze. I want to see.

"Hello, Samuel."

I exhale loudly. *Thank God.* "Hello, Governor. I was getting worried. I thought that maybe…well, you know. Anyway, you can let me out of the restraints. I'm not going to hurt anybody."

"Keeper, would you bring in the chairs?" the governor asks.

The largest blur moves away. The keeper. I hear footsteps moving toward the door. A moment later, the sound of chairs being dragged across the floor fills the enclosure. The sound gets closer as the chairs are placed in front of me, close to me.

"I know Zoo regulations have to be followed and all, Governor, but you can let me go. You of all people know I've changed. I'm not violent anymore."

More movement toward the door. The next sound adds to my confusion—jingling keys, followed by a motorized hum.

Someone has just inserted a key into the switch that slides the hard plastic cover across the viewing wall. This only occurs when an exhibit is closed due to the inmate being in the Repair Shack.

"Hey, what's going on?"

"Samuel, as I told you before, there is someone who has the special ability to help you. And that person is here now. Standing beside me. Please, sit down," the governor instructs his guest. My guest.

"Who's with you?" *Goddamn it I wish I could see.*

The chairs creak as they take on weight. And then there is only silence.

"Hello, Samuel."

A woman's voice.

"Who are you?" I ask.

"Samuel," the governor says, "you need to brace yourself."

"For what?" I stare hard at the two figures, trying to make out any details at all. None materialize.

"It's your mother," he replies.

"My mother?"

"Samuel, it's me."

My thoughts freeze like a Minnesota lake in January.

"I know this must be quite a shock, Samuel, but I had to come. Governor McIntyre said I was the only who could help."

No, this isn't right. Not right at all. It can't be her. Not now. Not here. Not after three decades of silence.

"Please, Samuel, say something."

The sound of this woman's voice stabs into my heart like icicles.

"Samuel," the governor begins, "remember when I told you I had access to your files?"

"Yeah."

"I didn't just look at your crimes. I looked at everything, starting with your birth. I know your story. Your mother left you as a child. I know how traumatic that must have been."

"What is this? What's going on?" I try to understand the direction of this visit.

"I tracked her down," the governor says.

"No, Governor, that's impossible. This woman isn't my mom. My mom's dead, because that's the *only* reason she would never have come back."

"Yes, Samuel, it's really your mom. I found her."

"Samuel," the woman begins, "I would've come to see you, but I didn't even know you were here."

I turn to the blur accompanying her voice. "No, you wouldn't have. You abandoned me." The harshness of life's little joke is crushing. "How could you leave your children with him?"

There is a long pause. I wait for the answer.

"Samuel, I was afraid for my life. Your father beat me. Raped me. I had to leave. But before I did, he told me if ever thought about leaving him, he would find me and kill me. And if you and Sheila were with me, he'd kill your kids, too."

"My life is your fault."

"Please don't say that," the woman responds.

"You didn't leave me a note."

"You were too young for a note."

Anger three decades in the making flashes through me. But I remain calm. If there was ever a time for calm, it's right now. "Governor, you said my visitor could get me out of here. What can she do?"

There is a brief pause. "Samuel, there are things about this place that you do not know. Your mom's visit is one of them."

"What does that mean? Enough of the games."

"Your mom's visit, Samuel, it's called a Level three visit."

"A Level three visit? What the fuck's a Level three visit?"

The woman begins to cry. I recognize the sound from my childhood. She cried a lot. Yeah, it's really her.

"Governor McIntyre told me that I was your last chance, your last hope," my mother begins. "He told me the horrible things that happen in here. Oh God, Samuel, I can't even imagine what it must be like."

"I don't care what you can imagine or what you can't. All I care about is how you can get me out of here. Governor, let's get this thing moving."

"Indeed we shall, Samuel. Indeed we shall. Come with me, Ms. Bradbury, and we'll get the paperwork going."

Chairs creak. I hear the sound of footsteps moving toward the door. The locks disengage.

"Governor, I'm not sure what this whole thing is about," I say, calmly, collected. "It has a strange feel to it. But it better be exactly what you promised. It better be about getting me out of here. No more talk, right?"

"No more talk, Samuel. Time to get you out."

The Truth

THE GOVERNOR AND MY mom left forever ago. My keeper released me from the confinement chair and told me to "hang tight." No problem. I'll just sit here and wonder whether I'm about to once again feel sunshine on my face, hear birds singing, and have someone say, "Good morning, Samuel," or endure an eternity of torturous hell as CZ1013. But hey, either way I'll be sure to hang tight while I'm doing it.

Through the blur, I pace back and forth. Fuck me, how long does it take to do paperwork? And then a troublesome thought hits me. *What if she does it to me again?* She already abandoned me once.

I continue to pace.

The locks disengage. My heart leaps into my throat.

"CZ One-Zero-One-Three," my keeper says. "Move to the chair."

I jump into the seat. After I am secured, the blurs of my guests return. Chairs are brought in, locks are engaged, and seats are taken. I hear crying. Why is she crying? I turn to her hazy silhouette. "Why are you crying? What the fuck is going on?"

"Samuel," the governor begins, "once in a while, a very special visit occurs in here."

"Yeah, we've covered that already, Governor. I have a Level three visit. It's very special, got it. So how does it get me the fuck out of here?"

"The paperwork's done. Your mom signed off on everything."

"Way to go, Mom," I say without emotion. "Let's get to it."

"It's not discussed with the exhibits of the Zoo," the governor begins, "nor are the details of the visit ever released to the media. But when an inmate has proven to be remorseful—truly sorry for his actions, as you have—and all indicators show the inmate would not be able to survive the full twelve months in the Zoo, early freedom can be granted."

"Why are we still talking?" I'm beginning to grow agitated. Very agitated.

"It can only happen," the governor continues, "if requested by the exhibit *and* carried out by a member of the exhibit's immediate family. As a representative of the Criminal Zoo, I signed off on the paperwork from the Zoo end and your mother signed off as immediate family. Now it's your turn."

"What exactly am I supposed to be requesting?" I ask. "I already told you I want out."

"You have proven to be truly remorseful, Samuel. Now I just need you to tell me which direction you want to go."

"Which direction I want to go? I want fucking out! Now!"

"Your mom has come today to give you your freedom from the Criminal Zoo. No more torture. No more pain. No more suffering. But not in the way you were thinking. You need to know the truth of an L-three visit, Samuel."

"Why are you playing games?" My pulse pounds in my head.

"There are only two ways out of the Criminal Zoo—period. One year served with Level two visits, or death."

A monstrous vise clamps down on my heart and gets tighter by the second. "I don't understand. What's this whole Level three visit shit, then?"

My mother continues to cry.

"Sometimes," the governor begins, "the right thing to do is the most difficult thing to do. Sometimes no matter how painful it is, one's own heartache, one's own pain, needs to be put aside for the benefit of another person. In this case, you."

"Quit fucking around, Governor. Tell me exactly what you're talking about."

"Sometimes death is a better option than living. I don't think you want to endure nine more months in here. And I guarantee you, it only gets harder. Your mom just gave you an out. If you want it."

I feel as if I have just been dropped into an ice-cold ocean and I am sinking into the depthless abyss, still strapped into this fucking chair. I don't say anything for a long time. I'm trying to completely understand what it is I'm being told. Finally I ask, in as tight a voice as I can, "This is a joke, right?"

No one speaks.

"Tell me this is all just a fucking joke!"

"This is the only way out," the governor says. "Samuel, you know you won't last nine more months. You can either end it peacefully, at your own discretion, or you can wait for another lunatic L-two to take you out. You've already had one. You will have another. And then another. Do you want to let someone else decide for you when you die?"

"You're saying my mom is here to kill me?" I am spinning in the haze. My mouth becomes dry, my skin is shriveling, tingling. I am nauseated. "You promised I'd get out of here!" I turn to the second blur. "I don't know what he told you, Mom, but you're supposed to help me, not kill me."

"Samuel, I—"

"I'll forgive you, Mom, for everything you've done. For leaving us with Dad. Get me out of here and then we can be a family again. You, me, and Sheila. We'll forget about the past and move forward. We can do it."

"Honey," she begins.

"No! No fucking *'honey'*! Get me the fuck out of here!"

"Your mom is here to free you, Samuel. For you, she is willing to commit the greatest sacrifice a mother could ever make for her child. Like Abraham was ready to sacrifice Isaac, she is willing to free you, despite the painful loss she will endure. Think about the magnitude of that sacrifice. Because of your mother, because of her willingness to let go of her only son, your time in the Criminal Zoo has come to an end."

"Fuck Abraham. I don't want to die." My heart breaks free of the vise and pounds against my chest wall. My whole body shakes. "You can't be serious. You're talking about putting me down like I'm a stray dog. I'm not a fucking dog. I'm a human being."

"Not in here, Samuel," the governor says. "In here, you're below a dog."

"You can't just kill me. That's murder."

"Samuel, trust me: this is the best way out. You simply go to sleep. Painless."

"*Letting me go* is the best way out!"

"I'm afraid that's impossible," Governor McIntyre says.

"Jon McIntyre, you are a fucking bastard. You gave me hope. Why did you do that? Why do you want to fuck with me so bad?"

"Samuel, you are a psychopath. Regardless of what you tell yourself, or how you try to justify it, the truth is you kill without conscience. There is no cure for what you have. You can never be set free."

"You're wrong. I'll never hurt anyone ever again."

"I'm sorry, Samuel. I really am."

My mom continues to cry like she cares.

"Bitch, why are you crying?" I ask her blur. "You're not the one everybody is trying to kill."

"Samuel," the governor interrupts. "Do you remember Dr. Kevorkian?"

"Who?"

"Dr. Kevorkian. He helped the terminally ill die with grace. Without pain. I can help you die painlessly and with dignity."

"I'm not terminally ill, you fucking idiot. I have the rest of my life in front of me. I have great things still to accomplish."

"In here?"

"No, not in here—I want the freedom you promised me, you son of a bitch!"

"You can't go through any more of this!" My mom's sobbing distorts her words. "I can't live with the pain, knowing you're still in here, someone hurting you every day. Cutting into your flesh. Butchering you as you sit strapped to a damned chair."

"*You* can't live with the pain? Are you serious?"

"Yes, I'm serious," the haze calling itself my mom says. "That's why I'm here. To end your pain."

I turn to the Jon blur. "You lied to me. I swear to God, if it's the last thing I do, I'm going to make you pay."

"I didn't lie. I just didn't tell you everything in the beginning," he says. "I should have. I'm sorry."

"You're sorry? *You're sorry* when you spill your beer on someone. *You're sorry* when you hurt someone's feelings. You don't say *you're sorry* when you forget to tell someone you came here to kill them."

"Let God decide your eternity," the mom blur says.

"Don't talk anymore, lady! You have nothing to say that I want to hear."

"Please, Samuel...I'm so—"

"Yeah, I know. You're sorry. The governor's sorry. Everybody's fucking sorry! But that doesn't really seem to be getting me anywhere, does it? This is far crueler than anything I ever did. I never gave a desperate human being the hope of renewed life, only to snatch it away. You're worse than I ever was."

"Samuel," the governor begins.

"Get out. Both of you, now."

"There was nothing else I could do, Samuel," the woman cries. "If there was, I would've done it."

"Leave me the fuck alone!"

"You're not thinking this through," the governor says. "We'll go, but understand, you have an L-two scheduled for tomorrow. And after you recover, you'll have another one. And another after that. L-twos and the Repair Shack…your life will be filled with nothing but pain and you know it. But you don't have to stay in here any longer. Not if you don't want to."

"We're done."

"If you realize the truth in what I am saying," the governor tells me, "all you have to do is call out my name."

Decision Time

I AM SUFFOCATING IN THE haze. The blur is heavy. So very heavy. I barely have enough strength, or desire, to inhale. I will face yet another L2 tomorrow. My suffering begins again, with no hope of reprieve. Maybe it's a "normal" L2. Maybe it's a crazed L2 bent on taking more of my body parts.

My freedom, dangled in front of me like the carrot in front of the donkey, has been ripped away. I have no reason to exist. Wait, that's not true. I do have a reason—to make everybody else feel better about their lives. Hurt so they can pretend they don't hurt as much.

I can't do it. I can't take one more L2. My life is over. One way or another, I have come to the end. The movie will never be made. How stupid of me to think life would ever work out that well.

I lie on my bed, unmoving, and dwell on this for a very long time. I know I won't sleep. I may never sleep again. Unless it's for eternity. The governor's final words stick in my thoughts. *If you realize the truth in what I am saying, all you have to do is call out my name.*

I sink deeper into my thoughts. Analyze everything. Maybe everything I thought is wrong. Maybe there never was a race of Gods. Maybe the billions of people who believe in a single God are right. Could He really exist?

The more I think about it, the more I want it to be so. But not the Old Testament God. No, I'm looking for the New Testament God. The one who is forgiving. The one who wants us all to live in His glory.

Certainly mankind would not believe in a fairy tale since the beginning of recorded time. There is no Santa Claus or Easter Bunny. There is no Tooth Fairy, no little Cupid flying around with a bow and arrows, spreading love. We learn the truths of these fictional characters by the time we enter grade school. Yet the majority of people—including some of the smartest throughout history—have strongly maintained the belief in some kind of a God, from childhood all the way to death.

No matter how advanced we become, a form of God continues to exist. Science has answered every other mystery in the universe, yet the belief in God cannot be explained away. People go to war for Him, lay down their arms for Him, die for Him. How can billions of people be wrong? Pretty farfetched to think this fantasy could stand the test of that kind of time. So if it's not a fantasy, it's reality.

And if the masses are right, then He exists. In some form or another, He's got to exist. Maybe He's the universe. Maybe He's pure energy. Perhaps our mortal minds aren't meant to understand His existence. But He must be *something*.

And then it hits me. Maybe my greatness lies not in this world, but in the next. Maybe this existence has groomed me, steel tempered by fire. Perhaps I'm supposed to go to the next level, stronger because of my experiences in this fucking hell on earth. Maybe I'm meant to go into the next life as a battle-hardened spiritual warrior and lead those who need a leader. I want this to be so. I choose to believe it.

Suddenly, there is no reason to fight for this shitty life. I will not exist merely for the sick, perverted pleasure of others. I will not be cut on anymore. I realize I have the possibility of moving on, going to the next level of existence. In the next life, I will be great. And the energy that is God, perhaps, I, too can become that energy.

So once again I am faced with a decision. A decision that changes everything. Before it was a red button. Push the red button and get out of the white nightmare. Now I'm in a nightmare void of all detail, permanent haze filled only with pain. So what am I going to do? Stay? Or push the button? Stay? Or push the button? Decision time.

I sit up, take a deep breath, and call out, "Jon McIntyre."

A Confession

THE DOOR CLOSES AND automatic locks snap into place, bouncing a metallic *click* off the walls. Like the sun fighting through cloud cover, fluorescent light fights through the haze. It is badly diffused, but I see it. This will be the last time I see light. The last time I think about the sun. The last time I think.

With a mortal mind, anyway.

I lie flat on my back, my feet strapped together and my wrists fastened to armrests extending straight out from each side of my body, in the shape of a cross. How fitting. I am uncovered, wearing only a pair of light pajama bottoms, yet I am warm. An antiseptic smell, like that in the Repair Shack, accompanies the warmth.

I am hooked up to the "Freedom Machine." That's what Jon calls it. In reality, it is a killing machine. Once the button is pushed, a series of drugs will be pumped in a specific order through an IV into my arm. The first drug is a mix of an anti-anxiety medication with a muscle relaxant. Jon says it will feel like I'm being submerged into a nice hot bath. The second drug, an anesthetic, will gently ease me into a deep sleep. The third and final drug is pentobarbital. I will feel nothing when my heart stops.

A blur approaches.

"Jon?" I turn to the blur. He is no longer Governor McIntyre. Not even *the governor*. Not anymore. He is merely a man. A feeble little mortal. That which I will ascend.

"Yes, Samuel, it's me."

"Where's my mother?"

"She's with the doctor in the hallway. She'll join you after I push the button."

Push the button. Another button ending one existence and beginning the next. Jon explained how it all works right before I was led into this room—a room I didn't even know existed two hours ago. "She can't bear to watch you push it, can she?"

"Think about it, Samuel," Jon answers. "She's committing the ultimate sacrifice. Sacrificing her only son so he can be free of pain and suffering."

"No, she's atoning for her biggest sin. Me."

"Either way, it is time. Samuel, are you ready to be set free?"

"I am ready to accomplish great things in the next life, yes."

"Of course you are. Oh, hey, I almost forgot. Before I push the button, I have a confession."

"A confession?"

"When I said you'd only been in here two and a half months, I wasn't entirely honest. In fact, I flat-out lied."

"What?"

"You've been here a lot longer than that. Actually, you would've been scheduled for release to prison in exactly ten days. Your time was almost up. You did it, Sam! You made it! Can you believe that? That's got to make you feel good."

"No, no, no." I shake my head. "Then stop. I know the rules. You can't do this without my consent."

"Sorry, buddy. I've waited too long for you."

"Jon, you're about to fuck up more than you can even imagine. Let me go and I'll let you live."

"What?" Jon sounds genuinely shocked. "Jesus Christ, Samuel. You're going to be a fucking nut job right up until you die, aren't you?"

"You don't know who you're dealing with, Jon. I'm not kidding. Push the button and we both die."

Jon laughs. "I love it! Right to the very end. Damn, Samuel, I'm actually going to miss you."

I cannot escape the truth. I am going to die today. But I am strangely calm. Because I'm about to be converted to pure energy. "I'm going to kill you, Jon."

"Another thing," Jon begins, unfazed. "Remember when I told you Allie's scream will haunt me for the rest of my life?"

"One last chance. Let me go."

"There is one other thing I will never forget. The guy who killed my wife said something into the phone just before smashing it. He said, 'Suck me sideways.' Like you said when I walked into your enclosure."

So he did know. Shit. This was all just part of his revenge.

"But don't kick yourself, feeling like you spilled the beans. I knew who you were a week after you got here. Remember all those stats I hit you with about missing persons and unidentified bodies?"

I look at his blur. Try hard to focus. I really want to see his face.

"They're true. But not in Allie's case. Her remains were finally identified, and I received the phone call right after you got here last year. She was found just outside your shithole little town. Since you were already here, we sat on the information." His blur leans toward me. "Sam, you killed my wife."

"It wasn't my fault. Blame your wife. She was the one standing in the middle of road."

"Nothing is ever your fault, is it? You're just the victim of a horrible life. Misunderstood. Wrong place, wrong time. Funny thing is, everyone in here says the same damn thing. Never their fault. Wrongly accused. All of you assholes are innocent. Yet you're still in here with me. And how do I know this? Because I sit here and have this same lame conversation with each of you before I push the button."

"Each of us? How many people have you killed?"

"Everyone I can." Jon laughs. "I'll bet I have a higher death count than Richard Ramirez, Jeffrey Dahmer, and Ted Bundy combined. If my stats ever went public, I would be one of the greatest serial killers our country has ever seen. In here, I can do anything I want." He pauses. "You thought you were becoming God. Who's God now, Sam?"

"You're playing with a power you have no understanding of."

"You know," Jon ignores me, "you'd be surprised how easy it is to take the will to live out of someone. Man. Woman. Child. Fill them with despair. Take all hope away. Putty in my hands, little buddy. And now it's your turn. But don't worry—you won't be the last. Not even close. I'm going to eliminate your kind, Sam. One press of the button at a time."

"I feel sorry for you, Jon. You're pathetic. You think this gives you power."

"Power enough to send you straight to Hell, where you will suffer for an eternity. Like you made me suffer. But I must admit, your suffering here has helped. I've watched you." He chuckles. "You know the lunatic L-two? The psycho who cut off your fingers? I hired him. He was working for me. I used him to push you over the edge. To make sure you were ready to agree to this little L-three visit."

"Death is not the end. It is the beginning."

"You lived like a rabid dog, Sam. And now it's time to put you down like one."

"You will free me. And I'll come for you. I promise."

"This is for all your victims. People you butchered. They didn't deserve this. Especially the little girl—the sheriff's daughter. She was just a child. For her, I now push the button. Like flushing the toilet."

Click.

I hear fluid squirting through a cylinder.

"Goodbye, Samuel."

Locks disengage and I hear the door open. I listen as someone enters the room. Steps toward me.

The Jon blur moves close to me. "Samuel, it's like I just turned on the light in a child's room and the monster disappeared."

"Samuel, go and be in peace." My mom's voice.

I am suddenly warm. So warm. And sleepy. And as my mom suggested, I'm at complete peace, in a strange place of comfort. "It's okay, Mom. I'll find a way back. I have a promise to keep."

I take in a deep breath, let it out. It seems to take a long time, like my lungs can't remember exactly how to do it. I think I can actually feel my heart slowing down. I am so very tired, more tired than I have ever been in my life. My eyes drift close.

A cheek presses against mine. Comforting. Soft. A clean smell. My mom. That's how my mom smells. She speaks. "Our Father who art in Heaven, hallowed be Thy name…"

I fight with all my being to crack open my eyes. She is pressed against me. But I can't make out any details. I wish I could see her one more time.

A hand, soft, smooth, trembling, takes my right hand. "Thy Kingdom come, Thy will be done on Earth as it is in Heaven."

The growing blackness is heavy, pushes me into the bed.

"…but forgive us our trespasses, as we forgive those who trespass against us."

"One last thing." Jon's voice. My mom's cheek pulls away. "Samuel, where is the girl's body?"

"And lead us not into temptation, but deliver us from evil." My mom's voice is still close, perhaps right next to the bed. "For Thine is the Kingdom, the power, and the glory. Forever and ever. Amen."

"I didn't kill her."

"What?" Jon says.

Warmth floods my entire body. The description of a hot bath is not far off. "Her hair. A keepsake. Proof of my reward from God. I accidently cut her forehead, but I didn't kill her."

"Cut whose forehead?" my mom asks.

"The sheriff's daughter," Jon exclaims. "Jesus Christ, Samuel, she's alive? Where?"

My mind is slowing drastically now. Thoughts are losing form.

"Where's the damn girl, Samuel?" Jon screams.

"I'll take you to her when I come back for you. So she can watch you die."

I am so very tired. But must fight to stay awake. One last thing to say.

"Mom?"

"Yes, Samuel?"

"You can't erase me."

Then there is only darkness.

Acknowledgments

YEARS AGO, DR. CINDY Kennedy and I visited about a double murder in the news. The victims were young girls. We agreed there should be a place where real justice existed. Where crimes committed against the innocent could be exacted upon the guilty. Dante's *Inferno* style. Cindy coined this place a "Criminal Zoo." Fast forward eleven years. *Criminal Zoo* is here.

I have learned that being an author is like being the captain of a ship. I get to drive. But it is the crew that launches the vessel, keeps it afloat. As the author, my name is on the cover, so I will take the blame for this terrifying story. But I will not take the credit. To begin, I want to thank my wife Tiki. You believed in me. Cheered me on. Gave me every reason to succeed.

To Pat Walsh and Defenestration Press, along with Tyson Cornell and Rare Bird Books, where do I begin? You guys took a chance on me. You guided me through the roller coaster ride of getting published and you made my dream a reality. Words cannot describe my gratitude.

Dad, JoAnn, Mom, and Alan, you raised me to never give up. You taught me that anything worthwhile must be earned. And all things are possible. Because of your lessons, getting published was the only acceptable outcome.

Stevie, Quinn, Tyler, and Jaxon, you guys grew up watching my struggles. During times of discouragement, you had only words of encouragement. How many times did we talk about "one day when I get published...?"

Stephen Lance, you suggested I give my manuscript to your wife, Karin. I followed your advice and she brought legitimacy to my work. Janet McDaniel, I greatly appreciate the reams of paper and enough ink cartridges to fill a dump trunk. Karen Klement, thank you for helping me get this endeavor off the ground. Dr. Eldon Olson, because of your knowledge and expertise, I was able to write through the mind of a serial killer.

To my siblings: Chimene, Cindi, Brandon, Jeff, Kristin, and Erin, your unending support made a difference. And to all my friends and family members, thank you from the bottom of my heart. Matt Dahl, we shared a lot of coffees talking about this. Thank you for getting involved. And Alli, night after night, you kept an eye on me as I wrote. I will never forget you.

Dan and Kim, Susan, Mr. Kurt Anthony, Kayce and Austin, Cassidy, Dave and Pam, Dawn, Cindy, Lynnetta, Dr. Anne Guiliano and Jim, Lil, Cam and Amy, Bekah, Dr. Chris Schreiber, Bud and Joan, Kayla, Allen and Jennie, Sheryl, Dr. Joe Dillard and Stella Fong, and to all others who hired me for personal training sessions, while I worked my night job as a starving author, you gave me a day job and an income. And to you Beth Connaghan, see what you started?

To the supporters, some mentioned above, Richard, Reggie, Robert, and Chris thank you for believing in me.

Hey Woody, Monte, Mel, Levi, Reps, Meyers, JR, and Justin... we did it.

And finally, to the universe. You brought these amazing souls into my life. I am blessed.